MORE

I NEED MORE

KIMBERLEY WHITE

Kensington Publishing Corp.

http://www.kensingtonbooks.com

DAFINA BOOKS are published by

Kensington Publishing Corp.
119 West 40th Street
New York, NY 10018

All Kensington Titles, Imprints, and Distributed Lines are available at special quantity discounts for bulk purchases for sales promotions, premiums, fund-raising, and educational or institutional use. Special book excerpts or customized printings can also be created to fit specific needs. For details, write or phone the office of the Kensington special sales manager: Kensington Publishing Corp., 119 West 40th Street, New York, NY 10018, attn: Special Sales Department, Phone: 1-800-221-2647.

Dafina and the Dafina logo Reg. U.S. Pat. & TM Off.

ISBN-13: 978-0-7582-2210-7
ISBN-10: 0-7582-2210-6

First mass market printing: September 2009

10 9 8 7 6 5 4 3 2 1

Printed in the United States of America

I NEED
MORE

BACKWARD

CHAPTER 1

Dr. Erika Johnson slid the glossy black sachet across the desk, her heart pounding so rapidly she thought it would jerk into a rhythm incompatible with life, like a funky ventricular tachycardia. She watched him closely as his long fingers, attached to perfect brown hands once capable of caressing her into a crazed frenzy, reached out to accept the packet. He slowly brought the documents to rest on top of the medical file he'd been reading. He adjusted his glasses, in no particular hurry to open the mysterious offering. She willed herself to breathe deeply and stay calm. She searched for the tiniest sign of emotion as he slowly unwound the black string, threw open the cover, and read the heading.

Dr. Brock Johnson's thick lashes flipped up to look at her. He spared this minimal reaction but gathered his composure quickly as he continued to peruse the legal papers. His hands rested on each side of the page, one finger stroking the edge as his eyes moved back and forth. His expression remained blank, giving no indication of how he felt about what he was reading.

Erika found his ability to shield his emotions maddening as she fidgeted, waiting for his response to her announcement.

But hadn't she fallen in love with this man of opposites? The hospital staff had warned her about the stoic doctor who wanted his patients cared for in very particular ways. She'd come to learn Brock wasn't stoic, but highly conscientious about the welfare of his clients. Rumors were he was stuck-up because he didn't associate with the staff at Christmas parties and after-work get-togethers. Actually, he was a man trained to be professional at all times and found it improper to socialize with those you were supervising. He was called mean because he never smiled. She uncovered he was bursting with love but needed a special woman give it to.

She watched him, more than his huge desk separating them, and tried to pinpoint exactly when things had gone wrong. It seemed so long ago when she'd walked into a patient's room, instantly feeling Brock's heat as he meticulously sutured a long scar across the man's forehead. She had cried many tears since that day, and didn't doubt she would shed many more.

"What is this about, Erika?" Brock's wording was precise and well measured, the tone a school principal would use with a child about to be reprimanded.

She'd been preparing for this showdown for a week. She swallowed hard and matched his tone. "I want a divorce."

His dark eyes challenged hers, struggling for dominance in her surprise attack. He didn't look away as he closed the cover on the divorce papers. "And you approach me with this at work?"

"I didn't want there to be a scene."

"So you ambush me?" His voice dropped an octave, and for Brock it was the same as if he had shouted.

"If my intention was to ambush you, I would've had my lawyer deliver the papers to your apartment."

"Lawyer," he repeated as if he didn't know the meaning of the word. "Were we supposed to have gotten lawyers?"

"At some point, yes."

"Not at this point," he countered. He cocked his right brow, challenging her.

There was a time when he could wiggle his dark brow and blink his thick lashes and Erika would melt. With a creamed-coffee complexion and dark facial hair, he was quite simply the most handsome man she'd ever met.

Brock pushed the divorce papers aside. "We'll talk about this later. I'll call you. We'll have dinner." He resumed his work, dismissing her.

"We're going to talk about it now."

Her forcefulness earned her another hitch of his brow. He braced the edge of the desk and pushed his chair back, just a few inches, as if he needed the room to exhale his exaspera-tion. "I don't discuss my personal life at work."

"It's my personal life, too, and I want to talk now." She shook her head, refusing to let hurt feelings play a part in this interaction. The day he left, her heart had shriveled and died. It had taken a long time to become reconciled with his deci-sion. Her newfound contentment with her life wouldn't let her back down. "We've been separated for seven months. It's time to make a decision."

"And your *vision* has suddenly cleared."

Erika's strumming heartbeat came to an abrupt halt, and her new problem became fighting through an episode of dizziness and not ending up unconscious on the floor.

He knows.

She took a deep breath, fighting guilt. Brock Johnson was a well-respected intensivist at Mission Hospital, leading his physician group in the care of ICU patients. Of course he knew about the eye clinic opening across the hall from her internal medicine clinic in the hospital's office building. It didn't mean he knew *everything*.

"You're *seeing* what our future should be with 20/20 precision?"

The office lapsed into silence. She hadn't been prepared to discuss this. She could handle only one issue at a time with a man as stubborn and controlling as Brock. Today, it would be the divorce. She refused to be intimidated by his double-talk and pushed ahead with her purpose. "The settlement's fair."

His expression was frozen, his eyes locked onto hers with an angry fire blazing inside his pupils.

"All I ask is to keep using your last name. I've built my practice as Dr. Johnson. I'd like to avoid confusion or having to rebuild my reputation because of switching back to my maiden name."

"Do you really think I'm going to sign this?" He shoved the packet across the desk, and it toppled over the edge into her lap. "You walk in here and present me with divorce papers without any warning, and the only issue you see is whether or not I let you keep my last name?" His voice dropped to barely a whisper when he said, "No."

Erika clutched the sachet with icy fingers. "What?" she asked, sure she hadn't heard him correctly. She knew he would be angry, but she didn't think he'd refuse to grant her a divorce. *He* had been the one to walk out on their marriage.

"I'm not signing your papers."

She took a deep breath, held it, and exhaled slowly before speaking. "This may not have been the best place to approach you, but it was going to happen sooner or later. We're separated. We only see each other at work. Our only conversation is about our mutual patients. We aren't in counseling. What did you expect to happen? Where else could this go?"

He seemed befuddled, as if he hadn't contemplated this

reality. He licked the corner of his mouth, deciding his next move. "I'm not signing your divorce papers," he said with hard conviction. "I'm not granting you a divorce."

"Why not?"

He wiped his forehead, and for Brock, who prided himself on keeping his emotions in check, this gesture was as good as him falling out of his big leather chair.

So she pushed. "Why are you trying to make this so difficult?"

"I can't talk about this right now. I have to get ready for morning rounds."

"I expected you to be mad I'd beaten you to filing, but I didn't think you'd play games." She spoke the words out of frustration of believing her feelings were being discounted again. The man who once put her happiness above everything in his life hadn't been able to have a meaningful discussion with her in seven months. She couldn't spend any more time trying to figure him out. She had to move on with her life.

"This may be some sort of a race for you, but I won't end my marriage without any thought because I'm in a rush to get to rounds."

"How much thought went into you leaving?"

His eyes shifted away from her. Being the first to break eye contact meant he was floundering.

A pang of worry moved through her. Brock was a formidable opponent for anyone who challenged him. He used his silence to retreat into his defensive shell, hiding his emotions from her. She'd given him the perfect opportunity to end it all, but he hesitated. Hadn't he suddenly become distant the week before he'd packed his bags and left their home? Asking for a divorce had caught him off guard, but it wasn't like him to be stunned speechless. Something else was going on. She'd suspected some hidden agenda since the day he up and ended their relationship without warning or cause.

She softened her voice and called his attention back to her. "Brock?"

After a long moment of intense contemplation, his gaze met hers again.

"Are you okay?"

He spoke with a passion long missing from their marriage when he said, "I'm not divorcing you, Erika."

CHAPTER 2

He refused to let her go.

He couldn't let her go.

Brock knew he *must* let Erika go. Wasn't this what he'd decided the first day? The moment he found out, his first thought had been of Erika and what it would mean to her life. He had struggled with his decision, continued to struggle with it now, but the right thing to do was to end his marriage with the hope that Erika would go on to live a happy, productive life. It was the reason he'd started to pull away from her. Not because he didn't love her. It had been difficult to watch her hurt as he withdrew his affection, stamping out the core foundation of their marriage, but in the end, it would shorten her suffering.

He watched Erika approach, her crisp white lab coat unable to hide the fluid shift of her hips. He could smell her sweetness before she reached him, his mind playing tricks because he missed the softness of her touch, the unspoken understanding of his quirky ways, the gentleness of her kiss, and the ever-present support she gave by holding him in her arms.

He had come to the realization he had to end his marriage, and believed himself emotionally ready to accept his fate— until she walked into his office the other morning announcing she'd taken the necessary steps to end their limbo. The divorce papers made it too real. He had almost choked as his breakfast pushed its way up into his throat. His love for her materialized with such force he had become irrational, refusing to sign the papers when he had promised her a long time ago he'd always give her whatever she wanted.

"How's my patient doing?" Erika's presence settled around him like a broken-in blanket, soft and fuzzy and warm. He wanted to wrap her around him and absorb the love she had once offered. She encompassed the opposite of all of his qualities. Her kindness was genuine and unlimited, freely given to everyone she encountered. She calmed him, and made him believe he was invincible. Her face was not only flawlessly beautiful, her expressions openly displayed each of her emotions. She had barged into his life unexpectedly, opening her heart to him without pretense, and he'd immediately fallen in love with her.

"He's stable. Neuro wants to keep him in the ICU for a few more days." They began to leave the unit, walking side by side, her nearness enough to weaken his knees.

"Any deficits from the stroke?"

They were all about business, no signs of the closeness they'd once shared. "Hard to tell until he wakes up."

She shook her head. "It was blood pressure related. He wouldn't take his antihypertensives. He kept telling me he felt fine. I kept telling him it's common to be asymptomatic with hypertension."

"You did all you could do," he assured her as he stood aside to allow her to exit the unit first.

"There's always more I can do."

Erika always thought there was more she could do for her patients. She took it hard when one became acutely ill. He'd witnessed her crying when her patients died. She offered a tiny piece of her soul to everyone she encountered, losing a bit of herself when those she cared about were hurting. His duty as her husband, as the man who loved her more than anyone else ever could, was to replenish her mind and body. How could he be contemplating reneging on his original plan and refusing her a divorce when his situation threatened to destroy her?

"Don't beat yourself up for what you can't control," he told her.

She glanced up at him, cleverly finding double meaning in his words. She stopped, turning to him. "Things don't always turn out the way we want them to."

"No, they don't." He itched to reach out and caress her lips, wiping away her frown.

"We shouldn't belabor this."

He glanced away, checking the hallway to find they weren't alone. "We'll talk. Later."

She watched him, clouds of confusion washing over the smooth planes of her face. "I'm going to hold you to it, Brock."

He pressed his lips together, afraid he was about to blurt out how he really felt. Instead, he nodded.

"I'm going to check on my patient. I want to speak with his wife. See how she's holding up."

The long-suffering wife. Afraid her husband was going to die, prematurely leaving her and ending their life together. It would kill him to see Erika hurting this way.

"Erika," he called as she walked away.

She turned to face him. Her gentle nature was palpable, warming the air and washing over him in soft waves. How could she be strong and determined, and so loving and forgiving at the same time? He knew it was selfish, but he couldn't let her go. He needed to be in her heart; he had to be the man of her dreams.

"Brock?"

He blinked, unable to clear his warring emotions.

She came to him. "Are you okay?"

He watched for her reaction as he lifted his hand and rested his palm against her cheek. Shocked, there was a hitch in her breathing. A moment passed and her body relaxed into his touch. If they had been alone, he would have pulled her in close, buried his face in her neck, and apologized for all the grief he had caused her. Instead, he leaned in and pressed his lips very softly to hers. When he pulled away, she was watching him, her lashes beating frantically. Before she could recover and ask any of the hundreds of questions flashing behind her eyes, he walked away.

"How are you feeling?"

"Physically? Fine." Brock slipped off the exam table and began buttoning his shirt. "A little tired sometimes, but otherwise okay."

"Get more rest. I can write you off from work for a couple of weeks." Dr. Hassan Kabul was already reaching into his lab coat for a prescription pad.

"No." Work helped maintain his sanity when everything else was so out of his control. It gave him a focus other than how much he missed his wife.

"I don't have to tell you there are support groups—"

"For husbands who have separated from their wives and now want them back?"

"No shit?" Hassan asked, smiling beneath his turban. His accent made his attempt to curse comical, but Brock hadn't been able to convince him to stop trying. According to Hassan, he was a full-blooded American now, and his accent had been left behind with all the dark memories of the brutality in his homeland. "I told you, a wife's place is next to her husband. What do your American wedding vows say? 'In illness and in health'?"

"Something like that."

"Erika would want to know what is going on. She would want to stand by you."

Brock shrugged into his lab coat. "Not a word about this to Erika." He knew doctor-patient privilege would make Hassan keep his secret, but he wanted the promise of a friend.

"Not a word from me." Hassan crossed his legs, balancing himself on the tiny stool. "Any decision about what you'd like to do?"

How many options did he have? "You act like I have a choice."

"There are choices."

Brock leaned on the edge of the exam table, his long legs stretched out in front of him.

Hassan continued, "I think we should move beyond the observation phase."

He froze, everything coming to an abrupt halt in his mind. "Surgery?"

"It was my recommendation from the beginning." He leaned forward, an earnest expression on his face. "My friend, you have testicular cancer. We should have acted seven months ago. You wanted time to get your life in order. Your tumor makers have changed. We have to move on this now."

"Surgery?" he asked again, not believing it had come to this.

"Radical orchiectomy followed by single-dose carboplatin adjuvant therapy." Hassan scribbled something in Brock's medical chart.

"Wait. You want to remove my testicle and give me radiation therapy?"

"It's the recommended standard of care."

His nightmare began in the shower eight months ago, after

making love to Erika. He'd had a hard day, and she'd been so sweet, greeting him at the door naked except for a short silk robe. His emotions were on overdrive, so foreplay was short. He would often play with Erika's body for hours, not making love to her until she begged, on the verge of implosion. This night was different. He was the one in a hurry. He wanted her more than he'd ever needed her before. He dominated her body, egotistically taking what he wanted. She bucked beneath him, encouraging his selfishness until he turned over his control, coming with an explosion he would never forget.

As an internal medicine doctor, Erika preached prevention to her patients. At home, they'd made a sexy game out of her monthly breast exam. But he was like so many other physicians, keyed in on his patients' health but neglectful of his own. He'd left Erika to sleep after their vigorous lovemaking while he showered, and that's when he'd discovered the small lump on the right side of his scrotum.

Hassan had been encouraging, assuring him it was probably epididymitis, an infection of one of the cords responsible for transporting sperm. He was treated with antibiotics and scheduled for a follow-up visit. The antibiotics didn't work. The lump remained, and he began experiencing swelling and tenderness. Hassan scheduled an ultrasound of his testicles, which warranted more testing, and eventually a tumor was confirmed. The mass measured two centimeters, which should have placed him at stage II, but the cancer hadn't spread to his lymph nodes, and Hassan labeled it a stage I seminoma—it was all a play on words, because the cancer had already grown enough to limit his treatment options.

Brock shook his head adamantly. "I can't let you remove my testicle. I can't do radiation." He couldn't deal with the side effects when he'd just decided to get Erika back. "I need a quick fix, doc."

"Being a doctor, you know there aren't any."

"Remove my testicle?" He laughed sarcastically.

"This cancer has a greater than 95 percent cure rate, but we have to do *something*. We can't just wait around hoping it will go away on its own." Hassan began writing in his chart. "I'm ordering more tests today. We'll get you scheduled for surgery next week."

"I can't—"

"Brock, you know what can happen."

He did. His father had died from the same disease.

"Next week, Brock."

"I need to do a couple of things first."

Hassan stood and approached his friend. "I'm in this with you, but we can't fool around anymore."

He dropped his head in defeat. The moment he'd found the mass, he knew his life was changing for the worse. He fit the profile. An African-American man between the ages of 15 and 35, with a familial history of testicular cancer was at the top of the hit list. At 35, he'd thought he'd managed to escape. At 30, Erika was too young to watch her husband die.

"If the surgery and radiation don't work?"

"Don't get so far ahead."

"Hassan, please." He already knew the answer, but male cancers weren't his specialty. Maybe there had been medical advances he wasn't aware of.

"We try chemotherapy."

"And then?"

"And then? We won't worry about 'and then' because the surgery will remove the tumor and radiation will keep the cancer from spreading to the lymph nodes."

"But if it doesn't?"

Hassan sighed. "Surgery. Radiation therapy. Chemotherapy."

Brock looked away, not wanting his friend to see his

weakness. The muscles in his neck were so tight he couldn't turn his head. The taste of bile lingered at the back of his throat. His mind raced uncontrollably and he was unable to filter out incoherent thoughts. The stench of industrial-strength disinfectants threatened to strangle him. He was scared. He was afraid of dying. He was afraid of losing Erika. But mostly, he was afraid of dying and leaving her alone.

"There's something else to consider," Hassan hedged.

"What?"

"You said you want to get back together with Erika."

"I can't do this to Erika. I can't saddle her with an invalid."

"Brock, my friend. You can go on to live a healthy, happy life."

Not without Erika. And he couldn't have Erika if he was half a man.

"You must tell Erika. Let her make her own decision. It is what you Americans do—let your women make their own decisions."

He managed to smile at his friend's peculiar personality. Hassan, a man who suffered prejudice every time he went near an airport, dismissed the rights of women.

"Seriously, you have to consider a future with her. If you decide you want kids later . . ."

"I won't be able to have any." If the radiation didn't zap his ability to produce sperm, the surgical removal of his testicle would severely limit it.

"It may become an issue."

Brock couldn't handle any more issues right now.

"Visit a sperm bank before we begin treatment," Hassan said matter-of-factly. "Secure your future ability to make a choice."

CHAPTER 3

"Good. It's done, then." Mark Garing was the opposite of what Brock had become. He expressed his feelings for Erika at every opportunity. He was affectionate and available, knowing how to manage his work and still have a social life. It was his warmth, when Brock's love had turned chilly, that had made Erika gravitate toward his friendship.

"Not quite," she told him.

"What do you mean?" He placed his arm across her shoulders, bringing her into him. He always sat next to her in the booth of their favorite restaurant, telling her he didn't like the table separating them.

"Brock said no."

"No?"

"No, he wouldn't sign the papers, and, no, he won't give me a divorce."

"How can he not give you a divorce if you're asking for it?" Mark lifted his drink to his lips, sipping it slowly as he gathered his thoughts.

Erika angled toward him. "I think he knows about us."

"Did he say something?"

She repeated Brock's cryptic statements. Mark was the

kind of man who grew on you, and before you had realized what had happened, you were falling for him. His kindness made him a good friend; his openness would make him a good lover. A friendly person, he'd come across the hall the day before he saw his first patient in the new eye clinic to introduce himself. He'd waited patiently, being a good but not intrusive friend, until Erika had shared the news of her separation from Brock. Two months later, he'd made his attraction known. Another month passed before Erika's lonely heart told her it was all right to start dating. After keeping their relationship discreet for four months, Mark was getting anxious.

"It sounds like he knows," Mark agreed. "Is that all he said?"

She nodded.

"What are you going to do? He has to give you a divorce," he added as an afterthought. "Once the shock wears off, he'll come around."

Shock was not what she'd seen on Brock's face when she handed him the divorce papers. She couldn't quite name what emotion had caused the fiery storm in his eyes, but she would. She would have to. She needed to know what he was thinking—feeling, because whatever was moving through his heart and mind was keeping him from giving her her freedom. His sudden public display of affection outside the ICU only helped to muddy the waters. She didn't know what was going on with him, but maybe it was the answer to this whole strange situation.

"That's your cell," Mark said, jostling her.

"Dr. Johnson," she answered.

"Erika, I've been called to see one of your patients in the ER," Brock said without formalities. "I just finished the consult. I'm going to admit him. Meet you in the ER?"

"Twenty minutes."

"Twenty minutes?" Brock questioned. "Where are you?"

"Out of the hospital having dinner. I'll be right there." She hung up before he could question her further.

"Let me guess," Mark said. "You're meeting Brock. It wouldn't be about the divorce papers, would it?"

She shook her head, already putting on her jacket. "One of my patients is in the emergency room."

Mark grunted, downing his drink.

"What? If something's on your mind, say it."

"Is there some reason Brock can't handle the admission?"

"I like to evaluate my patients when they're admitted to the hospital. I've always done it this way. The receiving doctor calls to notify me, and I go in to check on my patient."

"You can consult over the phone like all the other doctors do."

"Too impersonal. My patients count on me being there."

Mark nodded, his expression saying he wasn't convinced. "What do you think this is about?"

"I think your husband has said he won't divorce you, and now he's tightening the reigns. You said yourself he's suspicious about us. He's going to do everything he can to keep you close to him until he's ready to make his move."

"Brock will get over my asking for a divorce, and then he'll sign the papers. Remember, he left me. It was just a shock to him. That's all."

Mark shook his head, not convinced.

"Believe me, he wants this as much as I do."

"And how much do you want it, Erika?"

She angled toward him. "What does that mean?"

"Take him to court and force him to divorce you. He can't stop it, really."

"Make it as ugly as possible? No, I won't do it. Brock will come around. If he doesn't soon, I'll nudge him."

"And in the meantime, what about us?"

"I'm not quite sure what you're asking."

"We started dating four months ago." He ran the rough pad of his thumb over her cheek, across her lips, and down her neck, stopping in the cleavage underneath the dainty fabric of her blouse. "Do we stay at a standstill while we wait for Brock to 'come around'?" Another finger flicked at the button above his thumb. "Or do we get to know each other better?"

Mark had been patient about advancing their physical relationship, always knowing it would happen when she'd settled her marriage. With Brock's refusal came Mark's insistence.

"With everything so fragile right now, and Brock probably aware we're dating, I don't want to do anything to push him the other way."

Mark searched her expression, daring the truth to be other than what she'd stated. She was physically attracted to Mark, but she was a married woman. Her morals won out over her libido every time. Finding no deception, he pulled his hand away. He leaned in and gently kissed her cheek. "Call me when you're done *seeing your patient*."

In the emergency department, Brock had returned to his old stoic self, discussing Erika's patient's case with cold formality. She watched him, jotting down his orders in the chart, careful not to look at her directly. They concluded their business without any discussion of their personal lives. She stopped in to go over the plan of care with her patient, promised she'd see him during her rounds, and left the hospital saddened and confused.

She didn't know what she had wanted to happen. She told herself she hoped only for some explanation of why he had left her in the prime of their marriage when she was still discovering new things to love about him. If she admitted the truth, she wanted more. She wanted him to tell her he'd made a mistake—

not about refusing to sign the divorce papers, but to driving her to even consider dissolving their three-year marriage.

She got nothing from Brock. He gave her no hint as to how he was feeling about her, about their marriage, about her request for a divorce. His focus never wavered from giving the patient his best, and she wondered when he had stopped wanting to give her his best.

Erika arrived in the Oakland County, Michigan, suburb to a beautiful 3,000-square-foot luxury home—the home Brock had left for a tiny apartment in the residents' high-rise overlooking Mission Hospital. He traded a half-million-dollar home for a two-hundred-dollar-a-month apartment—another jagged piece of the mysterious puzzle, because they had worked so hard to buy their dream home.

She pulled the red Navigator into the attached two-car garage, next to the empty space where Brock's black Lincoln Zephyr should be parked. She'd long gotten over the void left by the missing car, and admonished herself for sitting in the SUV for twenty minutes reliving the day they went to the Ford dealership and brought the matching vehicles.

She entered the house that should have been a home, hanging up her jacket and leaving her melancholy at the door. She was immediately greeted by the aroma of homemade jambalaya. Not only had Brock left her the house, he'd left her his mother.

"You're right on time." Virginia Johnson scurried around the kitchen, the only hint of her 65 years being the slight limp caused by a prematurely needed hip replacement last year. She had survived the birth of three boys at home without anesthesia or a doctor. Her husband had passed of testicular cancer almost four years ago, and she'd managed to gather her inner strength and keep going. It had been a tumble down the stairs of the Memphis courthouse that physically crippled her and made her dependent on her youngest son.

"I hope you're hungry," Virginia said, moving into the nook of the kitchen where they shared most of their meals.

Erika didn't have the heart to tell her she'd eaten earlier. "We didn't bring you here to cook, Mom. I'm supposed to be taking care of you."

"I can't putz around this big house all day doing nothing. You kids work all day. I like keeping house. It's a perfect match. Go wash up."

"How did physical therapy go today?" Erika asked as she headed to the nearest powder room. She would have to ignore her full belly and eat at least one bowl of jambalaya. She'd done a good job of keeping her relationship away from Brock's mother. She didn't want to explain she'd already eaten dinner this evening.

"I made it through." Virginia hated her therapy sessions, but she went because Brock made a big fuss when she didn't.

Erika washed up and joined Virginia for dinner.

"Is Brock far behind you?"

She almost dropped the basket of fresh bread. "What?"

Virginia tended to forget minor details. Like the fact her son had left her daughter-in-law seven months ago.

"Brock called earlier. He said he was coming for dinner tonight." She beamed. "I fixed his favorite meal. I'm wondering if we should start without him."

"He didn't say anything about coming over when I saw him at the hospital."

"Well, you know he doesn't like to put his personal business on display at work. Maybe we can start on the bread, but wait for Brock for the jambalaya."

Erika sat speechless as Virginia prattled on about something cute her youngest grandson had told her over the phone. Maybe

Brock had changed his mind and now he was ready to sign the divorce papers. She pictured the glossy black packet tucked away in her top dresser drawer. Maybe Brock was coming by so they could sit down and tell Virginia together they would not be reconciling. Maybe he simply wanted to have dinner with his mother—he did at least once a week, but usually out of the house. Maybe he'd forgotten some important papers in the upstairs office they'd once shared. Maybe . . . maybe . . . maybe. Hadn't she promised herself there would be no more maybes? No more tearful hours spent trying to understand why Brock had done what he'd done.

"Sorry I'm late." The throaty tone of Brock's voice dripped over her like sweet honey.

She didn't need to turn around to know he filled the doorway behind her. He went to his mother and kissed her cheek before taking the seat between them at the head of the table. She hated he felt comfortable enough to sit there. She hated she didn't want to tell him to move.

He'd changed the aesthetic white lab coat for a gray jacket to match his slacks. The man knew how to wear a suit. The fabric melded against his biceps, his pants legs perched atop expensive slip-ons. Deceptively large, he appeared wiry until he took you into his arms and embraced you in his muscular protection.

"Hi, Erika," he said, his voice not betraying how the uncomfortable situation affected him.

"You didn't tell me you were coming by."

"I didn't think you'd be here . . . since you already ate dinner."

Virginia piped in, happy to have a miniature version of her family together, no matter the circumstances. "We're all here now. Let's eat. Say the blessing, Brock."

After dinner came peach cobbler. Brock and Virginia chatted away about nieces and uncles and cousins, reliving their time in Memphis. Erika picked over her bowl of cobbler, smiling politely when Virginia looked her way. She didn't have much appetite, and it had nothing to do with the fact that this was her second dinner of the evening. They had an agreement—Brock had walked out, his open invitation to visit the house had been rescinded. He had to call and clear it with her if he wanted to stop by. Dropping in without warning and eating diner together as a family was no longer on the menu.

"I'll clean up the dishes, Ma," Brock said, speaking to his mother adoringly.

He *never* offered to do anything concerning the kitchen.

"I am a little tired," Virginia said, pushing away from the table. "I think I'll go to bed early."

"Take the elevator up," Erika called after her, noticing the increase in her limp.

"Good night," Virginia called, heading for the stairs. The elevator had been installed specifically for her use, but she rarely took the tiny car upstairs. Taking the elevator meant admitting she was handicapped, and she'd never accept the label.

As soon as she was out of sight, Erika turned to Brock.

"Thank you for letting my mother stay here."

"I'd never ask her to leave. This is her home."

Brock nodded, spooning another helping of cobbler into his bowl.

"What's going on?"

He leveled a look at her.

"Brock? What's going on with you? You've been so up and down lately. You showed up here tonight for some reason. Are you going to tell me?" The more questions she asked, the more she wanted to know, and needed to say. "What you're doing isn't right. You're mom doesn't understand what's going on between us. Just when I think I know what you want, you tell me I'm wrong. I don't know what to expect from you. I can't explain what's happening, and it's making me very uncomfortable."

"Erika," he whispered, stopping her rambling.

"What?" she asked too harshly.

"I'm moving back in."

CHAPTER 4

The day Brock decided he needed to make love to Erika, he broke it off with the other woman he'd been seeing. He'd come to the realization after six months of dating he had to get as close to Erika as possible—mentally and physically. It became a compulsion, and his thoughts never ventured far from how their first intimate experience together would be. Every time she innocently brushed up against him or touched his hand during dinner, his mind scrambled and his body went haywire. He'd never wanted a woman as badly as he wanted her, and he was scared to death the actual experience wouldn't be as good as his fantasies.

He'd met the other woman while picking up his dry cleaning. They'd bumped into each other a few times, but that particular day a lingering glance made him bold enough to approach her. She was pretty and had a witty personality, was ambitious and sweet. He dated her for two months before meeting Erika at work over a shared patient. The other woman—he couldn't remember her name all these years later—would have been a good catch, she just wasn't Erika.

He'd never been a man to sleep with more than one woman at once. Even in college when his buddies teased him about his serial monogamy, he didn't stray from this rule. In his residency, he saw the effects of men and women who slept around indiscriminately, always crying on his shoulder, begging for a cure for genital herpes or HIV or AIDS, saying, "I never thought it would happen to me." It *wouldn't* happen to him. If he could control the odds enough to limit the chances, he would. One woman at a time and unwavering use of condoms was a good sound practice that carried him into his adulthood without disease to his wife's bed.

The other woman had been mildly distraught by his abrupt end to their relationship. They'd never promised not to date others, but her reaction told him she had assumed she was the only one in his life. He let her down as easily as possible, assuring her she was a wonderful woman who would find the right man for her. He ended all contact, not wanting to lead her on under the pretense of just being friends. Soon enough, she moved on with her life and stopped trying to contact him.

Erika became the focus of his life. He loved his work, and always would, but she helped him realize the hospital couldn't be his life.

The night he made love to her, he cried. Erika didn't say one belittling word. She held him in her arms, her soft touch caressing his temples until he fell asleep. She never questioned him, demanding why he had become so overwhelmed he'd sobbed for the first time since he was ten years old. Never had his emotions been so strong, or his heart so open. It broke him, bringing him to silent tears. She watched over him all night, in the morning simply asking, "Can I see you this weekend?"

The emotions had been magical, and the physical act magnificent. He'd never forget how soft her skin was, or the light scent of rich flowers on every curve of her body. His raw emotions caught her off guard, leaving her completely uninhibited as she openly showed him how good he made her feel. She made a lot of noise when she climaxed. He loved it, and it was enough to bring him over with her. "Let me know how I'm making you feel," he encouraged when she became embarrassed. "Louder," he demanded when he told her to say his name.

She kissed deeply, holding him tightly and filling him with her emotions. When he looked into her eyes, everything she felt for him was written there. The stark reality of knowing she cared about him so deeply made him thrust his hips harder, faster in an attempt to push his own overwhelming feelings away.

She touched him brazenly, demanding he experience as much pleasure as she was feeling. She moved beneath him, raising her hips up to meet every one of his thrusts. She wrapped her legs around his waist, pulling him in deeper, challenging him to give her his best—not merely what he thought was good enough.

He came twice, one right on top of the other, his sperm filling the condom two times before his body stopped quaking. He was drenched in sweat, his thighs ached, his back had a major kink, but he'd never felt better in his life. His body hummed with satisfaction, radiating from his groin through each of his limbs. His heart raced, filling him with an increased supply of adrenaline.

In the midst of the frenzy, Erika placed a chaste, tender kiss on his lips . . . and he began to cry.

He would never forget it. Never.

The day he proposed came as a complete surprise to him.

He received a call from his mother—his father was dead. He was extremely close to his dad, so even though Brock had witnessed the devastation of the cancer, he wasn't prepared to lose him. He rushed to his mother's side, catching the next flight to Memphis, having only enough time to pack a bag and call off from work.

The next morning, Erika stood on his mother's doorstep, distressed but ready to be strong for him. He pulled her inside, not knowing how much he needed her until he saw her. She didn't wait for formal introductions. She mixed in with his extended family, doing whatever she could to make this time easier for him and his family. In the evenings, when most had gone, she lingered, doing the little things that were important but often forgotten.

"Who is she?" his mother asked the first night as Erika cleaned up the kitchen.

"She's my girlfriend." He'd never referred to Erika by a title because she was so much more than he could label.

"Did you ask her to come?"

He shook his head.

"She just showed up? Came all on her own?"

He nodded, his eyes wandering toward the kitchen.

"Why?"

"To be with me."

His mother pursed her lips, her eyes narrowing with curiosity.

At the funeral, she appeared unobtrusively, sitting in the back of the church and respecting his time of mourning with his family. At the cemetery, after the casket was lowered in the ground and everyone had gone, Brock needed to stay and watch his father put into the ground. He needed the closure. He'd been slowly preparing for the inevitable since his father's diagnosis, but he still had to come to terms with the reality of losing his parent. After a little while, Erika approached him, taking a seat next to him as the last corner of the casket was covered.

He took her hand, turning to her and piercing her with his wary gaze. "Will you marry me?"

She gulped, not at all expecting those words from him.

"Please."

She blinked hard, and he knew she was looking for the words to provide him a quick out when he came to his senses and realized what he'd done.

"I love you," he said. "I've never said it, but you know it. I've known it for a very long time."

She watched him, stunned.

"I know my faults, and I'm a very realistic person."

Her lips parted, but she remained speechless.

"I'm not good enough for you, but I can't be without you. I need you to marry me, because this world isn't tolerable without you."

Brock remembered the day as if it had happened yesterday, and Erika was now wearing the same shocked expression she'd worn then. So he repeated himself, making his intentions loud and clear. "I'm moving back in."

"No."

"No?" He cocked an eyebrow, fighting an angry outburst.

"No."

"I still live here. We're still married."

"You moved out. I filed for divorce."

"I pay the bills here. I'm not signing your divorce papers." His tone was harsh and menacing, but Erika didn't back down.

"Why do you want to come back now?"

"This is my home." He meant it in more than one way.

"You're going to fight with me over property when *you* walked out? Unbelievable, Brock."

"The house—"

"I don't care about the house." She cut him off, and she knew he hated that. She paused, then softened her voice. "Why did you leave in the first place?"

He'd avoided telling her for months. Now he was going to have the surgery, and she should know, but he looked into her soft brown eyes and couldn't take advantage of her compassion. She didn't deserve to be saddled with him and his sickness. He needed to leave, but he couldn't go. He loved her, although he didn't deserve her, and he couldn't imagine living without her in his life.

"I made a mistake," he said.

"Are you saying you want to *come home,* come home?"

"I'm not divorcing you."

"Why not?"

He tried to think of a reasonable answer but couldn't.

"You left me. You won't tell me why. You won't give me a divorce. You won't tell me why. This isn't you. You're a lot of things, but obstinate and difficult you're not. Why won't you tell me what's going on?"

"I'm not ready to consider divorce, that's all."

"Then what? We've been apart seven months. What do we do now? What do you want to happen?"

"Not divorce."

"What?"

I can't let you go.

He had to let her go.

He loved her too much to force her to watch him deteriorate. She'd feel obligated to stay with him and care for him. He couldn't ask her to sacrifice her life for him. He was supposed to protect her. Her happiness was his responsibility. She'd nurse him to the end, never complaining, but being miserable. He couldn't stand it if she looked at him with regrets.

His ringing cell phone gave him the reprieve he needed to pause and put the conversation back on track. "It's not me," he announced, sliding the phone back into his suit jacket.

Erika hesitated, but the incessant ring made her answer. He

watched her closely, checking her reaction when she saw the caller's identification on the screen.

"I can't talk now," she said. A few "um-hmm's" and she hung up the phone, finding it difficult to look him in the eye.

"The hospital?" he asked.

She shook her head.

"Is something wrong?"

"No."

He suspected he knew the caller, but he didn't ask right out. He penetrated her with a stern narrowing of his eyes. He wanted to snatch the phone and return the call, getting indisputable evidence that Erika had moved on and was seeing another man. He'd suspected it for months but hadn't been able to catch her outright.

"It sounded as if you were trying to be cryptic."

"We were in the middle of an important conversation. Should I not have taken the call?"

He studied his brilliant wife, who was answering without answering, and throwing the blame back at him. She was right, and he was wrong—on so many levels—and it made his blood boil.

"Who would be calling at this time of night?" he asked, not expecting an answer but wanting one.

"Are you screening my calls now?"

"Just wondering who's calling my wife."

"You gave up the right to question my calls when you walked out the door."

She couldn't have hurt him more if she'd hit him over the head with a pot.

"Who does have the right, Erika?"

Her cell rang again. This guy was impatient and possessive. Possessive of another man's wife. He felt his insides come to a slow boil while acid poured into his stomach. He was so mad his temples throbbed, and he felt he was going to do something very irrational.

"Yes?" Erika answered, a little irritated with the caller. "No. No, I can't talk now. I will. I will. I will."

I will? His wife making promises to another man? His vision turned green, and without thinking, he snatched the phone from Erika's ear. She managed to hang on long enough to push the button to end the call. He didn't know this model of phone as well as he knew his own, so it took him a minute to find the sequence of buttons to display the last caller's identification.

"What are you doing?" Erika snatched at the phone, but he wouldn't let it go.

"I want to know who's calling my wife." He pushed frantically at the buttons, desperate to identify the guy.

"You can't barge in here and run my life." With those harsh words, she caught him off guard and grabbed the phone away. "Brock, I can't do this with you."

He'd never come this close to laying an angry hand on her. He never pushed or shoved or snatched anything from her before, and his level of jealousy scared him. "I'm sorry," he apologized sincerely.

"I can't do any of this anymore. We've fallen apart, and I had no warning and still don't know why it happened." She was breathing hard, her chest heaving. "I don't want you to move back in."

"You can't stop me." Suddenly, he felt desperate not to lose her. His emotions were all over the place. He was completely out of control.

"No, I can't. So you go ahead and move back in." She pushed back from the table, standing and gripping the back of her chair. "You move back in, and I'll move out."

CHAPTER 5

"You look like hell," Ginnifer said. She was the buxom nurse-practitioner working with Erika at the internal medicine clinic. She'd been a find, and Erika knew she couldn't have handled the expanding volume of patients without her. Besides being an excellent employee, Ginnifer was a great friend. She lived an unconventional lifestyle, sharing a home with two lovers. She was smart and dynamic, and all the patients and staff loved her sense of humor. She had been the first shoulder Erika cried on when Brock walked out of their marriage.

"You look like hell," Ginnifer repeated. "And I've had to correct three of your orders this morning." She flopped down in Erika's office. "What's going on with you?"

"I didn't sleep much. Brock and I are fighting."

Ginnifer closed the door to Erika's office and then returned to her seat. "About what?"

"I filed for divorce."

"No kidding?"

"He didn't take it well."

"He left *you*."

"I know. He won't give me a divorce. And he wants to move back in."

"He wants to get back together?" Ginnifer was delighted, always having liked Brock.

"Not as far as I can tell. He just wants to live back at the house."

"That sounds crazy."

"The whole situation seems crazy to me, and I don't want to try to figure it out anymore."

Nothing was crazier than the day Erika came home and found Brock packing his bags. The action was so incongruent, it took her an extraordinary amount of time to process what was happening.

"Do you have a convention this month?"

"No," he answered, pointedly not looking at her.

"Has something happened to one of your brothers?"

"No."

"Why are you packing? Did I forget something on your schedule?"

He stopped fiddling with the suitcases, straightened his back, turned to her, and shattered her world. "I'm leaving you, Erika."

She laughed. "Stop playing around. Where are you going?" She moved down the private corridor connecting the master bedroom to the master bath. She stepped inside her walk-in closet, flipped on the light, and began removing her suit. Even today she remembered every silly action, the sound of the light switch, the indentations left in the carpet from Brock's shoes.

"Erika."

If she could have stayed in the closet and never, ever have turned around, she would have. She froze, recognizing the serious, unwavering tone of his voice. If she didn't look at him, it couldn't happen. He wouldn't leave.

"I'm sorry," he'd said, as if that explained it all.

"Why are you leaving?"

She heard his soft steps approach. "I have to."

"Is there someone else?" Her voice was even. If there was another woman, it made sense. Somewhere deep inside she hoped there was another woman. She couldn't stand thinking he'd leave her because she hadn't loved him enough. He was her world and everything in her life was about loving him.

"No," he answered softly, his voice full of compassion.

"You don't love me anymore?" Her voice cracked then because she couldn't stand it if he'd fallen out of love with her. She needed him to love her as much as she loved him.

Brock laid his hand softly on her shoulder. "I love you. I'll always love you." He tried to turn her to face him, but she wouldn't move. "I can't be married to you anymore."

"Did something happen? Did I do something wrong?"

"It's not you, it's me."

She wanted to smack him then. She deserved better than a cliché. "Then let's work on you. Let's make you better."

"I have to go now." He leaned in close and kissed her cheek from behind. His hand lingered on her shoulder for a moment before he turned away.

Erika remained in the closet for hours. She couldn't move. She couldn't speak. She was terrified of going back into their bedroom and finding Brock gone.

"Erika? Are you all right, Sugar?" Brock's mom was waving a hand in front of her tear-stained face. "I've been calling you for ten minutes. I've been standing here for five. Are you all right?"

"Brock?" Erika screamed, running from the closet. She dashed next door to his walk-in closet, frantically flipping on the light and counting his suits. If he didn't take his suits, he would be back.

"Erika?"

"Seven are missing."

"Seven what are missing?"

She dropped to her knees in a heap and cried for what seemed like another hour. Brock's mother held her, rocking her and trying to calm her enough to find out what was wrong.

"Mom, Brock left me."

His mother laughed.

"He's gone."

"Now, that's absurd." Disbelieving, she climbed to her feet and limped out of the closet. A little while later she returned to where she'd left Erika. "He's not answering his phone. We'll wait until he gets home. He'll clear this all up."

"He packed his bags."

"You must have misunderstood. You know he's always going to some conference or another. You got your signals crossed is all." She gathered Erika in her arms. "We'll just wait a little while and call him back so he can explain."

They waited hours, but Brock never answered his phone.

"We'll talk to him about this over breakfast," Mom said, sounding less sure as the hours rolled by.

They waited seven months of breakfasts, but Brock never cleared it up.

Brock's announcement last night was as sudden as his leaving seven months ago. He wanted to move back in, but he never said he wanted to put their marriage back together. He was clear divorce wasn't an option, but what was he offering? She reran the dinner scene over and over in her head, making it through the day on autopilot. It was no wonder she was distracted and made a mistake that could have caused her to be harmed.

It was a relief when the nurse announced her last patient of the day. Erika wanted to go home and take a hot bath before climbing into bed and hiding underneath the covers. She didn't know if she would find Brock at the house, which was another source of anxiety. She didn't think she could make it through another dinner with him. Her emotions were all over the place, hating him one moment, but still loving him all the others.

Danny had become her patient on his nineteenth birthday on referral from his pediatrician. A year later she suspected a new onset of schizophrenia and referred him for psychological testing. The last year had been hard for Danny, trying to weather the growing pains of being a teenager while finding a healthy balance of medications to control his behavior.

"He's out of control again," Danny's mother said when Erika entered the exam room.

"Tell me what's going on."

"Don't talk about me like I'm not here!" Danny jumped down from the exam table and began pacing the room, mumbling under his breath. He was disheveled, his clothing soiled and wrinkled. He smelled as if he hadn't washed in weeks. His overly long blond hair was stringy and matted. When Danny went into crisis mode, his appearance was always the first thing to go.

"Dr. Johnson is trying to help you, Danny." His mother looked haggard and scared. His father left soon after Danny was diagnosed, and she'd been carrying the entire parenting burden. "He's been seeing things again," she said to Erika.

Danny continued to pace, mumbling rapidly.

"Are you taking your medications?" Erika asked him.

He whirled on her. "Those medicines make me feel sleepy all the time. And I can't hear the warnings."

"What warnings?"

"God tells me when the evil angels are coming," he answered, his pacing becoming more rapid in the tiny exam room.

"We should talk about other things we can do to help you feel better," Erika offered.

"You want to put me away again. I'm not going back to that hellhole." He began yanking drawers open, disregarding his mother's frantic pleas to calm down. Finding what he wanted, he grabbed a scalpel and turned on Erika and his mother. "I'll kill you if you try to put me back in that place! There are too many evil angels there! The devil is waiting for me!"

The scene quickly became chaotic. Ginnifer overheard the disturbance from the exam room next door, astutely realizing she should call for help before she tried to intervene. Erika pulled Danny's mother into the corner, huddling together while a scalpel-wielding Danny blocked the door.

She tried to console the mother because her wailing only seemed to upset Danny more. Her attention was divided between the two as she scolded herself for being so distracted she'd been careless. She'd witnessed Danny's violent tendencies before—in the form of his mother's broken arm. She'd seen the signs in Danny before, knew how violent he could get, yet she'd allowed herself to be placed in a vulnerable position. There were methods of verbal deescalation, of talking him down that had worked in the past, but Erika's mind was so scattered, she couldn't recall any of them now.

Bradley was the first security officer through the exam room door. He was a hawking man with an intimidating physique and a heart of gold. A retired police officer, he'd had to take early retirement because of a nasty excessive force lawsuit. He was older now, but still in good shape. A handsome man with a thick beard he used to hide his age lines, he was sweet on Ginnifer.

Bradley crashed into the room, striking Danny with the door and putting him off balance enough to wrestle the scalpel away. Once Bradley had the weapon, three more officers crashed in, subduing Danny. Danny fought with the strength of ten men while shouting curses at his mother for condemning him to the wrath of the evil angels. They handcuffed him because they had no other way to control him. He was wiry and strong, completely possessed by an irrational need to escape in order to save his life. As the three officers pinned him to the floor, Bradley called for another officer to bring a stretcher so Danny could be transported to the emergency room in the main building of the hospital.

"Everyone okay?" Bradley asked, his eyes trained on Ginnifer.

"We're good. Thanks for getting here so fast." Ginnifer joined Erika in picking Danny's mother up from the floor.

"I'm so sorry, Dr. Johnson. He's such a handful. I try to make sure he takes his medicine, but—"

"It's okay," Erika assured her. "You have a lot to deal with."

"They'll keep him?" she asked, referring to the inpatient psych unit.

"You'll have to fill out the papers."

Danny's voice rose over every noise in the room, shouting colorful curse words at his mother, threatening her if she had him committed again. Seeing how distraught it all made her, Erika ushered his mother out of the tiny exam room, leaving Ginnifer to work everything out with security.

"I saw security running for your office. Are you all right?" Mark rushed up to her.

"We're all okay," Erika answered, hoping his concern didn't appear too focused on her. No one knew they were dating, and she wanted to keep it that way for now. Things were complicated enough with Brock to add her relationship with Mark to the mix.

"My receptionist thought—" He exhaled deeply. "I'm glad no one is hurt."

Erika handed Danny's mother over to the clinic nurse, who hauled her away to meet with the psychiatric staff.

"I have a situation here," Erika told Mark.

"Yeah, right. I'll let you get things under control." He peered over her shoulder in the direction of Danny's loud protests.

Ginnifer appeared, ushering the last patients of the day back into their exam rooms. The ruckus had them peeking out of their rooms. The security officers' radios were squawking, heightening the scene.

"It's crazy," Erika told Mark. "I'll explain later."

He dropped his voice. "You're okay?"

"I'm fine." Still a little shaky, she offered a weak smile. "Really. Don't worry."

He watched her, reluctant to go until the scene had been cleaned up.

Two security officers burst through the door of the clinic, pulling a stretcher along with them. They made a racket, hitting furniture as they navigated through her waiting room. The room was filled with tables and chairs and other comforts. It wasn't designed for driving stretchers with uncooperative wheels through it. It wasn't until Erika and Mark started moving the chairs out of the way that she noticed Brock standing near the door.

"I'm glad you all are all right," Mark said, immediately going into concerned colleague mode. "I'd better get back to my patients." He left, acknowledging Brock with a small nod.

Brock stepped up to her. In the middle of all the bedlam, he made the chaos go quiet. His controlled presence brought calm, helping her to manage her emotions. Immaculately dressed as usual in dark blue slacks, off-white shirt, blue tie, and crisp lab coat, he loomed over her, wearing an expression of curiosity and concern. Watching the rough treatment necessary to get Danny controlled made her heart break.

"Security told me about the call," he said evenly. "Did he hurt you?"

"No."

"Danny again?"

"He stopped his meds. His mother brought him in."

"Erika," he breathed. He had told her to transfer Danny to another physician. One who could physically handle him when he became violent.

"I should get back. Security will need help getting him to emergency."

"And you're going to lift him?" Brock raised a brow.

"I want to medicate him so he'll calm down."

"You're shaking." He gripped her shoulders, letting his hands cascade slowly down her arms. The gesture relaxed her, despite the noises projecting from the back of the clinic.

"He's scared."

Brock watched her, his eyes going soft behind the gold rims of his glasses. His shoulders shifted as he exhaled. He knew how much she cared for her patients, and Danny's erratic behavior didn't change her feelings. "C'mon, I'll help hold him while you give him the injection."

CHAPTER 6

Brock sat in his Zephyr outside the nondescript building he knew was Michigan Cryogenics. He'd cancelled his other appointment, so this was his last chance to collect his sperm before he started radiation therapy. The risk of genetic defects and sterility made his visit a necessity. He struggled with indecision right now, but he had to secure the future possibility of having kids—if he could get Erika back, she'd want to know their dream of a family was still alive.

He'd been able to delay his first radiation treatment by pointing out to Hassan he had to undergo genetic counseling before he stored his sperm. His father had died of testicular cancer, and now he had the diagnosis. If it was inherited, he could pass it on to his kids—if he ever had children.

The genetic counseling had been inconclusive, finding he was at higher risk than the general population, as would be his children, at getting cancer. Without the ability to test his father, the counselor couldn't be more specific. As a physician, he wasn't a genetic specialist, but he'd known the basics, and he knew he needed his father alive for the testing to be conclusive. In a way, the counseling sessions had been a stalling tactic. The surgery was inevitable, but the idea of it was surreal. Even knowing his inherited risk, he'd never really believed he'd get the disease and have to get half of his manhood removed.

This would be his first visit over the next two weeks. He needed to store at least five ejaculates to increase his odds of success, because of the inconsistencies of a woman's ovulation cycle. Between gathering samples he had to remain abstinent for forty-eight hours. Abstaining was the easiest part of the whole ordeal. He'd been celibate for seven months, not once desiring another woman since leaving Erika. His gut tightened as an unwanted thought entered his brain—he wondered if his wife had practiced abstinence with the eye doctor.

Involuntary sterilization. Brock had stared at the words for hours after scheduling his first radiation treatment. The removal of his right testicle would leave him with one functioning testicle, but radiation therapy could cause temporary or permanent sterilization—he wouldn't know which, if either, would happen to him until after his treatment. He had to forget his embarrassment and his pride, and do this for Erika. Hadn't they talked about starting a family as soon as her practice was more stable? When his mother was settled and fully recovered from her hip surgery? They wanted two kids, maybe three, and had planned to raise them with old-fashioned values and grand ambitions.

The first time they'd discussed having kids was on their honeymoon. "You're beautiful," he'd told her. They were lying in bed nude, enjoying the sensation of bare skin to bare skin as he held her against his chest. "I want a daughter with your expressive eyes."

"And your determination and strength," she added. "We'll have two."

"The oldest must be a boy," he added, watching curiously as her petite frame slipped down the length of his body.

"Who is his father in every way."

A fissure of pride ripped through his heart. All machismo was gone when he was alone and intimate with Erika. It was about soaking up her compassion, reeling in the love she offered so freely. He fought to hold his composure as he drowned in unfamiliar emotions, while Erika, who enjoyed giving love as much as she enjoyed receiving it, was in a playfully giddy mood.

She gathered pineapple rings off the abandoned dinner tray with her fingers. "When should we get started?" she asked.

He folded his arms beneath his head, his eyes on the ceiling as he dreamed of their future. "We should get you settled in your practice first."

"We did get married suddenly." She giggled with happiness.

"You don't regret it, do you?" He held his breath as he waited for an answer. He'd known Erika was a perfect fit for him from the first time they'd had a conversation, but this was the first time he doubted his value to her. Hurting her, disappointing her would crush him.

"Hell, no."

It was the first and last time he'd ever heard her curse. He smiled at how awkward the word sounded coming from her, a woman with such a sweet disposition just entering a room made preexisting tension dissipate.

Something tightened around his penis. "What are you doing?" His head bobbed up to see her forcing the pineapple rings down the shaft, each breaking open enough to fit, releasing cold juices. She glanced at him with those soulful eyes, her smile replaced by something more primal, and he almost exploded at the intensity of it.

He became bone-hard instantly, stretching the fruit with his girth. The juice from the pineapples poured down his penis, pooling at his balls. Erika washed the sticky mess with her tongue. She took her time, angling her head and slowly eating away each pineapple ring. The scene was erotic, hot, and dangerous because it sent his mind to places it had never been, and he became desperate to release the tension riding him. His scrotum tightened, his penis throbbed, but Erika continued on with painful precision, ignoring his anxiety.

She ate at him with tiny nibbles, alternated with big bites, always coming close, but not quite putting her mouth on him. His fingers burrowed in the pillows, fighting the urge to grab her hair and drag her mouth to his penis, forcing the whole length of it down her throat. She unraveled him, unleashing every sexual fantasy he'd ever had. Pineapples would never be served the same again.

Finally, every ring was gone. She leaned up from his thigh just enough for him to watch her drag the back of her hand across her mouth. His restraint shredded into tiny pieces just as she lowered her head and sank her mouth down on him, letting her tongue guide the way. She tried to swallow the length of him, but she was still new at having him in her mouth, and it proved too much for her. She applied suction, hallowing her cheeks as she moved upward off his penis. When she reached the throbbing bulb, she released him with a smack of her lips, and he spewed like a geyser.

Now, a surge of guilt threatened to make him pull out of the parking lot. Here he was planning for a future with Erika when he had destroyed any chance of it happening. He'd left her because it was the right thing to do. If he was confused on that point, just sitting in the parking lot of a sperm bank should clear his head. He was sick, and even if he beat the cancer, there would be lingering effects.

He should leave her. Leave Erika to find the happiness she deserved. With someone else. *Like Mark Garing?* The thought made him flush with anger. He'd suspected it, and he'd all but proved it when he walked into her office a couple of days ago and found Mark there, comforting her when her patient had all but attacked her.

To an outsider, it looked innocent enough, a colleague coming to check out the commotion and maybe assist if he could. Camaraderie between the physicians at Mission Hospital. *Yeah, right.* He'd seen the way Mark looked at his wife. He recognized the admiration and desire for Erika—he felt it himself. Mark wanted his wife, but he would not get her.

Brock left his car, mindlessly hitting the button to lock the doors and arm the alarm. Frozen sperm had been shown to produce pregnancies for fifty years after donation. It could be stored indefinitely. With the way things were between him and Erika, he needed to know this clock wasn't ticking against him.

Armed with his physical assessment, verifying he was free from AIDS, HIV, gonorrhea, hepatitis, and syphilis, Brock entered the clinic. He handed over all the paperwork Hassan had completed and took a seat in an elegantly decorated waiting room. Sitting alone in the waiting area, he had second thoughts. The other patrons were paired by two, probably married couples seeking an alternative, looking for hope when all else had failed. They were so in love, so desperate, they were willing to raise a child half theirs. Doubts assaulted him again, and he rose to leave, but a nurse with a warm smile called his name, pulling him into the back before he could escape.

The consultation took place in a medicinal office with the nurse asking blunt questions in a professional tone. He'd always marveled at the way the nurses at the hospital could tackle the most controversial subject with patients without hesitation, while he and his colleagues hedged and vacillated before reaching the point.

"We like to run all the required tests here," the nurse said as she reviewed his paperwork.

"The director made prior arrangements with my doctor,

because of the press for time. This entire process had to be completed before my surgery."

"Surgery?"

He struggled with telling a stranger he was having one of his testicles removed. He couldn't say the words aloud. Instead, he pointed to the place in his paperwork where she could find the answer.

"I'm sorry," she said, her eyes revealing she truly meant it.

He saw Erika's face, devastated by his diagnosis and what his future would become.

"I see you've completed the mandatory counseling session, but our social workers are always available if you'd like to discuss this before beginning the process."

He could only imagine what expression he was wearing to make her offer additional counseling sessions. "No, thank you." He had to do it today, because he'd never gather the resolve to return if he walked away now. This was for Erika and their future. He had no room for hesitation.

After collecting a urine specimen for further testing of sexually transmitted diseases, he was given a short tour of the facility. He learned how his sperm would be frozen, labeled, stored, and monitored twenty-four hours a day. Finally, he was escorted to a private donor room on the other side of the facility. He was left alone with a sterile cup, a stack of magazines, and a television with plenty of XXX movies.

"Take as much time as needed," the nurse said, closing the door on him.

He locked the door and then dropped on the sofa, cup in hand. Just knowing the nurse was waiting for him to masturbate into the cup was enough to keep him limp. Ten percent of his sperm would die during freezing—he couldn't waste a drop, which added more pressure. It was all so medicinal. His sperm would be analyzed, and he could call in the morning for the results of how well his sperm swam. A cryopreservative would be added; then his sperm would be separated into vials and frozen in liquid nitrogen. He couldn't even think of what Erika would have to go through to be inseminated. He'd always pictured his wife getting pregnant with his child after they'd made love. Not this way with doctors and nurses providing the only skin-to-skin contact during the inception.

This venture was costing him a nice sum of money. There were fees associated with every step of the process, not to mention the monthly storage fee and withdrawal fees—if he ever needed to use it. He hadn't been able to drink for two days prior to banking, but he sure as hell was heading directly to his favorite bar afterward.

He flipped through a magazine, turning the pages in bunches. He had no interest in these women. They were too perfect, which made them phony-looking. He selected the first video in the stack, finding the scenes humorous and not at all arousing. If he couldn't provide a sample, he'd have to resort to a seminal collection device to force the sperm out of him.

He was too stressed. Stressed over his marriage, his medical condition, and knowing the nurse was outside the door waiting for him to jack off.

"This is for Erika," he said, closing his eyes on the television screen. He relaxed back into the sofa, stretching his long legs out in front of him and thinking of the pineapples again.

On their honeymoon in the Pocono Mountains, Erika had slid down the length of his body, her hands caressing his back, his ass, his legs, until she kneeled on the floor in front of him. She looked up at him with those big brown eyes as if she were asking permission to take him inside her mouth—and it had been the biggest turn-on of his life. Even now as he remembered her naked on her knees, his penis stirred to life. He unzipped his pants and took himself in hand, remembering lubrication and saliva was a no-no when obtaining a clean sample. This would have to be a rough ride.

Although she'd done it a few times, he could tell Erika wasn't comfortable with fellatio. He didn't press the issue, knowing she'd probably come around, but realizing it didn't make a difference in how much he loved her. But their honeymoon was different. Fresh from the shower, after making love twice, he'd been prepared to climb into bed and hold her tight until morning.

He watched with fascination as she blinked, waiting for him to begin, when she had taken the role of aggressor. She lifted his penis and placed it gently against her lips, leaning in when her lips parted. She played with him first, touching and stroking with only the tip between her lips. Then she lightly licked his crown, like tasting a candy sucker—similar to the way his thumb brushed the blooming head now.

She took in only an inch or two at first, sampling the feel of him rubbing across her tongue. Her hands encircled his shaft and, together with her tongue, made a slow, steady rhythm. He tried to recreate it now as he stroked his penis, slowly, up and down, with only his palms touching the sensitive skin.

Erika took another two inches, using her tongue to circle the head. She'd been holding out on him—or practicing. He didn't care which. He was only happy he'd married her. She kept giving him reasons, and seeing her on her knees, watching her take his penis inside her mouth was one of the best. He mimicked her actions now, remembering every detail of their first married night together.

She worked him, quickly learning how much power she had over his pleasure. She took him as deep as she could, struggling with her gag reflex, and never realizing how much it excited him to see her fighting to get him all inside. She pulled back to the tip, lavishing it with her tongue while she watched him with the deep brown eyes.

His penis began to pulse—then and now—and he pumped uncontrollably—then and now. It had freaked her out a bit and she started to pull her mouth away, but he couldn't let her. His fingers tangled through her hair, bringing her back down his shaft. She picked up the pulse throbbing up and down his penis, and chased it with the tip of her tongue.

His legs had started to buckle. The muscles of his thighs were quivering now, and he increased the speed of his stroke, using both hands—one to apply pressure, one to pump him.

Erika sensed the nearness of his climax. She pulled away, taking the heat of her mouth with her. She looked up at him and asked, "What would you like to do to me next?"

He exploded—now. Back then he had pushed her onto the carpet and sank his penis deep into her until she placed her hands on his shoulders and told him to slow down. He was barely able to separate reality from the past, but he grabbed the sterile cup in time to place it beneath the arch of his sperm.

Brock wasn't about to evict Erika from their home. She'd threatened to leave if he moved back, so he stayed in the dingy apartment on the hospital grounds. But that didn't stop him from going back to the house every chance he got. He couldn't shake the way Mark had been looking at her, and he wanted to find out exactly what it meant.

"Ma, we have to go or you'll be late for your therapy appointment." Brock waited impatiently at the bottom of the stairs for his mother to come down. She insisted on using the stairs, ignoring the elevator he'd had installed in the back of the house for her usage when she refused to take their downstairs master bedroom suite.

"I'm coming."

He watched in amazement as his mother descended the stairs. She was dressed in a gray jogging suit, but her face was all made up, and her hair had been done too. There was less gray and more curls.

"Close your mouth, son."

"Why are you dressed up for therapy? I thought you hated PT."

"I do. So I might as well dress my best for it. It makes me feel better."

It didn't take long to figure out why his mother had obtained a sudden love of going to therapy. His name was Titus, and he was the therapist's assistant. He appeared to be around his mother's age—60, maybe—and he also appeared to have a thing for women five years his senior. Brock watched from the sideline, quietly observing the ratio of talking and flirting to working out. A couple of times he'd started to cross the room when Titus found it necessary to work out his mother's muscles.

He watched the show, reserving his objections until he could speak to Erika about it. She'd gotten possession of the house and his mother when he'd moved out. Surely, he could hold her responsible for his mother's flirtatious behavior. He wanted his mother to have a full life, but not with a man neither of them knew anything about. He couldn't wait to get his mother home, narrowly following the speed limit. When they arrived, Erika was in the kitchen cooking dinner. His mother practically bounced up the stairs to her bedroom with her bum hip, limp and all.

"You didn't tell me the assistant therapist has a thing for my mom," Brock said, leaning against the kitchen counter.

"What?" she asked, amused.

"Older guy with graying temples, wears his pants too loose and his shirts too tight." The older man actually had a solid build for someone his age.

She smiled at him and he thought it was genuine. "Are you upset? Your mother is entitled to have a personal life. It's kinda cute."

"What do we know about this man? And what do we know about what's going on between them?"

"This is the first I've heard about it."

"Can you talk to her about it?"

She realized his seriousness. "I'll talk to her, but I won't pry into her business."

He crossed his arms over his chest. "I wouldn't want something going on with them right up under my nose and not know about it until it was too late."

She glanced at him, and reading him correctly, she turned her focus back to the stove.

"Men like to take advantage of a woman if he feels she's vulnerable," he pressed. "Especially if the woman is lonely."

"I'll look out for your mother."

"How's Danny doing?" He switched the subject quickly, wanting her to make the connection.

She filled him in on the young man's progress. "He'll be an inpatient for at least thirty days."

"You must have been scared. Was that the new ophthalmologist in your office?"

"Dr. Garing."

"You didn't introduce us."

"It was crazy." She answered him coolly, giving him no hint of emotion, which was odd for a woman as expressive as Erika. The vigorous way she stirred the bubbling pot told him she was nervous.

"What was he doing there? Is Danny his client too?"

"No." She turned away, checking something in the oven. "He heard all the noise and came to see what was going on. Like you did."

"Bradley called me because you're my wife. Why did he come?"

"I guess he came to help."

"He didn't say?"

She shook her head, her back still to him.

"You were talking when I came in."

"Maybe he did say. There was so much confusion."

"Yeah." He watched her move across the kitchen, checking pots and avoiding his gaze. "Mark Garing, he knows you're married, right?"

"What?" She laughed nervously.

"Does he know you're married?"

"He knows."

And now I know the character of the man I'm dealing with. "Does he hang around your clinic a lot?"

"What? No. What's with all the questions about Mark?"

"I like to know what's going on in my wife's life." He glared at her, searching for any evidence to confirm his suspicions. "I don't want this situation to become more complicated."

"Complicated how?"

"Any other woman might see seven months as a long time to be apart from her husband. She might not be as strong as you are. She might be vulnerable enough to let an opportunistic man work his way into the middle of her marriage."

She turned to him, putting down the cooking utensils and focusing her attention on him. "Any other husband might not leave his wife in limbo for seven months. He might make a decision and let her move on with her life . . . no matter what direction it would take her in."

"Well, it's a good thing we're not those people."

CHAPTER 7

"I can't see you anymore, Mark."

"Wait." He shook his head, clearing his confusion. "What's going on?"

"Brock knows about us. I don't know how he found out, but he knows."

"Good, he knows. Now he'll give you the divorce."

They were sitting together in the living room of his simple but luxurious condo, surrounded by browns and blacks. His furniture was overstuffed and comfortable, made for the consummate sports watcher, and Mark loved them all, finding his glory living in a lively sports town like Detroit where every sporting event from kid's soccer to the NFL was celebrated daily. They were drinking wine under soft lights, and Erika had known as soon as she arrived he was a man with things on his mind, ready to take their relationship to the next level even if she was hesitant.

"He's still not signing the divorce papers. He wants to move back in."

"He wants you back?"

She shook her head, not answering because she wasn't certain what Brock wanted.

He refilled her glass before his own. "He's playing games with you. The man walks out without any explanation and he thinks he can come back without one. Tell him he's right about us and divorce his ass. Take him to court and sue the bastard. Whatever you have to do to get rid of him."

His light features grew dark, and she felt dwarfed by his height, which matched her own, but projected on a larger scale representing his anger. She watched him above the rim of her glass, surprised by his hostility. He'd always been gentle and kind, never speaking negatively of anyone. This sudden flare of aggression made her uneasy. She wondered if she really knew him. After what Brock had done—leaving her without warning or apparent cause—she began to doubt her ability to read people, which left her vulnerable to the world's mercy.

"I can't sue Brock," she told Mark.

"Why not?"

"It's too complicated with us all working together and his mother living at the house. It would get messy, possibly affecting all of us." She paused, taking a sip of her wine for courage. "And seeing you makes it more complicated. We all work under the supervision of the same medical director. If Brock tells anyone we're seeing each other while I'm still married, I don't know what the repercussions will be."

"Brock is too arrogant to tell anyone his wife is moving on without his approval."

"You don't know him well enough to criticize him."

"I know his kind. He didn't know what a good woman he had until he lost you. Now he sees how much I appreciate you and he wants you back. Don't fall for it." He set his glass down on the coffee table with a thud. "Are you defending what he did to you now?"

"No."

"It sounds as if you are." His anger flashed again, his features hardening as he struggled to keep his fists open, exercising his fingers until he was able to calm himself.

"I can't defend Brock because I don't know why he did what he did. I'd never feel leaving without a reason is the right thing to do to anyone you're in a relationship with—especially your wife. I wouldn't be having this conversation with you if I believed otherwise."

The caring Mark she'd grown fond of returned. "You're protecting me?"

"I'm looking out for both of us. Seeing each other is too risky right now. You've been at Mission Hospital less than a year. Five years into practice, I'm still considered a new doctor by many of the physicians at the hospital. I don't want to lose my clinic because I couldn't separate it from my personal life."

He quietly contemplated what was at stake.

"Brock's mother still lives with me, so it's not like I can have you over for dinner. And I have to settle this with him—find out why he won't give me a divorce. I'm sorry, Mark, it's just too much going on right now for me to start another relationship. It isn't fair to you."

"I was the one holding you when he left you hurt and confused."

"I won't ever forget it."

He leaned forward, resting his elbows on his knees. "I won't let you do it, Erika. We can back off a little and be more discreet, if you want. But I won't stop seeing you because Brock is making waves. He was bound to find out about us, and now he has. He walked away when things got rough. I'm not going anywhere."

Erika was shooting her best game of golf ever, but she wasn't enjoying one minute of it. She'd decided to hit the greens early with a six-o'clock tee time. She planned to concentrate on her swing and gain a few yards. The weather was sunny and warm, and she lavished in the scenery provided by the lush pine trees and pristine greens. The course was over 5,000 yards of beautiful rolling hills and tree-lined drives. She managed to avoid all the sand traps and water pitfalls, even the infamous ninth-hole pond. She was taking it slow, allowing two other groups to play through.

She had tried to get Brock interested in the sport when they first started dating, but he didn't take to it. His height made swinging awkward, even with the extended clubs. He was a racketball man. He worked out his frustrations on the court, hitting the ball as hard as he could, running up and down until he was drenched with sweat. She appreciated what the sport did for his body, making it hard and well-toned, but she couldn't keep up with the pace. They'd agreed they would not share their hobbies.

The one time they'd played together, the ball ricocheted off the wall with the force of a rocket, striking her in the knee and leaving her hobbling for a week. It was her earliest memory of Brock's tenderness. His handsome features were always knotted in a scowl, causing most to scurry away when they saw him coming. The first time she'd seen him, she'd glimpsed the sensitivity he closely guarded, but he didn't expose his true nature easily. When the ball smacked her, her knee buckled and she went down on the court. She heard his racket hit the floor a second after he arrived at her side. He lifted her in his arms, carrying her to the car and driving her to the nearest Urgent Care Center. With them both being physicians, the exam was unnecessary, but he was so worried—pacing the waiting room and asking the nurse every five minutes how long it would be before she was seen by the doctor—she didn't argue about seeking medical help. He couldn't apologize enough, or do enough to make it up to her. He lavished her with attention, stopping by her place every day after work to feed her and make sure she had everything she needed.

She witnessed his softer side, and she needed that man to reappear long enough to explain what was going on in her marriage.

"How'd you do?" Ginnifer asked when she joined Erika for lunch.

She'd introduced Ginnifer to the sport during a conference held at a PGA golf course resort. Ginnifer had taken to it immediately but was impatient with learning the nuances. She played for fun, not at the professional level Erika enjoyed. Regardless, they met at the private course once a week during the warm months for nine holes of golf and lunch at the clubhouse.

"Came in under par without a handicap."

"And you look cute as hell too. Bravo."

"Couldn't get out of bed this morning?"

"Frick nor Frack wanted to let this warm body go." She grinned, shimmying her chest.

"You're outrageous."

She shrugged, pausing to sip her raspberry iced tea. "Bradley came on to me again, thank you very much."

"Me? I didn't encourage him."

"You got stuck in the room with a schizophrenic waving a scalpel around. You know he must have loved getting the call. Can you imagine his face?"

Ginnifer had ordered their usual—turkey on rye with side salads and raspberry iced tea—so it didn't take long for their order to arrive.

"So why don't you give up Frick and Frack and go out with Bradley? Settle down and have some kids."

"Kids! Are you joking? Can you see me with kids? *Honey, go ask one of your daddies to fix the leaky sink.* Please."

"You're worse than a polygamist, you know." Erika couldn't imagine sleeping with more than one man at the same time. She and Brock hadn't been intimate in seven months, and she still hadn't been able to sleep with Mark. She had to be certain it was over with her husband before she invested her heart or gave her body to another man.

"You're worse than a nun. When are you going to get back out there? You've served Brock papers—and don't think I didn't see him come running the other day—so start dating again."

Erika had tried to explain her one-man-at-a-time philosophy to Ginnifer before, but she received only a blank stare of confusion in return for her hard work. She didn't bother to try again. "I thought you were cheering for Brock and I to get back together."

"I am, but it doesn't mean you can't have a little fun while you're waiting for it to happen. Do you think he's been celibate?"

"He has," she answered too quickly. She couldn't let her mind begin to imagine Brock giving his body to another woman. It would be the thing to break her resolve and send her hurdling over the edge of sanity. She'd managed to weather the past seven months, with the help of her friends, but she couldn't stand it to find out this had all been about Brock's desire for another woman.

"How do you know?"

"I know. If he'd been with another woman, I'd know."

Ginnifer studied her determination and wisely left the subject alone. "As a matter of fact, Mark came running too," she said, watching Erika carefully. "They're both really handsome. Maybe you should have some Frick and Frack in your life."

She laughed, breaking the tension. It felt good to be out

with Ginnifer, joking and having a good time. "I can't handle Frick right now. Frick and Frack together would kill me. I'm not a threesome kind of girl." She swallowed a bite of her sandwich before she spoke again. "I don't know how you juggle Rhon and Will."

"I was honest with them from the beginning. That's key. Will is younger and he can get a bit jealous if Rhon and I are too loud. He's the one who came up with the schedule. Sunday, Monday, and Tuesday are Rhon's. The beginning of the week is most hectic and stressful for me and he's older, more laid-back. Wednesday, Thursday, and Friday belong to Will. By the middle of the week I need some excitement, and it doesn't conflict with his school schedule. Saturdays they share me."

"Which is why you couldn't get out of bed this morning."

She shrugged. "Rhon's day starts at nine."

"I don't know how you do it."

"It's not easy living with two men. Imagine having two Brocks at home."

"Right now I'd settle for having one."

"What?"

She'd spoken without thinking.

"You want Brock back?" Ginnifer asked, glowing with hope.

"I never wanted him to leave."

"Yeah, but do you want him back?"

She swished her iced tea around in the glass, trying to find the correct answer. "I don't understand what's going on with him. He just up and left, but he won't give me a divorce. It doesn't make sense."

"Forget what Brock wants. What do you want?"

She closed her eyes and dropped her head back, exhaling deeply. "I don't know. I still love him, but he left me. I can't just forget what he did." She hesitated, looking at her friend.

"What aren't you telling me?"

"I've been seeing someone."

"You never said a word! And you let me go on about getting a Frick and Frack when you're already well on your way. Who is he?"

Erika leaned in, lowering her voice. "Mark Garing."

"Umm-hmm. I thought he was a little too nice to the staff, bringing donuts all the time. The nurses think he's undercover, but I knew better."

"They think he's gay?"

"Yee-aah." She cocked her head as if asking why Erika hadn't noticed.

"He's not."

"Oooh, tell."

"We haven't slept together. I can't be with another man until everything is settled between me and Brock."

"Back to Brock. You didn't answer my question. Do you want him back?"

"I don't know. Some days I miss him so much I can't stop crying. Other days, I hate him for breaking my heart. I just don't know."

"But you filed for divorce."

"One of us had to do something. We can't be married but not together forever."

"So you did it to get a reaction out of him?"

"No, when I served him, I really believed I wanted out."

"What happened between then and now?"

She thought back to their interaction outside of the ICU. Him kissing her in public had been so uncharacteristic, she'd analyzed it to death. She knew Brock, and she knew he was hiding something. He had kissed her innocently enough on her cheek, but it felt different. It felt as if he were being forced to say good-bye when he never wanted to leave her.

"So what was it?" Ginnifer asked again.

"There's something going on with him. I don't know what it is, but there's something wrong. Maybe if I knew what it was, and could assure myself he's not in any danger, I could walk away and put an end to this for both of our sakes."

"Then you know what you need to do?"

"Yes, find out."

CHAPTER 8

"Stay away from my wife." Brock had carefully contemplated the repercussions of confronting Mark, and he decided he didn't give a damn. He'd completed his five visits to the sperm bank and his surgery was two days away. He wanted his house in order before going into the hospital. He wouldn't be able to pop into Erika's clinic then, and he needed to know Dr. Garing was keeping his distance and staying in his own office down the hall.

Mark moved around Brock to close the door to his office. It was the end of the day, but the receptionist still lingered in the outer office, readying things for the next day's work. Mark returned to his desk, relaxing back in his chair and making a steeple out of his fingers.

Brock wanted to break them off—one at a time. "Stay away from my wife."

"I heard you the first time. I'm trying to figure out who your wife is. Could it be the woman you dumped without explaining why? Is it the woman I've been comforting the past seven months while she tried to work through her confusion? Or is it the woman I've been dating for four months, trying to help her piece her emotions back together?"

Brock couldn't argue his wrongs, but he didn't like another

man being this familiar with his wife. "Stay away from her. Stay out of my way."

"Why? Have you decided you aren't through with her yet?"

"This is between me and Erika. If you don't get out of the way, you'll be hurt. I'll see to it."

"And you think threatening me will get Erika back? She cares about me. How could coming here help you?"

Did Erika really care about Mark? The possibility made Brock's stomach tighten. Could she have put her feelings for him aside and fallen for another man? He never thought Erika capable of dismissing their relationship as if it never meant anything, but he never expected her to file for divorce either.

"Let's handle this man-to-man," Mark said. "You left her. I would never leave her. You move out of *my* way."

"Erika and I aren't done."

Mark sprung from his chair, showing his first real hint of anger. "You can't run back to her because you don't want another man to have her. You don't know how to treat her. Get the hell out of her life and stop hurting her. Can't you see what you're doing?"

"Don't talk to me about my wife like you know her better than I do."

"Don't you be so cavalier, you arrogant son of a bitch," Mark shouted. "I'm building something with Erika because I care about her. You run up in my office threatening me like a pitbull fighting for a piece of meat. Erika is more than that. *Erika is everything.* But she's not a prize in some contest you're trying to win. Not once have you mentioned being in love with her." His eyes narrowed and he pounded his fists on the desktop. "*You* stay the hell away from her, or *I'll* hurt *you*. Believe that."

Brock didn't walk away because Mark scared him. He left Mark's office without another word because he hadn't realized another man was in love with his wife, and it shocked him. A crush, maybe some casual dating, okay, but he hadn't suspected Mark loved Erika. Erika might not know it, hell, Mark may not know it, but Brock saw it written all over the man's face.

Brock learned something else during his visit. Mark's vicious response went beyond his threat or his shouting. Brock was a man and he knew men. And he knew his wife. Erika wouldn't be involved with such a volatile man . . . Mark hadn't showed her this side of himself.

Erika is everything.

"Everything," Brock repeated, knowing it to be true. He gripped the steering wheel, driving a little too fast to the house he'd once shared with Erika. He knew what he had to do, and no matter what the consequences, he would.

He didn't use his key. He parked his Lincoln in the garage next to Erika's car, testing the temperature of the hood. She hadn't driven for a while—the engine was cool. He rang the doorbell, praying his mother would be asleep at ten at night.

"Brock?" Erika was dressed for bed, with the robe he'd given her two anniversaries ago cinched at her waist and her hair wrapped tight beneath a scarf.

"I need to talk to you."

"Now?" She looked up at him and saw something that didn't make her wait for an answer before opening the door to him.

They walked through the foyer into the great room, but it was open to upstairs where his mother slept in one of the three upper-level bedrooms.

"Can we go somewhere more private?"

She eyed him strangely but led him into their bedroom. She took a seat in the sitting area. He stood over her, too nervous to sit down.

"What's going on, Brock?" she asked just as her cell phone rang.

"Don't answer it."

"It could be important. I'm on call."

"It's not about a patient."

"How do you know?"

"It's Mark Garing." He knew it was Mark, because if he'd been Mark, he would have called and warned her about her crazy husband barging into his office this afternoon.

Her face dropped with guilt.

"I went to his office today."

She ignored his directive and crossed the room to answer her phone. She held an uneasy, cryptic conversation. After assuring Mark she was fine, she rushed him off the phone, promising to call later. If there was any way he could stop her, she'd never make that call.

"He's a friend," Erika said.

"I know what he is. Are you in love with him?"

"With Mark? No."

"Tell me the truth."

"I don't lie to you."

He squared his shoulders, ready to do what he'd come for. "Do you love me?"

Her face contorted in confusion. "Is this because I asked for a divorce?"

"Do you love me, Erika?"

"You have no right to question me. You left me."

"Do you want a divorce? Even if I don't?"

She looked beaten and weary. "What's going on with you? I know something is wrong. You wouldn't have just up and left without a reason. Talk to me."

"I don't want a divorce," he admitted.

"You've said that before. You haven't told me what you do want."

He wanted her. God, he wanted her more than anything. His entire reason for coming was selfish, but he loved her too much to care about his motives. He'd come for two reasons: to keep her from divorcing him, and to make sure she'd never leave him.

"I love you. I just can't be with you now."

"What are you talking about?" Anger made her nostrils flare. "Why did you come here tonight? Did you do something to Mark?"

He cursed, hating her concern for another man.

"No divorce," he ground out.

She turned the curse word on him. "You're making me crazy! You know what? I don't care what you want anymore." She charged to her dresser, yanking the drawer open so hard it fell off track and hit the floor. She dropped to her knees, fury fueling her as she tossed the contents around the room. She snatched up the glossy black packet and rushed at him with it. "You're going to sign these papers right now! No more of this, Brock. I'm tired. I'm tired of trying to figure you out. I'm tried of worrying about what you want." Her shouts became a choking sob. "I'm tired of trying to love you."

He grabbed her up in a bear hug, his size no match for her struggles. He held her tight, letting her strike him until she exhausted herself. When she was done, and had melted into a limp mass, he picked her up and carried her to the bed. He wiped her tears away, kissing her gently as he removed the scarf from her head and combed out her locks with his fingers. He peeled open the robe and stripped her of her gown, slowly, patiently, watching the confusion and love intermingle in her expression.

"You're tired of trying to love me?" He wiped away her

tears. "Just love me tonight." His lips went to her neck and she pulled his belt from the loops of his pants, her tears forgotten. "We'll figure out the rest tomorrow," he told her. Tonight, he wanted to make love to her as a whole man, because in two days, he wouldn't be.

She was seven months' wet for him, and he was seven months' hard for her. He ran his fingers through the soft curls between her thighs, promising he'd taste her later. She pulled him on top of her, going for his mouth with unbridled desperation. He kissed her hard and deep while he grasped his raging erection and slipped it inside the tightness of her vagina. He worked her good, slow and thorough . . . trying to make a baby.

He was so out of his mind with love for her, he wanted it all, and he wanted it now. She couldn't be inseminated at a clinic. He needed her to get pregnant with his child this way—while he was loving her. A baby would take a complicated situation and make it more complex, but he wasn't thinking straight. He needed to love Erika and know she needed to love him. He needed to know she wanted him to be the father of her children. He had to know she loved him that much.

"We're going to make a baby," he told her, working his hips in tight circles.

Her passion dissipated enough for her to come to her senses. "Use a condom. I'm not taking the Depo shots anymore."

He didn't have a condom, and he didn't want one. "Forget the condoms."

Her body froze beneath him.

"No condom." He continued to work his hips, adding sensuous kisses to her breasts. He palmed her cheeks, looking deep into her soul. "Make love to me, Erika."

She cared about him so much she agreed, easily falling back into rhythm with his hips. It was good—much better—

than he could remember it ever being. She was tight and wet and hungry for him. He'd always envied her ability to openly express her emotions, regardless of the consequences. She was never guarded about how she felt, and was an expert at exposing herself while making love. She took him quickly to the final phase of his orgasm, joining him at the last second before he filled her. He pumped hard through his climax, ensuring she received every drop of his sperm, because this was how he wanted her to become pregnant with his baby.

"Where are you going?" he asked, encircling her wrist.

"To clean up." She smiled down at him.

"Don't go anywhere." He pulled her back down on the bed, enfolding her from behind. He slipped his hand between her thighs, measuring how much of his sperm had been lost. He'd learned the value of every ounce when he masturbated on the Michigan Cryogenic couch. His finger dipped inside her sweet walls, sampling her wetness, and she shivered. He added a second finger, and kept them there, falling asleep atop the comforter with Erika in his arms.

He awoke a few hours later when Erika tried to disentangle herself from his hold.

"I have to go to the bathroom," she pleaded with a cute giggle when he tried to stop her from leaving the bed.

The master bath was down the hall, past the twin walk-in closets and a linen closet. The master suite was large, running beyond the length of the house. He listened to the faint sound of running water and wondered which sink she was using—his or hers. She returned to the bedroom with a warm cloth and began cleaning him, stroking his cock until it sprang to life again. When her touch became too intimate, he removed the cloth from her and finished the job himself. He couldn't have her discovering the cancerous lump on his right testicle—not now, and not this way.

He tossed the cloth away and pulled her into his arms, pressing his erection into her back. He turned her chin, meeting her mouth in a sensuous kiss, spurring them to go at it a second time. He caressed the lines of her body, admiring the lush curves making her a woman. He buried his nose in her neck and inhaled her feminine fragrance. He lifted her thigh and placed it over his, nudging his penis back inside her plush walls where it belonged.

His original horny energy had been spent, so he could love her for a long time. He palmed her breasts, working his penis into her from behind as she moaned. His fingers danced across her belly and separated her curls until they found her swollen clit. He massaged her with slow swipes of his fingers until she panted and begged for more. His nails bit into her thigh as he spread her wider, leveraging more penetration with the thrusts of his hips. She began to piston, pushing her lush ass into him. He mimicked her motion, pulling her body tightly against his. He was whispering nonsensical words in her ears when he came, her following a split second later.

"I love you," she said, instantly falling asleep.

An hour later, Brock realized how much his body had missed Erika. She was curled up against his chest, her thigh wrapped around his and her fingers gripping his thigh. He shifted, trying to find a comfortable position for his brutally hard penis. Having her entwined with him brought all her intimate places in contact with his skin.

Seven months had been too long and his body had grown oversensitive to her presence. Each soft breath she took rippled over his skin, setting him on fire. He inhaled, deeply absorbing the fragrance of their previous lovemaking, and the smell of it made his balls tighten and lift. He licked his lips and found remnants of Erika's sweetness. The sight of her plush breasts pressed into his side forced him to stroke a finger over her nipple. She moaned at his touch and his manhood throbbed.

"How long have you been awake?" he asked her.

"A while."

"Did you do this to me?" He rotated his hips, and his jutting erection sliced through the beams of moonlight intruding on their night by pushing in through the slivers in the patio blinds. This is how possessive he'd become of Erika—he didn't want to share her with the moon or the stars.

"I might have had something to do with it." She tilted her head up to look at him, wearing a telling grin. She wanted to play.

"What are you going to do about it now?"

"Hmmm."

"Why don't you climb up here while you're thinking?" He pointed to his erection, which was ready to be a willing participant in their game.

She straddled his thighs, waiting patiently for his next demand.

"You're a very mischievous woman." He placed the tip of his finger in his mouth before he pressed it into the nest of soft curls at the top of Erika's thighs.

She wiggled her hips, angling to put pressure against her slit.

"Don't move," he growled. He was hard enough to explode without penetration, and he wanted this to last a long time. When she settled, he buried his finger a little deeper, careful not to brush her engorged bud, then traced her slit from top to bottom with an agonizingly slow stroke.

Erika moaned, thrusting her hips forward, and pressing her hips down onto his finger.

"Don't move. Lock your hands behind your head. I want to look at you."

She moved quickly to give him the view he desired. Her

breasts were full and heavy. He tested their weight in his hands, his fingertips gliding easily over the soft flesh. He touched every inch, ignoring the hardness between his thighs as he teased Erika into matching his state of readiness. He saved her nipples for last, plucking at the twin buds until they were hard and ready to burst.

"Up," he told her, pressing his hands into her thighs until she came up on her knees. Now he had access to her plump bottom. He took the globes into his palms, kneading them until Erika's thighs quivered. She would fight her excitement and let him manipulate her body even though she was glistening wet—because he'd told her not to move. He pushed her limit, letting his finger venture into the crease between her ass cheeks. She'd never let him explore her, always letting her fear overwhelm her at the last minute. Tonight she let him gently, delicately stroke the puckered hole. She found what he'd told her to be true. The area was ultra-responsive to his touch, igniting new sensations and taking her to an unprecedented level of readiness.

His hand went back to her slit, leaving her panting. Her chest was moist with perspiration brought on by her struggle to control her need.

"You're dripping wet," he told her. He placed his longest finger at the entrance to her cavern and pushed. He stopped at the first knuckle and a violent shiver went through Erika's body, but she never dropped her hands from behind her head. He added a second finger and pushed farther, farther, and farther until his palm was pressed into her soft curls.

Controlling her pleasure, knowing he mastered her body and directed the release of her orgasm made his erection weep. He gritted his teeth, but not controlling his needs as well as Erika, he used base words to illicit what she wanted from him.

"I can't . . . wait any . . . longer," Erika ground out. Fine tremors racked her body while her thighs tensed, caging his waist beneath her.

"Then take what you need," he told her, pulling his fingers away quickly, shocking her with their sudden removal.

When she grabbed his erection, his back bowed off the bed. He was turned on by how badly she wanted him. Her touch was aggressive as she frantically placed the tip of his penis at her opening. As badly as she wanted him, his size kept her from impaling herself too quickly. She moaned, falling forward to rest one palm in the center of his chest while she used the other hand to fit him inside.

He almost exploded before she could take him all in. Her eyes were closed, her features twisted in pleasurable pain. He fisted his fingers in her hair and brought her to him for a kiss. His lips moved slowly, thoroughly over hers—a direct contrast to the frenzied movements she was making with her hips. She pulled away, preferring the vehement thrashing of their bodies to the tenderness of his kiss.

She came quickly, without warning. Her entire body shook. She let out a loud cry. Her walls tightened around him, rhythmically milking the length of his shaft. Before he could thrust his hips, he was filling her with the volcanic explosion of his climax. Exhausted, she dropped down on him, her cool, wet body extinguishing his heat. He held her close, refusing to let her move.

He had come to Erika in a panic, his ego more than a little bruised after his meeting with Mark. Possession drove him. Desperation filled him. He couldn't let her go. No matter what the *right* thing to do was, he loved her and he needed her.

But he'd messed up things so badly between them he didn't know exactly how to fix it. She was asking for a divorce. Mark was waiting for him to give her one. He was ill, his future uncertain. His method of winning her was irrational, but he wasn't in a place to be sensible right now. So he held her tightly, not wanting her to move, or have the opportunity to wash away his seed, because his irrational, desperate, possessive mind told him the only way to get Erika back was to give her his child.

He awoke early the next morning, not necessarily wanting to explain his presence to his mother. Not until he could explain it to Erika, or himself. Erika wasn't beside him, but he heard running water from the master bath. It was early, but he remembered Erika and Ginnifer golfed on Sunday mornings.

He left the bed and eased down the hallway, thinking to surprise her. They could make love in the shower like they used to before she dressed to hit the golf course.

"Good morning," he said as he entered the bathroom.

"Hi." She downed a pill with a big gulp of water.

"Headache?" He kissed her as he held her from behind, admiring how right they looked together in the mirror.

"No." She held up the blister packet with two tiny pills—one of them missing—and his heart sank down into his stomach. "Plan B. I had Ginnifer bring it this morning. She's waiting out front. Today's our golf day. Remember? Do you want me to cancel so we can talk?" she asked, reading his expression wrong.

He shook his head, unable to speak. She'd taken the morning-after pill. He turned away, pressing his lips together against a string of violent curses. His temper flared in unjustified anger. There would be no baby.

His mind shifted, seeing his rage for what it truly was: hurt. He was devastated by her rejection. His world began to spin, everything was out of his control—his health, his marriage, his disproportionate love for Erika. All the intimate wishes he'd shared with her during sex were enough to excite her and heighten the encounter, but she didn't really want to make a baby with him.

"We should still talk," she said, her concern worrying her brows.

"I'll call you."

She turned to him, making him face her. "I'm glad you came. Last night was good. Like you haven't been away."

He leaned in and kissed her forehead.

"Brock?"

"You better get going. I'll leave before my mother wakes up."

CHAPTER 9

"He shredded it," Erika squealed in disbelief. She was standing in the middle of her bedroom, fresh from nine holes of golf with Ginnifer. The glossy black packet lay on the floor, and every sheet of the divorce document was confetti in the middle of the bed, the bed where they'd made love last night.

She stomped out of her bedroom to the backyard where Brock's mother was working in her flower garden. "Mom, did Brock call today?"

Because of her bum hip, she had to plant the flowers in pots, which she expertly arranged in the backyard. Brock had purchased hundreds of dollars of gardening equipment, including a miniature greenhouse. They had originally planned to put in a pool, but the greenhouse gave his mother a little piece of Tennessee living and a lot of happiness.

"No, Sugar. I'm supposed to call him later to let him know if I want him to carry me to my therapy tomorrow."

"I'll get you to therapy," she said absently.

"Is something wrong?"

"No, I need to talk to him when he calls." She went back into her bedroom before dialing his number. He didn't answer at home, or his cell. He wasn't available at the office. He never returned her pages. She called his apartment again, not realizing how angry she was until she started leaving a message.

"I don't like it when you're controlling." She turned her back on the mound of confetti. "We're supposed to talk, discuss things like a real married couple. You can't make all the decisions without consulting me. Call me back."

Brock never called, but Mark did, and she gladly accepted his invitation to the Detroit Institute of Arts. African-American art from the Walter O. Evans collection was on display and Mark was interested in her experiencing it. Erika welcomed the diversion. She was not as proficient in the arts as Mark was, but she enjoyed learning from him, and he liked sharing her interests. He had played golf with her several times, even though he couldn't seem to get a handle on the sport. He liked to watch, he told her. He was a visual man, enjoying activities through observation.

Mark met Dr. Evans during a residency rotation at the Kresge Eye Institute, and he admired the man immensely. He often spoke of their brief encounters, and how they were powerful enough to influence his career decisions. As Dr. Evans had done, Mark was slowly building his collection of African-American pieces.

The afternoon was easy, providing a welcomed respite from the turmoil of her marriage. Mark toured the museum with unbridled enthusiasm, pointing out the works of Jacob Lawrence, Elizabeth Catlett, and Romare Bearden. The art beautifully displayed the joys and struggles of African-American life, helping Erika put her troubles into perspective. The paintings and prints were Mark's favorites, but Erika enjoyed the sculptures. The colors, textures, and patterns inspired her to redecorate her home. She and Brock had spent many hours decorating room by room until they had created their dream home. Now it was a place with smothering memories, and changing to an artsy-fartsy theme might not be bad.

"Brock came to see me yesterday," Mark said as they strolled through the museum. "Did he tell you?"

"He did."

"He was there when I called, wasn't he?"

"This is why I told you we needed to stop seeing each other. This entire situation is a mess. I don't know what's happening with me and Brock. I don't want to jeopardize your feelings, or your job."

He pulled up short, glaring down at her. "What is happening between you and Brock? Why was he at your place so late last night?"

"I wish I could give you an honest answer to your question, but I can't. I don't know why Brock came by. If anything, everything is muddier than it was before."

"I was up-front with him. I don't intend to let you go because he can't figure out what he wants but gets upset when he thinks about you with another man."

"I wish you wouldn't have talked to him."

"He stormed into my office. How was I going to avoid it? Besides, I wasn't going to back down to him. This is about his pride, and jealousy—not about being in love with you. You have to see it."

They started toward the exit, the bitter conversation putting an end to their outing. The truth was her feelings were so strong, she couldn't see anything clearly. She couldn't separate what she wanted from what was best for her.

"Is he still refusing to give you the divorce?"

"He shredded the divorce papers. I found them piled in the middle of my bed."

"He takes you for granted. He knows you won't press the issue." He caught her hand, bringing her into his hard chest, shielded by the parked cars in the museum lot. "Brock is playing games with your life." He used his finger to secure a clump of curls behind her ear. "It's time to move on, Erika. I'm standing right here, and I want to be more than your friend. I want to help you get over your baggage and realize I'm here, waiting to prove how desirable you are."

"Mark, you're wonderful. I couldn't ask for anything more in a friend."

"Friend? Friend, but not a lover?"

"A lover, too—if I was looking for a lover. I'm married. I have to see how this is going to play out between Brock and me. I thought I was ready, but I'm not. I'd like to keep you as a friend, but I can't promise you anything more. I don't want to take advantage of you, and that's why I suggested we stop seeing each other."

"Every time we have a conversation about what's happening between you and Brock, you're always concerned about what he wants and what he's doing about your relationship. When are you going to focus on your wants? Your needs? Brock doesn't deserve you. I know it, and you know it."

"Maybe not, but this isn't about him deserving me. This is about me being a married woman and honoring those vows. It might sound crazy today when people get married with the safety net of divorce if it doesn't work. I've never been that way. My marriage was supposed to last forever. Divorce is immoral. It's not something I take lightly."

Filing for divorce had taken seven months of uncertainness and crushed emotions. She'd become physically ill when she left the lawyer's office. It took three weeks after filing to gather the nerves to present the papers to Brock . . . and her concerns had been justified because her actions had started a storm of troubles.

"You're married because he's refusing to give you a divorce.

Think how things would have been between us if he would have signed those papers the day you gave them to him."

Mark was right. They would have advanced their relationship and probably have been pretty happy.

"He *didn't* sign the papers, and I'm still a married woman. I would've never started seeing you if I'd known this was going to happen. But the truth is, I can't date one man and be married to another. It isn't morally right. It confuses our friendship. It isn't fair to you. It jeopardizes all of our jobs and our reputations."

"I hear you, Erika, but it doesn't change the fact I'm crazy about you."

"I know." She took his hand. "I'm sorry."

"Admit you feel something for me."

She didn't understand the point, or why he'd want to torture himself, but she wouldn't lie. "There was chemistry between us."

"You're trying to play it safe, but safe won't make you happy. I won't walk away because Brock is playing games. I'm going to remain your friend, and when you're ready, I'll be waiting for you. No questions asked. You just come to my door, and I'll know why you're there."

Mitchell Lexington was a man's man. He drank too much, partied too hard, gambled every chance he got, owned private suites at every local sports arena, and was a connoisseur of beautiful women. Shaq-sized, but not as good-looking, his personality made up for any shortcomings he might have. Despite his wealth and boisterous personality, he was a family man with six kids and a pregnant wife at home.

He'd made his fortune with twenty-six Ford dealerships around the country. Lexington Lincoln was the largest, monopolizing half a city block in metropolitan Detroit. It was at this dealership—during its growing years—that he was brutally attacked and ended up in the Mission Hospital ICU where critical care fellow Brock Johnson saved his life.

Mitchell and Brock had been friends since the day Mitchell walked out of the hospital. They'd bonded during his hospitalization and continued the friendship with occasional couple outings. Over the years, Mitchell's wife had more children, becoming a full-time housewife and mother. She and Erika were still distant friends, but Brock and Mitchell had grown closer over the years. The last time she'd seen Mitchell was the day she and Brock picked up the Zephyr and Navigator from his dealership. He'd called once or twice after Brock left her, but his friendship was more with Brock, and they eventually lost regular contact.

Erika wanted answers, and Brock wasn't returning her phone messages, so she started digging for the truth at the best possible place—with his best friend. And she knew just where to go to find him. She dressed the part, tucked in her mother-in-law for the night, and made the trek to the city.

"Erika," Mitchell barked, "what the hell are you doing in a titty bar?"

"I need to talk to you," she shouted over the music, ignoring the half-naked woman draped over his knee in the VIP booth.

A popular pro football player sharing the VIP booth offered his unsolicited comment, "You must be new, because don't much talking go on up in here."

"Chill out," Mitchell said, handing the half-naked women off to the ball player. "She's a good friend." He turned back to her. "Can I catch you tomorrow?"

"Yeah, I'll have coffee and catch up with your wife while I'm waiting."

His eyes widened. He lumbered his big body out of the

booth and scooped her up by the arm. He escorted her through the club to a back office, making her wonder if he had a personal investment in the strip club. He closed the door on the bass-bumping music. "You're cold. You didn't have to go there, bringing my wife into it."

She crossed her arms over her chest. "What's going on with Brock?"

"You talk to him?" He pulled a cigar from his suit pocket and nervously chewed on the end.

"He's not giving me answers, and now he's not taking my calls. Nothing but radio silence all day."

"You got to talk to him, Sugar," he said, sincerely using the nickname Brock's mother often called her.

"Tell me why he left me."

Mitchell shook his head. "Can't."

"What's going on with him?"

Mitchell looked away.

"Is he seeing someone else?"

"Brock? Naw, he's straight. He wouldn't do that."

"He's got to be in trouble," she said, thinking aloud. Her voice was thin, and shaky. "Is he in trouble?"

"Talk to Brock."

"Brock won't tell me!" she shouted. "Do you know what's going on?"

He stroked her arm, then helped her to sit down on a lumpy sofa. "Relax, Sugar."

She was choking back her tears now. "My marriage is falling apart, Mitchell. I'm doing everything I can to save it, but I don't know what I'm fighting."

He rubbed a paw across his chin. "Go home. Get some rest. This is not the place for you. Coming to me wasn't the right thing to do."

"You know, don't you? You know what's going on?"

He nodded. He wouldn't lie. "I know."

She latched onto his sleeve. "Tell me. Please."

"I can't. Brock is my friend."

"*I'm* your friend."

"You know I love you, Erika, but I can't betray Brock's trust. He made me promise to keep my mouth shut. I owe him my life. I can't go back on my word."

"Mitchell . . ."

"Brock loves you, be sure of that. I don't agree with what he's doing, but he's a man and it's his choice—not mine. Go home, Sugar. I'll follow you to make sure you get there safely."

"I'm not leaving until you tell me what's going on with my husband."

"I'm not going to tell you anything, but I will call Brock and tell him to talk to his wife. I'll do what I can, but I can't go back on my word to him."

"Should I leave him?"

"I'm not going there with you," he answered, unwaveringly.

She was becoming hysterical. "Should I forget about him and start moving on with my life?"

He watched her with sympathetic eyes.

"Is he with someone else? Is he in trouble? Does he still love me? Why won't he talk to me? Where is he right now? Should I move on? Should I sue him for divorce? Is that what he's waiting for? Does he want me to shoulder the guilt so he's pushing me away until I do what has to be done? Why did he show up last night if he didn't want to make this work?"

Every question she wanted Brock to answer tumbled past her lips in one long, slurred string of half-comprehensible words until Mitchell took her arm and shook her. "Sugar, stop it. You're asking the wrong person. Talk to Brock."

"Brock won't talk to me! Haven't you heard anything I said?"

"I'll talk to him. Try to get him to talk to you. Right now, let me get you home."

She jerked away from him and stormed out of the club, rushing to get away before the tears of frustration started. She had completely broken in the back room of a strip club, after all these months of struggling to keep it together. Mitchell was a man of conviction, just like Brock, and she knew no amount of cajoling would get him to budge off his loyalty to a friend. Coming to the club had been an act of desperation. She was losing it, but before she did, she had to realize the hard truth: Brock was playing games with her heart . . . and he didn't really want to save their marriage.

The shredded divorce papers had been replaced by a white envelope wrapped in a dainty red bow. Erika ignored the gift, walking in a large circle around the bed. She showered and dressed for bed after checking on her mother-in-law. She returned to her bedroom and sat in the easy chair, watching the envelope. She knew there would be something inside it to reduce her to tears again. She'd read the card Brock's mother had left on the kitchen counter next to the crystal vase of yellow roses. It was a sweet declaration of Brock's love for his mother, along with a round-trip ticket to Memphis. She would leave in the morning. The return date was over three weeks away. A telephone message from Brock's oldest brother confirmed the plans.

Erika replayed Brock's visit the night before. She'd foolishly believed he was home for good. Less than a day later, she couldn't rouse him on the phone. She leaned forward, gingerly taking the envelope off the bed. She slipped her nail under the flap and ripped the delicate paper for an anticlimactic ending. Inside was a complete golf package for two. Her heart leapt . . . if they went away together, they could work out their problems—whatever they were—and start all over again.

All her hopes were crushed when she deciphered Brock's wild handwriting.

Take Ginnifer on a much-needed vacation. Enjoy.

Anger made her rip the vacation brochure into pieces. She silently cried out her frustration, the embarrassing scene at the club keeping her in check. She was a strong woman. No man would break her. No matter how much she loved him, her mind was not for his destruction. She was on the floor, gathering the pieces to do a little shredding of her own when she remembered Mom's tickets to Memphis. She gathered the slips of paper and pieced them back together. The dates of the golf package over-lapped most of the days Mom would be in Memphis.

"He wants us out of town," she whispered. She searched her memory, desperately grasping at bits of conversations they'd shared last night.

Her anger was replaced by numbing fear. Her fingers grew cold and tingly. Brock knew she couldn't leave the clinic without much planning and plenty of notice—and take Gin-nifer with her? They covered each other for vacations. His ac-tions weren't rational—as if he had come up with the idea of sending his wife and mother away too hastily. Brock was a man of concentrated details. Throwing the twin vacations together, avoiding her calls—it was too uncharacteristic of him. As if he were too stressed, or confused, or scared to re-alize he wasn't acting logically.

Nausea made her stomach roll. *Brock is in trouble.* He still loved her, he'd confessed to it last night. She loved her husband. She wasn't going on any vacation. Whatever was bothering him was her problem too. She loved him that much. No matter what, she would find him, and she would bring him home.

CHAPTER 10

Virginia Johnson loved each of her three children, and if asked she'd say they were all special. But Brock held a special place in her heart. His birth had been the hardest on her body, so she and her husband decided he would be the last. Knowing there wouldn't be more made her hold a little tighter to Brock. She tried to shield it from the other children, but she indulged him, encouraging his pursuit of anything that made him happy as if it were her own.

Brock's father had been a good provider for his family. He was a better husband, and Virginia had taken his death harder than she thought she would. After all, she hadn't had time to prepare. His cancer had spread throughout his body before he even received his diagnosis. He quickly righted his estate—he had managed to put away a modest amount. The boys were called home and told the truth in frank terms. Decisions were made, and before Virginia knew it, she was sitting vigil at her husband's deathbed. As much as she loved her life with her husband, she hated watching him die.

The time after her husband's death was lonely, and once she broke her hip, she was lonely *and* dependent on the kindness of strangers to care for her. Brock stepped in, nobly volunteering to care for his mother as her health deteriorated.

Virginia harbored some guilt about Brock having to care for her and bringing her into his household when he was barely more than a newlywed. "How can I ever repay you for every dinner you've cooked, load of laundry you've washed, and scrape you've bandaged?" he'd asked, kissing her on the cheek. Erika had been equally as gracious, treating Virginia as if she were her own mother.

Virginia was always critical of the girls Brock brought home during his teen years, so he'd shied away from bringing women around when he got older. What a delightful surprise Erika had been. She walked into the front door without a formal invitation and barged right into Virginia's heart. The family embraced the city girl, teaching her the ways of Southern women. Unlike Virginia's other two daughters-in-law, Erika was a career woman, and it took Virginia a little longer to acclimate her to the kitchen. When Brock invited Virginia to live in their new home, Erika had insisted, accompanying Brock when he drove to Memphis to collect his mother's things.

Virginia's memory wasn't as good as it once had been, but she was still sharp. Her children attributed it to old age, but her doctor had discarded the idea, blaming it instead on a delayed grief reaction—she hadn't completed mourning her husband, and until she did, the lapses in memory would continue. She passed on her doctor's recommendation of grief therapy.

She might not be as sharp as usual, but she understood what Brock was doing to Erika and she didn't like it. But he was her son and she loved him. Erika pretended to be unaffected, hiding her tears whenever Virginia witnessed her sadness. Virginia understood what it was like to lose someone you loved before you were ready. She knew Erika's pain. Watching Erika trying to hide it rekindled her own grief.

Virginia looked out the window of the plane, the city below obscured by clouds. She wondered what this little impromptu trip was all about. She hoped Brock wanted time alone to win his wife back, but Erika hadn't given indication of that being the case. Her youngest son was suffering, and he hadn't come to her. She could've lived with that reality if he'd gone to his wife. Instead, he had walked out on them both.

After Virginia had prayed over her husband's grave, caught up with old friends, and spent much-needed time with the grandkids, it was time for a good old-fashioned Sunday evening family dinner. She and her daughters-in-law spent two days cooking and baking while the boys gathered enough furniture from all their homes to accommodate the growing brood. Her heart sang with memories of good times and fond remembrances of her children growing up. She could have never prepared herself for how her world would shatter from memories of her husband's death when her oldest son said, "Ma, we need to talk to you about Brock. He's sick."

The primary care clinic closed each day from noon to one o'clock for lunch, and Erika didn't waste one minute hurrying across the medical campus to Brock's apartment. She'd gone to his office first only to find he had taken three weeks' vacation. She didn't bother to ask his closed-mouth secretary where he had gone or when he'd be back because the woman had been personally selected by Brock for her Fort Knox–like abilities at securing information. Besides, Erika wanted to hear it directly from Brock. The mystery of her failing marriage was becoming more complicated, and she demanded an explanation.

None was coming, however, because Brock's apartment

was empty. She rang the bell until a resident recognized her and graciously allowed her access to the locked building. She banged on Brock's door for fifteen minutes before another resident informed her he hadn't seen Brock since the evening before. Defeated, and more than a little angry, Erika returned to her office.

She wouldn't give up the fight for her marriage. Her love could sustain a hit, but her patience was growing thin. If not for the nagging feeling in the pit of her stomach that something was very wrong with Brock, she would have forced herself to realize her marriage was over and move on. They may not have the bond married couples of fifty years had, but their love for each other was strong. Divorce didn't fit in their equation. They were a young couple with kids and grandchildren in their future. She couldn't count the times they had sat together on the patio dreaming of a future in a small town where they would open a joint practice and raise their children with old-fashioned values.

Their courtship had gone slowly, every step meant to advance their relationship with longevity in mind. Even their wedding was a practice in old-fashioned rituals, wrapped in family values. The celebration began with the arrival of both families and ended six days later when Erika and Brock said their vows. She was a new doctor, so many of her friends from med school were still in the area and attended. Brock was skyrocketing to the top of his practice and had many friends in administration who joined the celebration.

Their official colors were burgundy and black. Erika wore a fairy-tale dress with layers of pink-blush satin and lace. Brock stood tall and proud at the altar in a black tuxedo with a burgundy tie. Their parents were honored, their siblings saluted, and their friends appreciated. Their ceremony was the legal bonding of their love, but it was formality, because they had already given their vows in the candlelit privacy of Brock's bedroom the evening before.

"I will cherish you, and give you everything you need to be happy for the rest of my life," Brock promised, stroking the hollow of her lower back as she lay nude across his lap. "Anything you need, you ask me for it, and I'll do whatever it takes to get it for you. I'll never stop loving you. It isn't possible because you're engrained into every fiber of my heart and soul."

"And I'll love you for the rest of your life, and well after I die. I'll always support you, and I'll be your soft place to fall." She knew he adored that about her: She was soft where he was hard.

"Are you okay?"

Erika looked up to find Ginnifer standing at her desk. "How long have you been here?"

"A minute." She flopped down in her favorite chair. "Asking if you're okay is getting old. I love Brock to pieces, and you know I think you two are the perfect couple, but this situation is not healthy for you."

"I'm not ready to give up on him yet. If I could just discover what he's hiding, I could make an informed decision."

"No luck?"

She shook her head. "Mitchell wouldn't tell me anything. He admitted something was going on but said he promised Brock he wouldn't tell me."

"What about his other friend? The doctor?"

"Hassan. I didn't bother to ask. He and I have never really hit it off."

"Why not?"

"His culture says women are homemakers—not doctors—and he's always been afraid I would be a bad influence on his wife."

"Who cares what he thinks about you, or your career? You

just want some information about your husband." Ginnifer stood and approached the door. "Sounds like he's intimidated by you, if you ask me. Use it against him. Barge into his office and get in his face. *Make* him tell you what the hell is going on with Brock."

Erika pondered the suggestion only a minute before she made her way to the elevator and to the urology clinic, but when she barged into his office, the secretary informed her he was performing surgery at the suburban branch of Mission Hospital. The way the medical assistant concentrated on avoiding her eyes made her spine ripple, and her second sense signaled Hassan's involvement. "Find Hassan, find my husband."

The worse thing Mark Garing could have done was fall for a married woman, but the heart wants what the heart wants. After one too many failed relationships, he'd relocated to Michigan to restart his career and jump-start his life. He'd had more than his share of money-grubbing, opportunistic, lying, cheating women. After the last fiasco, which involved an overanxious police detective, he'd moved thousands of miles away from his past and started all over again. He had vowed to be emotionally open and available, not revisiting his past relationship troubles on the next woman he met. Who knew the next woman he would fall for would be Dr. Erika Johnson— Mrs. Brock Johnson?

He fought the attraction hard at first, assuring himself sharing a friendship was more than enough. And then he'd been forced to watch as Brock ripped her world apart and crushed her heart. It only made her more attractive—all that vulnerability in a woman as beautiful, intelligent, and strong-willed as Erika. She was perfect . . . except she was married.

He gave up fighting his heart and began fighting Brock for

what he wanted. This situation was new for him, and more than a little uncomfortable. He'd never been placed in a position to have to fight over a woman. His past relationships were problematic, but if another man was involved, he always found out too late to make a difference.

With Erika, he had waited patiently in the background, knowing Brock's arrogance would cause him to make a monumental mistake. He waited four months before Erika confided in him about considering moving on with her life. He had jumped on the statement like a starving dog on a meaty bone. He eased into her life, always up front about his intentions. He had been elated when she'd finally agreed to go out on a date. And their first kiss? It gave him shivers even now to think about it.

He hadn't made love to Erika yet. Whenever they were together and their emotions ran high enough to broach the subject, something always made her hold back. She was an honorable woman, and no matter what shambles her marriage was in, she wouldn't cheat by sleeping with another man. Mark adored her more for holding on to her convictions, so he didn't push. He quietly waited for Brock to screw up again.

He didn't have to wait long. Brock refused to grant Erika a divorce, but he hadn't made a move to repair their relationship. His latest stunt of disappearing had pissed Erika off so badly she was considering suing him for divorce. She was tired of the yo-yoing. She wanted out. And he wanted her out too. But she was see-sawing again, not sure if she was ready to take permanent steps to sever her relationship. She was so torn, she'd broken off their relationship, afraid she might hurt him. Her kindness was irresistible.

He hadn't been planning anything deceptive when he scheduled a surgical procedure for his patient at Mission Hospital West. The medical center had recently expanded to a full-fledged hospital with a ten-bed surgical suite. The hospital was closer to his patient's home, making it more convenient for his wife to visit. Mark had made the appropriate requests until he was granted privileges at the hospital and scheduled the laser procedure.

Fate had placed him at the desk in the recovery room when Brock rolled out of the OR suite reserved for VIPs and important hospital employees.

Erika slammed the phone down on the receiver. Between each patient she'd made calls, searching for Brock or Hassan. She didn't know how she knew, but they were together on this "vacation," and Hassan would never leave his wife behind, so the vacation wasn't a vacation.

"Can you cover for me?" Ginnifer rushed into her office, purse slung over her shoulder. "There are only two patients left to be seen."

"Of course." Alarmed, Erika stood up behind her desk. "What's wrong?"

"Rhon just paged me. Will was cooking dinner and sliced off his finger. Rhon's driving him to the ER."

"Here?"

"No, Mission Hospital. It's closer to our house." She rambled on, jumbling her sentences together. "Rhon was hysterical. Will is hurt and he's trying to calm Rhon in the background. Can you imagine Frick and Frack in the ER? Can you cover the last two patients? I have to make sure it isn't anything serious."

"Ginnifer." Erika crossed the room and hugged her. "I'll cover your patients. Go. Call me as soon as you know something."

Ginnifer offered a tense smile and scrambled out of the office. She teased Rhon and Will mercilessly, making jokes about their bizarre living arrangements, but she truly loved them both. Erika gladly covered for Ginnifer—they were a good team and always had each other's back. After seeing the last patients in the clinic, she stayed behind to review test results, but her mind kept wandering. It was quiet in the clinic once the staff left. She shut off most of the lights while she finished her documentation, creating a relaxing atmosphere that was disrupted by her worries about Brock.

"Erika?" It was Ginnifer calling her cell.

"How's Will?"

"He sliced his pinky down to the second joint, but thank goodness he had the presence of mind to wrap it in ice and bring it with him to the hospital. He's in surgery now."

"How serious is it?"

"He's stable. Very embarrassed. Rhon is a wreck. After Will gets out of surgery and is in a room, I'm going home to clean up the mess. I don't think Rhon can take seeing the blood again."

Will, the younger of Ginnifer's boyfriends, was responsible for keeping the house. He was a college student, the only child standing to inherit a whopping trust fund, still trying to "find himself." Ginnifer supported his efforts to secure a stable future—she had no illusions about him leaving their triad one day.

"He's going to need occupational therapy before he regains full use of his finger. People don't realize how valuable a pinky is until they lose it."

"I'm glad everything is turning out okay," Erika said.

"Guess who I ran into while I was in pre-op?"

"Who?"

"Hassan. I remembered our conversation and did a little intimidation of my own." She paused, lowering her voice. "Erika, Brock's here."

CHAPTER 11

The cardiac monitor displayed the nervous beating of Brock's heart for all to see. He was embarrassed about being in such a helpless position with his coworkers to witness. He stared up at the ceiling, subconsciously processing everything going on around him. He had asked for local anesthesia, but Hassan refused, saying the operation was "too big" for a local. Brock suspected Hassan did not want him awake to question every move.

The nurse tied a tourniquet around his upper arm, smiling pleasantly as she stabbed his vein with the needle and threaded the catheter. She connected the IV tubing, laced the tubing into a machine, and wished him luck before moving away from the bedside. Another person appeared, clippers in hand, to shear off the fine hairs covering his abdomen. Others appeared, each efficiently doing their part to ready him for surgery.

He hid his fear behind complaints of discomfort. The stretcher was too narrow for his broad shoulders and didn't provide enough cushion for the swell of his behind. The room was too cold. He was having hunger pains. Anything he could grouse about to occupy his mind. The staff smiled, silently indulging him, obviously accustomed to dealing with patients in this state of mind.

The anesthesiologist strolled up to his stretcher and asked the standard questions about his medical history, placing a red ID band around his wrist to warn of his allergy to penicillin. Brock could hear him berating the staff a few minutes later about not identifying the allergy. He was considered a VIP, and everything had to be just right, or there would be hell to pay. Brock knew this threat fell on death ears. It wasn't like the staff gave shoddy care unless you were rich or famous.

A specialist would perform the surgery, but Hassan would scrub in and assist—observe—the procedure. The doctors visited his bedside before dressing for the OR, going over the procedure one last time before they disappeared through the great white doors. There was some comfort in having his trusted friend in the operating room with him, but Brock couldn't stop wishing Erika was at his side. Many of the OR staff knew he was married to Erika but were polite enough not to inquire about her whereabouts. Brock didn't doubt the news of their breakup had spread to this campus.

The anesthesiologist was his agreeable self again when Brock next saw him in the OR suite. The man chatted about nothing in particular—anything to get Brock talking while he pushed the first drug into his IV line. "Here comes the Versed," he said. "You're going to feel it. I heard you're married to Dr. Erika Johnson. I met her once, a long time ago. Beautiful woman. Very nice."

"Yes," Brock answered, his hearing a little fuzzy, "she is."

"Dream of her when I put you to sleep, and I might have trouble waking you." The man laughed, and Brock smiled at the inside joke. You couldn't dream when you were under anesthesia—the drugs bypassed the stage of sleep where dreams occurred.

"She is a dream."

The anesthesiologist continued to push the drug.

Brock flinched when the burning sensation moved up his arm. "I love her very much" were his last words before losing consciousness.

Piercing pains in Brock's gut made him howl, awakening him badly from the anesthesia.

Hassan leaned over his bed. "Everything went well," he said before giving the nurse a verbal order that sounded like gibberish to Brock, although it shouldn't. He was asleep again within seconds.

This time he did dream. Good dreams about his first date with Erika, their first kiss, and their wedding day. His heart fluttered now with the same nervous excitement it had when the preacher announced them husband and wife. He began to bargain . . . if he survived, he would make up for the hurt he'd caused his wife . . . if he were still a whole, functioning man, he'd make love to his wife every night. Whatever it took, no price seemed too high to get Erika back in his life. If he had any doubts about whether he wanted to save his marriage, they disappeared when he opened his eyes. Surviving the surgery made him regret his overzealous worrying about the the hit his illness would have on his marriage. Erika was strong, and he was too. Together they could get through anything.

"Welcome back, Dr. Johnson," the nurse greeted him. "You're on the medical unit. I just want to check your vital signs." She smiled politely, maintaining her quiet compassion when demanding patients were ringing call lights, waiting for her attention. She recited his blood pressure and heart rate as she jotted them in his chart. "Do you know where you are?"

"The hospital," he croaked, his throat dry and sore. "Mission Hospital West."

"What's today?"

He answered that correctly too.

"Tell me your first name."

"Brock."

She smiled down at him. "Can I get you anything?"

"Water. Please."

She rolled the bedside table up and poured a glass of water before leaving him. He felt a strange compulsion to call her back as he suddenly didn't want to be alone. He tamped the irrational urge down and sipped the cup of ice water. He pushed the table back, knowing he had to look but being terrified at what he would see.

He could feel the cool sensation on his scrotum and it wasn't pleasant. He stalled, gathering the sheets and blankets in his fist before pulling them back. The white gauze dressing on his lower abdomen was slightly soiled with blood but otherwise unremarkable. Just seeing the bandage made his stomach pain return, but he fought through it, needing to see the rest of the damage to his body.

His eyes ventured lower, sneaking a peek as if he were ogling a stranger. His penis sat limply on top of a mound of dressing meant to suspend his balls to help with the obnoxious, deformed swelling. *Balls?* He had only one—no plural. With the edema, the malformation wasn't noticeable, but he knew. He wondered about the biopsy results of the tumor. It would tell him if all the cancer had been removed, or if it had spread to other areas of his body. Knowing 95 percent of testicular tumors are malignant, he suddenly didn't want to know the results—or what the results would mean to the rest of his life. He had lost half of his scrotum, and his ability to father a child was questionable, while the chances of the tumor being malignant were good. And on top of everything, he had done the stupidest thing he'd ever done and left the love of his life. The realizations hit him all at once, and he felt as if his chest were being crushed. His lungs were tight, pushing against the air instead of embracing it.

Brock covered himself and rang the nursing call light. When she didn't immediately respond, he pushed it over and over and over again. Turning his fear into agitation, he called out, making a ruckus that didn't fit the severity of his illness.

Two nurses rushed into the room, one a man who connected with him on a level only another man could. He spoke to the other nurse, "Call the doctor and see if we can get Dr. Johnson something for anxiety."

Minutes later, the nurse pushed Ativan into his IV line, and the anxiety was washed away on a smooth, warm current. Brock's body responded immediately with the relaxation of his muscles and the unclenching of his abdomen. His mind remained disquieted, racing with thoughts of how he'd lived his life up to this point.

His father's diagnosis of testicular cancer knocked him off the pedestal his parents had built for him. They thought the world of their youngest son becoming a doctor, moving to Michigan to be a part of a renowned intensive care program. His mother's proud eyes turned on his in desperation, pleading for a cure. With all his knowledge and experience, he couldn't save his father, and he was forced to watch his father wither away. He believed he was useless, unable to save his own father. His mother's pain was worse. She suffered silently, keeping vigil at his father's bedside until he didn't even know she was there.

Brock had few regrets in his life, but the ones he did have were enormous.

Mixed into this period of confusion and self-doubt were shining moments. Times when he was able to slow down and concentrate on peeling back the layers to Erika's heart. She had allowed him to openly express his inadequacies without ever telling him there was nothing he could have done. She let him grieve the way he needed to until he was able to come out on the other side, whole again.

As much as he wanted to spare her the pain of his illness, he couldn't deny how much he needed her to help him survive. He'd done all the things Hassan had instructed, methodically submitting to lab tests, marching off to a sperm bank, and visiting a genetic counselor, but all the while he'd been empty inside, afraid all his efforts were useless because Erika wouldn't be there to share the rest of his life.

"Erika," he whispered, the Ativan lulling him back to sleep. "Someone please call my wife."

CHAPTER 12

Erika Hendrix was born to James and Susan Hendrix exactly thirteen months after her sister Corrine. Surprised, but overjoyed, her parents welcomed another baby girl. Because the girls were so close in age, they were often mistaken for twins. Both adorable with cherub cheeks and curly brown hair, they blossomed into two beautiful young women—with very different personalities.

Erika and Corrine's rivalry began in middle school and continued to this day. Corrine felt she was entitled to certain liberties as the big sister. Their parents didn't want to show favoritism, so what went for one went for both. Corrine's one-sided rivalry turned to jealous hatred in high school. She was the most popular girl in school. The girls all wanted to be her friend, and the boys all wanted her. Until Erika entered ninth grade and joined the cheer squad. The boys who had been pushed aside by Corrine found Erika's welcoming personality refreshing and began to use Corrine to get introductions to her little sister.

Living in a middle-class neighborhood, Erika and Corrine were better off than many of their friends, but Erika realized early that life would be hard if she didn't do something to secure her financial future. She decided to become a physician when her high-school counselor told her she couldn't.

"The odds of a negro woman making it out of this neighborhood and finishing college are slim. Only the best are invited to go to medical school," the counselor explained when James and Susan showed up at the school the following Monday.

"Negro?" Susan asked, disgusted by his choice of words.

The counselor cleared his throat. "I'm sorry. African-American?"

"You don't tell my daughter what she can and can't do," Susan barked, coming to the edge of her seat. "Erika told you she wants to become a doctor. Help her become a doctor. Do what you need to do to see she gets the best possible chance to reach her goal."

"Mrs. Hendrix—"

James touched his wife's forearm, stopping her from making her next comment. He slid to the edge of his seat, his voice low and menacing. "Erika doesn't need your help, sir. She is bright and beautiful and ambitious. She will become a doctor because that's what she wants. Her mother and me will help her get through medical school. You just stay out of her way."

As Erika watched her high-school–educated parents with barely a middle-class income defend her, she vowed she wouldn't let them down. No matter what it took, or what sacrifices she had to make, she would become a physician.

The next morning, Erika and Corrine were assigned another counselor.

"I don't want to change counselors just because Erika messed it up," Corrine whined.

Their parents eventually relented and allowed Corrine to stay with the counselor.

Erika excelled in her studies. Corrine had her first child by twelfth grade.

Erika missed not having the closeness of a big sister and often wished for a big brother. She substituted many in the role in her life, but none of them sustained. The more successful she became, the more distant Corrine grew. Eventually, Erika went off to college, sailing through her classes and anxiously awaiting the challenge of med school.

It was in her final year of premed that her latest big-brother substitute, Ali, tried to derail her life. They had been distant friends for two years, becoming closer during their final year of undergrad education because they had so many classes in common. She considered him a big brother, and often told him so. He enjoyed the title and unearned trust, and moved in to take advantage.

Alleging "date rape" on campus didn't always lead to justice so when Ali trapped her in his dorm room, pinned her to the bed, ripped off her clothes, and slapped her into submission, she didn't report it as a crime. Emotionally battered, and physically bruised, she returned home the following week for Thanksgiving break and tried to mend herself. Her mother noticed she was quieter than usual, but Erika told her it was because she was studying so hard. Her father noticed she was jumpy and didn't like to venture too far from home. "I want to spend my vacation with my family," Erika told him, but he remained skeptical, constantly questioning her about her life on campus.

By now, Corrine had two babies and was living place to place with whomever the man of the month might be. Their parents often kept her children, and Corrine wasn't shy about running in and out of her childhood home as if she still lived there. Erika was stepping out of the bath, soaking her bruised body, when Corrine burst through the door. She didn't notice the closed door because she was too busy making up excuses to their mother about why she needed the babies to sleep over.

"What the hell happened to you?" Corrine shouted, revolted more than concerned.

"Shh." Erika grabbed a towel and wrapped her nudity, trying to close the door before her parents could hear.

"What's going on?" James asked, appearing out of nowhere. He'd been waiting, searching for answers to her withdrawn behavior, and Corrine had provided an opening for further interrogation.

"Somebody beat Erika up," Corrine answered.

"What? Erika, is that true?"

"It's true. She has bruises everywhere under the towel. She didn't tell y'all?"

"Erika?" her father asked.

She looked at her father, needing his safe protection, but was ashamed to admit she'd gone to a boys' dorm unescorted.

"Erika?" he asked again, somehow knowing there was more to the story than a squabble or a fight.

"I didn't want to worry you and Mom."

"Can you take this to another room?" Corrine asked, jumping from foot to foot for dramatic effect. "I've got to pee."

The police were at a loss. After all, this wasn't a random attacker grabbing her from an alley and forcefully raping her. This was an intelligent young man, med-school bound with an influential family.

"We could notify the college," the officer told Erika's parents, "but I don't know what good it would do. Other than ruin Erika's reputation on campus. Did you say you went to his room willingly?"

After many hours of arguing, Erika convinced her parents not to contact the college. They agreed as long as she agreed to attend medical school close to home. She finished her undergrad degree, commuting every weekend and moving off campus, "As far away from that boy as possible," her mother said.

Sometime after Erika returned to school, her father went on his first business trip ever. The day after he returned home, Ali came to class with a broken arm, crooked nose, and various bumps and bruises. He never dared look her way again. And her family never again spoke of either incident.

Erika locked the experience away deep in the back of her memories until the second time she and Brock made love. He was especially lustful this night, not having seen her in the two weeks since their first time together.

He lifted his head from her belly. "Erika, why are you fighting me?"

The question caught her completely off guard. She hadn't realized she'd been resisting his efforts to seduce her, let alone outright pushing him away.

He moved up next to her, taking her in his arms and covering her with the bedding. "Tell me what's going on?"

She didn't answer right away, trying to decide if she should confide her greatest shame to him.

"You weren't this way the first time we were together— guarded like you don't trust me."

"It's not that I don't trust you." She'd never want him to think she was skeptical of him.

"You've given me your body, and now you want to hold out your heart? Talk to me, Erika. This relationship is about us. If you have a problem, we both do. How am I supposed to make love to you every time I see you if you're uncomfortable?" His smiles were so rare his grin made her tension fade away in a smile too. "Whatever you tell me is between us. What has you so upset?" He asked so tenderly she didn't measure what the consequences would be of telling the Ali story.

"I had a bad experience once. I didn't realize it still bothered me until now." She hadn't had many boyfriends in her life because she believed in serial monogamy. No one from her past had ever stopped in the middle of sex to discuss her feelings. Probably because their intentions on having a relationship started and stopped there, and her emotional state was of no consequence to them.

"Tell me exactly what happened with your 'bad experience.'"

"Date rape," she squeezed out, using the term aloud for the first time.

Brock shook his head, bringing her closer into his chest. "You haven't talked about this before?"

"No."

"No one from your past has asked?" He tensed a little when he waited for her answer.

"Never came up."

"It's coming up now. Talking about it will help you work through it. Start from the beginning and don't leave out any details."

She inhaled deeply. "Ali invited me back to his dorm—"

"Erika, start from the beginning. What time did you wake up that morning? What did you have for breakfast? Start at the top, don't skimp on the details, and keep going until I feel like I was right there with you when it happened."

She did as he asked, searching for the smallest of details until she had pieced together the entire day. Brock wanted to know the particulars about everything—weather, smells, clothing, lighting in the dorm. He pushed past her barriers, forcing her to do the same. Holding it all inside, trying to forget, had not helped her forget at all. It had only weakened her with an unnamed fear. Discussing it with Brock was hard, but it did help her work through the trauma of it.

"You've gone quiet on me," Erika said when she'd finished.

She had turned within the circle of his arms sometime during her reverie, and now her bare back was pressed solidly against his naked front. She felt vulnerable, sharing her secret while nude and their relationship being so young. She started to move away from him. He gave her room to reposition but didn't let her escape the safety of her arms.

"Do you feel any better?" he finally asked.

"Yes, and no."

"No?"

"You're purposefully not sharing your reaction with me."

The muscles in his arms twitched. She'd correctly read him, and he was uncomfortable about it. He'd often mentioned how uncanny it was she could interpret his moods so easily. "I am shielding from you," he admitted.

"Why?" She was afraid to hear the answer but needed to know the truth.

"Because I'm so angry right now I want to hunt down Ali and kill him."

She'd been worried he would blame her for getting herself into the situation. Or consider her damaged goods—and he was too busy with his practice to spare his free time fixing her.

"I can't kill Ali," he said, turning her to face him, "but I can help you hurt a little less."

Erika recalled every touch, every whisper, and every caress Brock had used to help her forget the brutality of another man. From that evening on, he was never far away, always using a subtle touch, the inflection of his voice, or his dominance to assure her she was under his protection. As she stood in the hospital doorway watching him sleep, she wished he was that man again—fierce protector—because her fear was smothering, threatening to make her run from the room.

RESUSCITATION

CHAPTER 13

"Erika," Brock whispered, uncertain she wasn't the vision of a dream. She was so beautiful—inside and out. She stood in the doorway of his hospital room, clutching the door and watching him with worried eyes. She wore a simple black pantsuit, but the soft fabric hugged the flare of her hips and dipped into the cleavage of her breasts. Tiny, brown, wispy curls dotted her forehead, hiding the shocked rise of her brows. Her lips were slightly parted, and he found them tempting, an invitation to kiss away her fear.

She stepped gingerly into the room, her hand clinging to the door until the last possible moment. She surveyed him, giving his body the kind of complete scan only a medical professional can do. She moved slowly, sitting down next to his bed. "Why are you here?"

He tried to hold his eyes steady, to give her truth in his emotions as well as his words, but his shame made his gaze slide away to the bulge beneath the blankets situated between his legs.

"I—" He didn't know what words to use to tell his wife he may be dying. He was a man. He sucked it up and started acting like it for the first time in many months. "I have testicular cancer."

He thought she would fall out of the chair. Her upper body weaved. She lost the glow behind her bronzy skin and turned ashen gray while her lashes beat wildly, trying to temper her reaction.

"I had the tumor removed today." He watched for her response as he told her about the operation. "Inguinal orchiectomy. Right testicle removed. Gone. They won't have the results of the biopsy for a week. Hassan said the surgery went well." He stopped because he realized he was nervously rambling through the myriad of expressions flickering across Erika's face.

Her lips moved, but he couldn't hear what she was trying to say. Her eyes narrowed and she sprang from the chair, grabbed his bed covers, and ripped them back from his body. Every gory detail of the surgery was on display for her to digest.

"I love you, Erika," he said, hearing the pleading quality of his voice but not being able to curtail it. His emotions were strong and he needed to convey his feelings to her. "I didn't want you to have to go through this, but I realized—too late— I can't do it alone. After watching my mother struggle with my father's illness . . . I couldn't inflict the same pain on you."

She was shaking her head, moving away from him. "Is this why you left me?"

"I didn't want to see you suffer like my mother had to. I love you too much."

The nurse bounced into the room, not reading the emotional heaviness until it was too late. She hurried, hanging his antibiotic IV and exiting quickly.

Erika didn't speak until the door *whooshed* closed on its hinges. "You left me because you wanted to save me from your—your—"

"Cancer." It didn't surprise him Erika couldn't say it. It had taken him weeks to pronounce the word. "Yes."

"You never stopped loving me?"

"God, no. I've told you I never stopped loving you."

"You did this for me. You went through this alone to save me?"

"I did." He itched to reach for her, but she was still standing a safe distance away. "But I can't do it without you. The only reason I want to try to beat this is so I can spend my life making you happy."

Her lips parted, but again, no words came.

He knew she was deciding. Deciding whether or not to believe him . . . and to take him back into her life. His voice took on a noticeable edginess as he scrambled to sway her decision. "You are everything to me, Erika. I was an ass. I should have trusted you to love me as much as I love you."

He saw her fading, going to the place in her mind where she could lock him away without guilt. "I should have come to you from the beginning, but I wasn't thinking rationally. What I did is inexcusable, but I have to ask you to forgive me, Erika, because I need you right now."

He sank low, using everything in his arsenal to keep her. He knew it was emotional blackmail before he said it, but he was desperate, and there was no way he could survive without her. "You know what it's like to feel like a helpless victim—alone and scared."

Her eyes narrowed, clearly understanding his meaning. He had supported her as she relived her attack, and now he needed her to support him. It had been hard for her to tell him about her college date rape, even harder to work past the pain and learn to trust him with her body. In his mind, she had to forgive him. She owed it to him not to leave.

"Why are you talking like this?"

"I can't lose you."

"No. Why are you struggling to complete a sentence?"

He hadn't noticed. He was so caught up in trying to convince her to love him again he hadn't realized breathing had become a fight.

Erika kicked into doctor mode, pressing the button on the machine standing next to the bed to take his blood pressure. "Your pressure is low, and your heart rate is too fast." She tugged at the collar of the hospital gown, exposing a large portion of his chest. "Are those hives?" Before he could gather enough oxygen in his lungs to answer, she was reading the IV bags hanging above him. "This is a derivative of penicillin."

Erika grabbed the call bell, frantically pushing for assistance. She informed the nurse of the problem as she wrapped the blood pressure cuff around his arm. Without asking, she snatched the nurse's stethoscope and concentrated on taking the reading. The nurse moved quickly to shut off the IV. It didn't take long for the room to fill with other medical professionals.

Brock's response to the penicillin worsened and breathing became almost impossible. Everyone moved around him, concentrating on an area of his body, dissecting him with their actions.

He searched the room until he found Erika backing a doctor into a corner. With her back to him, he couldn't make out all of her words, but she was jabbing her finger at the man while he silently nodded. The snatches of the conversation he could hear were powerful admonishments. Erika accused the doctor of malpractice, raising her voice when she said: "You almost killed my husband!"

She turned to him, and the doctor scooted from the room. He was getting lightheaded and dizzy. Before darkness claimed his vision, his eyes met Erika's. She was angry, but most of all she was worried. He relaxed into the darkness, knowing his wife was fighting for him because she still loved him.

* * *

At four in the morning, when Erika could barely hold her eyes open, Brock turned the corner, fighting off the respiratory distress and bypassing the need to go on a respirator. Hassan stepped into the room to assure her his latest set of arterial blood gases proved his oxygenation was good. He was moved to the Intermediate Care Unit, a step down from the ICU, but a step up in intensity of care from the general medicine floor where he was originally assigned. She watched him sleep, breathing easily with a contentment reflexive of her submission to his will, and for a flickering moment, she resented him.

Erika eased her tired muscles and weary bones from the chair and stomped up to Hassan with her last bit of energy. "If you ever keep anything from me concerning my husband's health again, you'll have to deal with me. And after I'm done with you, I'll do everything within my power to see you're no longer an employee of Mission Hospital."

He'd never witnessed her anger and didn't understand the full force of her wrath. "Brock is my patient. I have to do what he asks."

"I know your beliefs about men and how women should stay in their place, but you're in my country now, and you'd better learn how to function here, or I'll be the one to teach you."

Ginnifer was right. Intimidation did work on Hassan, and it felt good too. She ended her tirade by pushing past the stunned man. She burst into the corridor and ran into the solid wall of Mitchell's chest. She had called him to join her at the hospital after speaking to her parents on the phone and breaking down into tears. The only way she could keep them from driving to the hospital so late at night was to promise she'd find someone to come and be with her. They loved Brock and had called her cell four times before she convinced them he would make it through the night.

Mitchell steadied her. "You okay, Sugar?"

"You should have told me."

"Couldn't do it, but I thought you should know. How's he doing?"

"Better. He'll beat the anaphylaxis."

"He'll beat it all," Mitchell said with the conviction she should have felt. "He just needed to know there was a reason to."

"I never gave him reason to doubt me."

"Sometimes you don't have to do a thing. Sometimes a man just needs to know his woman is down for him no matter what."

She folded her arms across her chest, trying to process all she'd learned and see everything from Brock's point of view. She didn't know what she would have done if placed in his position, but somehow his choice seemed wrong. She was too tired to process his reasoning now. She was still stunned by his diagnosis—and the fact he'd almost died from receiving the wrong antibiotics.

"You look beat. Why don't you go home? I'll stay."

"I should be here when he wakes up." She watched Hassan slink from the room, avoiding eye contact with her as he moved in the opposite direction down the hall.

"You won't be any good here if you can't stand up. It's been a long day, and I know you didn't get any sleep the other night. So go home and get some rest. Come back in the morning. I'll be here until you get back."

With a little more prompting, Erika left Brock in Mitchell's care. She visited him once more, placing a gentle kiss on his forehead while being careful not to wake him. Before going to her car, she visited the hospital chapel and said a prayer. She dropped to her knees when she remembered the testicular cancer had started this mess and said a longer prayer, begging for a negative biopsy result.

The drive home was too quiet, especially when she knew there would be no one at home to welcome her. She was bone tired when she climbed into bed, but her mind continued to race, trying to see clearly through a thick fog.

She was on the verge of losing Brock forever, and she had never suspected the depth of the secret he was keeping. She would rather lose him to divorce than cancer. She had been right: Brock had walked away from her because of a problem in his life, but she no longer wanted to be right. She wanted things the way they were seven months ago.

She rolled over, noticing she had less than two hours of sleep before she had to return to the office. She closed her eyes and willed herself to sleep, but her will was no match to the tumultuous sadness attacking her heart. She cried tears of fear, confusion, and anxiety. The man she depended on to provide her strength now needed her to be strong enough for the both of them, and she wasn't sure she could do it.

CHAPTER 14

Mark sent a message to Erika: *I need to see you,* cleverly encoded as *I'd like to discuss one of our mutual patients.* Within the hour, his secretary told him Dr. Johnson had a busy schedule, but she'd drop by at lunch. She appeared in his office just after twelve looking worn and tired.

"I got your messages," she told him, dispensing with any small talk. "I'm letting Brock come back."

"Back home? Or back into your life?"

"Both."

"Why?" He was out of his seat, rushing up to her before he realized he'd left his desk.

"Brock is my husband, and he needs me right now."

"How long have you rehearsed that line? Enough times to convince yourself it's true?" He took her hands in his. "Listen, Brock left you. He walked out on you and his marriage. You're not obligated to him because he's sick."

Her eyes narrowed, and she took a step away. "I *am* obligated to him—I'm his wife. What do you think I'm going to do?" She shook her head, closing her eyes to gather her thoughts. "Mark, I told you I was going to try to make it work with Brock before I even knew he was sick. This doesn't change anything. If anything, he needs me more than I could've imagined. I'm not going to leave him. I'm sorry if it hurts you to hear it, but I still care about him, and I owe it to him to see if we can make it work."

"*Owe it to him?* What about what you owe yourself?"

"My marriage vows mean something to me. I made a commitment to my husband, and I'm going to keep it."

"What about how I feel about you?"

"It can't matter."

"It matters to me."

"It shouldn't. I'm a married woman. We should have never crossed the line. We did. I'll take the burden of the blame for it, but now we have to do the right thing. I'm going back to Brock. You find a woman who is available to be with you."

"Just walk away? Just like that?"

She nodded.

"What about our friendship?" He wanted her as his lover, but if he could maintain their friendship, there would always be a chance he could win her back.

"It won't work. There's too much history between us. It would be disrespectful to Brock. We have to stay away from each other."

He had cared about Erika for many months but never understood the depth of his feelings until he realized he was losing her for good. A sharp pain pierced his heart. He didn't like losing—especially when it came to Erika. He'd made a big mistake, falling for a woman who hadn't cleared up her baggage with her husband, but his heart wanted what it wanted. There was no logic, rhyme, or reasoning to it. He cared for Erika, and it hurt him deeply to know he could never have her.

"I wish I didn't have to be so blunt," Erika said, her voice softening. "I don't know another way to be clearer. I like you, Mark. You're a great guy. I just can't be with you."

She waited for him to respond, but he was too stunned. His mind drummed up scenarios in which he could trick her into loving him. He couldn't lose her to Brock. They belonged together, but Brock was scamming her into going back to him. The man had no boundaries. He'd do anything to win their rivalry. He watched her walk away, realizing he loved another man's wife more than he'd ever loved a woman in his life.

After the hurt wore off, anger gripped Mark's heart, and every bit of it was directed at Dr. Brock Johnson. He had fought dirty, using his illness to guilt his wife into taking him back. The man didn't deserve Erika. She was a queen, but Brock treated her like a child's discarded toy, giving her attention only when someone else wanted her.

As Mark sat alone in the darkness of his apartment nursing a drink, his heart began to demand vengeance. He didn't know Brock well, and Erika only spoke of their breakup and how it affected her. She never talked directly about what kind of man Brock was, although Mark had formed his own opinion from the information he had gathered and Brock's appearance in his office demanding he get out of the way. He thought Brock arrogant and selfish, a man who had been spoiled to believe he could have anything he wanted, whenever he wanted.

Over the past two days since Erika broke it off with him, he'd began to ask around Mission Hospital about Brock. By all accounts, he was a good doctor. Even his residents seemed to like him. No one had a negative thing to say about his doctoring skills.

Mark began to dig deeper, squirreling into the networks of people who weren't physician colleagues. Many of the nurses found Brock quite difficult to work with, calling him nitpicky when it came to certain things with the care of his patients.

He was considered quiet, aloof, and unfriendly—always about business and never taking the time to spend a minute to get to know the staff. Mark learned a good number of the management staff was intimidated by the broad-shouldered man who always wore a stern expression and rarely smiled.

Mark capitalized on what he learned. With boxes of donuts and bagels in hand, he made it a point to visit the inpatient floor where Brock's patients were usually admitted. He didn't know how he would do it, but he would turn Brock's short-comings against him, showing Erika just what kind of man she'd committed herself to.

He wasn't a bad man. In fact, he prided himself on being a good man. He was tired of lying down. Tired of being the good guy while the loser got the girl. Too many of his relationships had ended before he was ready, always being told he was too boring, or too busy, or too proper. His sister told him he had a habit of falling for the wrong type of women. This time he had fallen for the right woman, but the right woman was with the wrong man.

His digging kept bringing him back to Mission West. He "got turned around" at Mission Hospital West one day, ending up on the nursing unit where Brock had been admitted. He got to know the staff, befriending them with catered lunches until they felt comfortable gossiping around him. He learned every detail of Brock's stay, including the interactions between the doctor and his wife. With carefully phrased questions, he learned Brock had had a setback and was expected to stay in the hospital for several days.

"It's sad," one of the residents told him. The young woman had been flirting with him for months, but he had no interest in her. "Dr. Johnson must be distraught."

"Who wouldn't be?" Mark played along.

"Yeah, I mean testicular cancer when he's so young? He and his wife don't have any children, do they?"

Mark battled his surprise, keeping his voice even. "No, they don't have a family."

"Wow." She shook her head in despair. "It's really sad."

He made an excuse and quickly hurried away from the resident. Since Brock was initially admitted for twenty-three-hour observation, he'd assumed the operation was minor, maybe a cosmetic nip of the love handles. He'd never guessed cancer. As he made his way across the glossy floors of the hospital, his mind raced, trying to understand what Erika must be feeling. No wonder she had decided to stay with Brock.

For a fleeting moment, he wondered if he should back off from pursuing her. It wasn't fair to steal a sick man's wife. He didn't know how serious Brock's condition was, and for all he knew, the man could be dying.

He remembered the feel of Erika in his arms. The way their lips fit perfectly together for tender kisses. He thought of their potential. They had so far to go.

Brock had been given his chance, and he'd squandered it away. Mark was sorry he was sick, but it was no reason for Erika to give up her happiness. He'd have to change his strategy and not go all gangbusters trying to get her back, but he would not give Erika up.

CHAPTER 15

The day Brock came home Erika's mind was still wrapped in confusion. In a matter of days, she'd learned her husband wanted to put their marriage back together but might be gravely ill with cancer, limiting how much time they would have with each other. His illness was enough to handle, but toss in the turmoil of their rocky relationship, and it was enough to make her head ache.

"You need anything?" Mitchell asked her after accompanying Brock inside.

"I'll be fine." Brock held out his hand to her. "Now that I'm home." Other than walking a little gingerly, there were no signs of how he felt physically. He was equally as guarded with his emotions, wearing a doe-eyed smile whenever he looked at her.

Erika pulled away from Brock, still not completely comfortable with his transformation, and walked Mitchell to the door. "Thanks for bringing his car back."

"No problem." He grasped her upper arm, bringing her out on the front porch with him. "What the hell is wrong with him?"

"What do you mean?"

"The silly grin he's wearing. The moony looks he keeps

giving you. Brock hates it when I call him a metrosexual. What's with the I-love-everything-and-everybody-and-the-world-is-a-wonderful-place routine? Is he still doped up?"

"He's going through a lot."

"He lost one of his balls, not his mind. If he keeps acting like this, I'm taking him to see a shrink."

"It's the shock of it all. It's his way of dealing with the stress. We won't get the biopsy report for another five or six days. Once we're over that hump, he'll be his old self."

Mitchell watched her doubtfully, unaware he was adjusting his jeans. His sympathy pains had begun the moment they arrived at the hospital to bring Brock home, and apparently they were in full force.

"I'd better get back inside." Truth be told, she was hesitant about being alone with Brock. She didn't know what to say to him, or how to act. Were they supposed to go back the way they were seven months ago before he walked out on their marriage? Or should she confront him with her fears about his health and her anger at him for keeping it from her? It was much easier to advise her patients, being emotionally removed from the situation. She reminded herself to act selflessly, putting her husband's needs first.

"Still mad at me?" Mitchell asked, breaking her reverie.

"Yes."

He laughed heartily, pulling her against him for a tight squeeze. "You know you love me. Give me a call if you need anything, Sugar."

"I will."

She watched Mitchell bound off the porch knowing, as he did, she couldn't stay angry with him. It hadn't been his place to divulge Brock's secret, as much as she'd wanted him to. She hoped Ginnifer would be as good a friend if she ever needed it.

Mitchell backed out of the driveway and cruised down the street, his custom sound system leaving jazzy ribbons behind.

Brock's hands lightly dusted her shoulders, resting familiarly against her. "Come inside, Erika."

She hadn't heard him approach. She'd been standing on the porch under the pretense of watching Mitchell go when truly she was stalling—uncomfortable about being alone with her own husband. She willed herself to turn around and follow him inside. She fought the urge to bolt off the porch, race to the garage, jump into her car, and drive away as fast as she could.

"Hey." Brock's finger smoothed down the back of her neck. "Erika?"

"Give me a minute?" She sounded as if she were choking. She needed to analyze these new feelings. Where was the woman who loved Brock so much she was on the verge of falling apart because she didn't understand why he was rejecting her? He was here, now, and she was avoiding being alone with him.

"Come inside with me," he insisted.

"I want to get some air."

"Then we'll sit in the backyard. Or on the deck outside our bedroom." His fingers tightened on her shoulders.

She didn't move. He was reading her, and he knew she was afraid and contemplating running. He wouldn't let her. She was smothering. She needed time to digest what was happening. She was so out of control of her life. Major decisions had been made about her future, and she didn't have any say at all. A week ago, she'd been certain about what she wanted. Today, her stomach was tightening at the prospect she just might get it. Her chest heaved, the air around her too heavy to bring into her lungs. She needed to get away.

"Do you remember our first kiss?" Brock whispered near her ear. His heated breath tickled across her nerve endings, warming her to the bone. His hands left her shoulders and slipped around her waist as he stepped into her, pressing against her back. "Do you?"

"Yes." Thinking of it made her relax.

"I had tried to kiss you about a ka-zillion times, but whenever I moved in, you'd pull away. By the time we had our sixth date, I was beginning to wonder what was wrong." He placed his chin on her shoulder. "I asked you about it. You told me you didn't think I was ready." He laughed quietly, and she did too.

"You should have seen the look on your face. You would never admit you had no idea what I was talking about, but the look on your face told it all."

"But I did figure it out, and I did everything I needed to do to get ready." He twirled her around in his arms until she was facing him. "And then I came to you."

"I was speaking at the elementary school. Teaching the kids about hygiene."

"I couldn't wait any longer."

"You were standing by my car when I came out. You crossed the parking lot so fast I thought there was an emergency."

"There was."

Brock wore a designer suit that day, deep blue with a gray shirt and a tie mixed with the colors. His creases were crisp and his shoes polished. His face had the same expression of concentrated determination it had the first time she saw him, standing at a patient's bedside suturing a very difficult wound. His eyes were locked on hers, his arms coming up to embrace her before he reached her. The teacher she'd been walking with inhaled sharply as Brock scooped Erika into his arms and kissed her.

It wasn't the quick, proper kiss Erika had expected. Brock pulled her flush against his body, unaware and unconcerned about the tiny spectators or the teaching staff watching. His lashes flickered upward to read the shock in her eyes before he pressed his lips to hers. All the passion and longing he'd been harboring were communicated in his kiss. He entered her mouth slowly, savoring his first opportunity to experience this intimacy with her. He crushed her when she touched her tongue to his. When he released her, she was wobbly, so he helped her inside her car to sit and catch her breath. He closed the door, leaving her speechless behind the steering wheel. He walked away with a backward glance, but no words.

"You called me arrogant because I didn't say anything," he reminded her.

"I'm sure it wasn't the first time someone did."

"I didn't say anything because I couldn't. I was affected by that kiss the same way you were. One kiss changed my life."

"Really?" He'd never told her that before.

"I'll never forget it. Whenever I get stressed out, or nervous, or scared, I relive our first kiss in my mind, and everything becomes a little easier to handle."

She melted against him a little bit but remembered it was her turn to be strong enough to support him.

"Let's go inside, order takeout, and not worry about anything."

Suddenly, she felt silly for having any doubts. Brock hadn't changed. This was the man she'd fallen instantly, thoroughly in love with. "Yeah," she said, "let's go inside."

After the first round of Chinese, Brock disappeared quietly into the bathroom. He was trying so hard to keep her mind off his illness. While they ate, he kept the conversation light, repeating the antics of his nieces and nephews as told to him by his mother. She was having a good time in Memphis but missed them both.

Erika sat stiffly on the sofa, listening for any sounds from down the hallway. She wanted to join Brock in the bathroom, to see his scars and the damage to his scrotum. He wasn't ready, and she would respect him. As difficult as it was for her finding out days ago, Brock had been living with his diagnosis for months. Now he had to live with her reaction to it.

She thought about their first kiss again. Her life had been changed the moment she walked into that hospital room and saw Dr. Brock Johnson at work. The kiss had been the icing on the cake. Their first time making love had sealed the deal. She knew then she wanted to spend the rest of her life with him. He always marveled over her flying down to support him at his father's funeral, but she couldn't imagine being anywhere but by his side.

"Erika?" Brock was standing over her in rust-colored silk pajamas. "Where are you?"

She took his hand and placed it against her face, pressing the gold wedding band into her cheek. "I'm glad you're home."

He grinned. "Let's go to bed."

She showered and met him in bed, the shredded divorce papers all but forgotten. She cuddled up to him and they watched the news together. The way they used to. Before he had been diagnosed with cancer. Before he had left her. He was quiet but not sulky. She attributed it to his being uncomfortable with the changes to his body. She had pictured a romantic night of making love when they got back together, maybe out on the veranda underneath the stars, but she didn't push. It would take time for his body and his mind to heal.

"Erika?" Brock whispered once the lights were out and they were lying next to each other trying to fall asleep.

"Yes?"

"Did you sleep with him?"

The question shocked her. They were beginning to fall

back into their rhythm. Mark hadn't been on her mind at all. It must have been on Brock's all day. "No."

"You're my wife. Stay away from him."

Where was the "I love you" she expected? How about, "I was wrong and I'll never do it again"? Instead, he was giving orders, charging back into her life and taking over without showing any remorse.

"Erika? Stay away—"

"I'm not seeing him anymore."

He shifted, making the mattress dip in his direction. He remained on his back, although he could never rest that way. No matter how he got into bed, he always ended up on his left side because it was the only way he could fall asleep. The bedroom had been arranged so he could lay this way and still face her. The cancer had interrupted even the smallest areas of his life.

Insignificant things that were seemingly unimportant would impact him greatly. Not being able to sleep on his left side for a few days would only make him a little cranky, but it was a reflection of what was to come. She'd done the research. Every two months for the next year and every three months for the second year, Brock would need to undergo a battery of tests: physical examination, chest x-ray, and lab work for tumor markers.

There was also the emotional turmoil related to getting the biopsy result. The radiation treatment promised to be another physical and emotional hurtle. Brock was a strong man who liked to be in control of his life. Being sick did not suit him. It would be a difficult situation for anyone to be in, but he would need her support more than the next man.

With the radical orchiectomy and external-beam radiation therapy, Brock's chances of recovery were good—the 5-year disease-free survival rate being about 98 percent. It was something to hang on to. Two minor humps with the biopsy and radiation, and then they could go back to normal.

Brock rested his hand on her hip. "Thank you for coming to the hospital."

She closed her eyes, her tension fading a small degree.

"You saved my life. In more ways than one."

CHAPTER 16

"I want to know how you got my wife to start seeing you in the first place." Brock stepped into Mark's office unannounced among the protests of his receptionist. Upon hearing his accusation, she faded back, closing the door behind her.

Mark was cool, looking up from his work with an expression that made it impossible to read his thoughts. "There were no tricks involved. You left her. I was always there."

Brock thought he must be having a bad reaction to the new antibiotics because he'd been irrational all day. It started the minute Erika left for work. As he tried to rest and allow his body to heal before it was assaulted again with radiation therapy, he couldn't stop imagining what Mark must have done with her—to her. Regardless of her telling him they hadn't had sex.

On the pretense of getting a few changes of clothes from his apartment, he drove to the Mission Hospital campus. After packing a bag and talking to the manager about ending his lease, he found himself stalking the halls of the hospital on the way to Mark's office.

"Erika told you we're back together." He tilted his chin down, studying the man over the rim of his glasses.

"We've talked about her current situation."

He didn't like Mark's wording, or his cool demeanor. "Now I'm talking to you. I want to make sure you're clear."

"You're so clear I can see right through you and what you're trying to do." Mark's anger flared, forcing him to rise from his seat.

Brock had seen this display before, and it still bothered him to think Erika might have been on the receiving end at one time or another. "What do you mean?" He'd promised himself he wouldn't engage Mark in a debate over Erika's loyalties, but here he was doing all kinds of things uncharacteristic for him.

"You were perfectly fine with dumping Erika until you found out someone else wanted her. Now your pride won't let her go. So what do you do? You use your cancer to guilt her into going back to you."

How did he know about the cancer? Had Erika confided in him?

"Who told you—"

Mark shrugged, coolly contorting his face into a taunting smile. "I know all sorts of things about you and what kind of man you are."

"Then you know you shouldn't challenge me on this. Don't interfere with my marriage. Erika and I are back together."

"Yet you're standing here threatening me." He tsked, shaking his head in triumph.

"I'm coming to you man-to-man. I know you have feelings for Erika. It's hard for you to let go. I understand, but the best man has won. Time for you to move on."

"Erika's confused, but I'll be here to help her sort out every question she has. Every conversation you have with her, you'll be wondering if she's going to come to me for help making a decision. At night, when you're lying next to her in bed, you won't know if it's you or me she's dreaming about."

"You're pathetic. I'm trying to help you. Keep you from making a fool out of yourself."

"No, you're here because you know your relationship isn't as tight as you want me to believe. While you're laid up, my office is right down the hall from hers. When she gets tired of taking care of you, I'll be there taking care of her. Whether she needs conversation, to be held, or stroked, I'll be ready and available. *Whatever* she needs—emotionally or *physically*— I can give it to her. Can you promise her that?"

"I need to be able to make love to my wife."

"One minute," Hassan said, pulling Brock into a room used for office storage. "You shouldn't be driving. I am not surprised you are not able to bed your wife."

His phrasing made Brock cringe.

"I told you to get some rest. No work for three weeks."

"This is about sex with Erika, not returning to work."

Hassan looked uncomfortable. "You can do whatever your body tells you it's ready for. We do not want your plumbing to get jammed, as it were."

He'd had enough experience deciphering Hassan's sometimes cryptic English to know what he meant. A buildup of sperm in his scrotal sacks—sack—might be a bit painful right now.

Hassan lowered his voice when he asked, "Have you had an erection after the surgery?"

"Not yet."

"You may have to put some effort in achieving your . . . goal."

Again, Brock knew what he meant, but he was tired of masturbating for the cause.

"And your abdominal incision? Is it healed after only three days?"

He looked away uncomfortably.

"So I ask you, *can* you bed your wife yet?"

Brock hated his logic. "I have to be able to make love to Erika. We're back together now. If I don't do everything right, she might leave."

"There are other things you can do until your abdomen is completely healed. Other positions to try." Despite what Hassan called his sexually repressed cultural upbringing, he'd chosen a specialty requiring him to have frank discussions about sexuality and erections and other very male concerns, although Brock imagined plenty of women had similar questions concerning their husband's illness. Hassan had learned to handle his embarrassment well and answered Brock's questions honestly. "We talked before the surgery. Men react differently to what you're going through. There are support groups—"

"Enough with the damn support groups, Hassan. This is about saving my marriage, and losing Erika is not something I conjured up in my head. Give me a script for Viagra."

Hassan sputtered a hundred reasons why he wouldn't do what he asked. "You may need to do some self-practice to aid in achieving your first erection. After jumping over the big hurtle, it should come easier."

"What about a scrotal implant?" He pitched his voice lower. "I don't like the flapping skin." As the swelling began to subside, he noticed the lopsided difference between his full sack and his empty one.

"Come to my office. I'll give you some information to read over." He hesitated. "Most men find the difference small—"

"Use another word," Brock growled.

"Most men get used to the change and don't want the operation. The technology for implants is advancing, but the plastic still can be harder than normal . . . most women prefer the natural change in a man's anatomy. You should—"

"Go home and discuss it with my wife."

"It's what you Americans like to do."

"And no Viagra? Go home and masturbate is your best medical advice?"

Hassan shrugged, fighting a smile.

"You're not funny." He snatched open the door to the supply room. "And you're becoming too American."

Hassan ignored his foul mood. "Let me examine you while you're here."

"For what? You've already given me the answer to my question." He was halfway down the hall before he turned to meet Hassan's worried expression. He pushed away his frustration and spoke calmly to his friend. "I'll see you in a couple of days." He had an appointment to obtain the results of his biopsy.

Hassan hurried up to him, righting the angle of his turban. "There are other ways to satisfy your wife."

Right now I can't satisfy her in all the ways Mark can. And that was the problem.

"Man, what's wrong with you?"

Brock rolled his eyes at his longtime friend, reaching for the iced drink in front of him.

Mitchell snatched the glass away before it reached his lips. "Are you supposed to be drinking while you're taking pain killers?" Before Brock could answer, Mitchell signaled for one of the dancers lounging at the bar with the DJ discussing tonight's lineup. She switched over, her hips in full bloom, and took the drink away. She also took a slice of Brock's pride about not being a healthy male with her.

Brock enjoyed coming to the club when it was closed. The space was dark and quiet, allowing him to think without others looking to him for answers—or to spin a medical miracle. He hadn't visited the club during the show since he'd become engaged to Erika. He hated the way the married men lusted over women the same age as their daughters, tossing money onto the stage in hopes of scoring a lap dance, or a little something extra in the parking lot. Since Mitchell had taken ownership, the prostitution had ended—at the club anyway. He treated the dancers well, even giving them a health plan. He immediately remodeled the broken-down club, although the back offices still needed work. Most importantly, he hired a woman who was great at marketing and had connections with all the rich and famous. The makeup of the clientele was slowly morphing, and with it, the cost of admission was climbing. Like everything Mitchell invested in, the club was a gold mine.

"Why don't you go home and talk to Erika? She's down for you. You should have seen the way she barged up in here. She's a soldier in the Brock Johnson army, and she'll go down swinging to save your sorry ass."

He rested his chin in his hands, feeling he'd earned the right to be upset. "She's thinking about deserting."

"The eye guy?"

"He won't stay away from her."

"And?"

"And his clinic is right down the hall from Erika's. I can't watch her every second of the day."

"You don't have to." Mitchell exhaled loudly, clearly not having the patience to advise his friend in what he saw as a simple matter. "Look. Do you think my wife is down here at the club every night watching me?"

"Your wife doesn't know you own a strip joint."

Mitchell laughed, but it was short-lived and not humorous.

"She knows I hang out here. We don't discuss it, and she doesn't want to know what goes on here, and do you know why? Because she knows I love her too much to ever leave her, and if I want to keep her, I have to keep it in my pants. She'd know right away if I was with another woman. She'd know, and she'd scoop up my kids and be out. Without a word to me."

"Erika said she never slept with Mark."

"You believe her?"

He nodded. She wouldn't lie to him . . . but it wasn't enough because Mark was waiting.

"You mean to tell me you left her for seven months, didn't tell her why, acted a complete ass, and she never slept with another man? And now that you're back together you're afraid she's going to jump into bed with the eye guy?" Mitchell shook his head. "What kind of pills did the Arab put you on, because they're causing you to lose your mind. You're being paranoid. For no reason. Go home. Be good to Erika. She won't go anywhere."

He pushed away from the table, not wanting to try to explain how complicated the situation was to his friend with the golden touch. He could never understand what it felt like to be half a man trying to satisfy a woman special enough to equal two.

"I don't know who you are right now, but you've changed. They cut off your stone and turned you into a punk. My friend Brock doesn't cower for anybody. He fights for what he wants."

Brock unpacked his bag, finding comfort in returning his clothes to his vacant dresser drawers. When he was closer to 100 percent, he would pack up his apartment and move everything back home. There were so many things on his plate right now—moving back home, explaining everything to his mother, getting the biopsy report, radiation therapy . . . oh yeah, making sure his wife was still in love with him.

Before Erika made it home from work, he managed to throw together dinner. He ordered pizza—Pizza Papalis deep-dish pepperoni—and tossed a salad. He wasn't a cook and didn't pretend to be, but he could open a bag of premixed salad greens, add the toppings, and chill a bottle of wine. He set the table and rushed off to change.

As he stood in the shower, his back to the spray, he kept his ears open for Erika's return. He didn't want her to see him naked yet. Her surprise attack at the hospital only gave her a glimpse of bulky bandages. Those had been removed and replaced by sleek gauze pads and waterproof tape. The belly wound he could live with. It would heal over and leave a slight scar that would fade in time. His missing scrotal sack was another matter.

Hassan had discounted his fears, not understanding his aggressive need to have an erection. He clearly didn't like the idea of scrotal implants, although he didn't seem to want to veto the idea if it was what he really wanted. Masturbate and discuss the situation with Erika had been his advice, and Brock didn't find it helpful.

Leave it to Mitchell to be uninhibited and blunt about it, tossing around words like *stone, ball,* and cahones. With Mitchell, it seemed all right, one of the trials a man sometimes has to suffer, but no one in the locker room looks below shoulder level anyway, so who cares kind of thing. It wouldn't be so nonchalant a situation with Erika.

The truth was, he was half a man. He'd spent days at the sperm bank preparing for this reality. He'd taken care of conceiving but never contemplated the change in dynamics when it came to making love to Erika.

He had to be in control of all aspects of his life, but none more than in his bedroom. Even when they were decorating the house, he'd let Erika make all the decisions—except in furnishing the bedroom. He sought her input, but the final decisions were his. The tan, brown, and red color scheme with the huge bed and plush sitting area were his choices. Even the patio furniture on the attached veranda were his selections.

He dared look down, but not too long. He remembered his anxiety attack in the hospital and didn't want to relive it. He'd gotten the prescription for Ativan filled at Erika's insistence, but she didn't truly understand why he might need the relaxants. He didn't want her to find out firsthand. He turned off the warm spray and stepped out of the shower. He patted his groin area gingerly, careful not to touch the achy parts. Noticing the time, he quickly jumped into his pajama bottoms. He rarely slept in the matching tops, but he thought it would be smart so as not to draw attention to the rest of his body.

"You're dressed for bed already?" Erika was standing in their bedroom when he exited the bathroom.

"I'm a little tired." He leaned in and gave her a quick kiss. "I must have overdone it today."

"Hmm." She kicked off her shoes, bent to pick them up, and took weary steps to her walk-in closet.

He eyed her suspiciously as she reappeared and went into the bathroom. He'd expected her to come in the door, breathing hard and ready to fight after Mark told her about their afternoon meeting. Instead, she looked beaten and overtired.

"Hard day?" he called, raising his voice over the water.

"With Ginnifer and I both leaving the office early last week, we fell a little behind. Trying to catch up on paperwork between patients meant no breaks and no lunch."

He eased down the hall and slowly pushed the bathroom door all the way open, giving her time to object if she didn't want his invasion of her privacy. "I ordered Pizza Papalis and made a salad. You should eat and go to bed early."

"I will." She offered a shy smile. "Give me a minute?" She closed the door as easily as he had opened it, and the sting of the simple action took him by surprise. She'd found another way to shut him out.

CHAPTER 17

"What did you do all day?" Erika forced a casual tone as she speared lettuce onto her fork. She'd devoured her first slice of thick, gooey pizza. Since she was no longer starving, she found it hard to contain her anger.

Brock topped off her glass of wine as he answered. "Stopped by the apartment to discuss ending the lease with the manager. It's cheaper to keep the place until the end of the term than to break it. I'll see if one of my residents is interested in subletting. I picked up a few things while I was there. I hope you don't mind."

She shook her head, encouraging him with the wave of her fork to go on.

"I was getting a little stir-crazy, so I stopped by to see Hassan and Mitchell before I headed home." He lifted a third slice of pizza onto his plate. It amazed her how much food he could put away. He enjoyed gourmet food, as well as beer and hot dogs, eating them both with the same fervor. Pizza Papalis pizza was a one-slice meal, and anyone who claimed they could eat two slices in one sitting was suspect, but she'd witnessed Brock eat four and then ask for dessert.

She gulped her wine, gathering her courage and settling

her anger before confronting him. "You told me to keep away from Mark, but you think it's okay for you to terrorize him?"

"Terrorize?" He had the decency to look surprised. "Did he say I terrorized him? It didn't quite go that way." He laughed and it wasn't humorous. "Dr. Garing has his facts wrong. I went to him like a man, and I asked him like a man not to interfere in our marriage."

"You'd already given me that command. Why drag him into it?"

"Command?" he repeated, testing the word for its meaning before going on. "Temper your tone at my dinner table."

She was so outdone she couldn't speak for an entire minute, a long minute where Brock gazed at her, silently challenging her to debate him. "You know what?" she began, ready to do battle, but suddenly a futuristic picture of sitting in Hassan's office flashed before her. Not knowing what Brock's health held, she didn't want to spend their time together arguing about Mark.

Brock's glare was so heated she thought the lenses of his glasses would melt. Having stunned her, he didn't hesitate to make his point. "I haven't dragged Mark into anything. In the middle is exactly where he wants to be. Don't be fooled."

She silently counted to ten before she said anything. "I overdid it today. I think I'll go to bed early." She pushed back her chair, thoroughly regretting she was leaving behind a great-tasting salad, and headed for the bedroom. It pained her to miss the lettuce more than her husband's company.

Once in the bedroom, she reached back to unzip her dress, but Brock's fingers pushed her hand away, replacing hers. "I shouldn't have been so harsh."

She realized for the first time Brock was very good about skirting around his apologies. "To me, or to Mark?"

He tensed, but tempered his words. "I'm only concerned about you."

"This is as much my house as yours."

"I know." His fingers caressed as he slowly slipped the zipper down her back.

"Don't talk to me like I'm your child. Don't tell me what tone to use in my house."

"Understood."

"You know I don't like you to make my decisions."

"I do." He kissed the exposed skin of her shoulder.

Her libido started calculating how many days they'd missed making love during Brock's seven-month absence. She forgot why she was mad at him when his lips pressed against her spine, his tongue wiggling into the tiny space between each bony process.

One finger traced the path of the zipper. "I don't want to fight with you about Mark. Thinking about it makes me crazy. When I imagine what you did—"

She turned to face him, stopping him from traveling down that rocky road. He had walked out on their marriage, but she had brought another man into their relationship. There was enough blame to share in their marriage-gone-wrong, but knowing it didn't make her feel less guilty.

"Then we shouldn't talk about it anymore," she told him. "Don't go to his office again. Don't throw our marriage up in his face. This can't be a macho thing. We all work in the same building. Be the bigger man and keep the peace."

Brock nodded, but the lustful look in his eye made her wonder if he'd heard anything she'd said.

"I made it more complicated by seeing Mark, but you started it all by leaving. I'm trying to make it right with him. Don't cause trouble on purpose."

He snapped out of his lusty fog. "You're trying to make it right, how?"

"I apologized."

He waited for more, but she didn't give him anything. One thick brow ticked behind the rim of his glasses. For a man who shielded his emotions better than Fort Knox protected gold, he might as well have screamed at her. "Should I worry about losing you to this guy?"

"No."

His body stiffened, but he didn't push the issue. Behind his stony expression, his mind was whirling with questions and doubts. She saw it in the set of his jaw, behind the dark facial hair molded to his determined chin.

"No, Brock," she repeated, seeking to ease his concerns. "Through it all, I never stopped loving you. You don't have to worry about losing me to anyone—except you." If she ever walked away from him, it would be because he screwed up. Never for another man, because no other man could replace him.

"I didn't mean to make your day harder." He moved behind her again and began unfastening her bra.

"What did Hassan say? Did he examine you?"

His fingers faltered but quickly picked up rhythm as he tried to hide his uneasiness with the conversation. "The biopsy wasn't back yet."

She let him push the straps of her bra down her arms and toss the scrap of material onto a chair before she faced him. "I want to be there when you get the results."

"I can go alone."

"I'm going. Don't argue. From here on, we do this together."

She'd learned to read the subtlest gestures of his body over the years, and now his broad shoulders dipped a little, relief being evident. She reached up and stroked the waves of his dark hair.

"The other night . . . when we were together . . . I didn't get to look at you. It's been so long."

Her skin sizzled as he righted the error. He removed his glasses, placing them on the nightstand. His eyes moved over her, slowly and thoroughly roaming every curve of her body. His gaze was so intent she felt it as a gentle caress, leaving thousands of tiny goose bumps behind.

"It's too soon," she said, using her most reasonable voice, although it clashed with the brazen emotions flitting across his face.

With him watching her this way, she hoped he was about to tell her Hassan had given him the go-ahead to have sex. She needed to be intimate with him again—to solidify their relationship, to satisfy her body, to settle her mind. She didn't dare hope. Her sight locked above his collarbone, because the terrain below was too tempting. She knew the jock strap was there to give him the support he needed until he healed, but she also knew the size had been a tailored fit because his cup did literally run over.

"Maybe," he answered, not batting his long lashes, "maybe not."

She tilted her head in question.

He didn't break eye contact as he slipped his fingers into her panty line, pulling her to him.

"I need to shower." She sounded breathy and very, very anxious.

"You go shower while I figure out if it's too soon." He didn't let her go. He cast his dark eyes low as he pulled her panties down her legs, kneeling for her to use him as a brace while she stepped out of them.

He got up slowly, prompting her to ask, "How is your incision?"

"Tender. Healing."

"We shouldn't—"

"But you're so ready." He pressed her panties to his nose and inhaled deeply, reminding her with stark clarity how freaky he could be in the bedroom. His behavior in the bedroom was such a complete contrast to his normal propriety, it excited her beyond belief. There had been many times a randy phone call, dirty promises, or a scandalous touch had sent her over the edge, climaxing before he even undressed her.

"The last thing we want is to open your incision before it has a chance to heal." The voice of reason. *Where had it come from?*

"The first thing we want to do is f . . ." He rarely used the four-letter word, but when he did, he meant it. He repeated the word, finishing it with unrestrained gusto. The grin tilting his lips upward said he really meant it right now. The F-word moved through her, one letter at a time, stirring up every sexual nerve ending it passed as it took the long route from her ear to her brain.

"You're ready." He tossed her panties onto the chair with her bra. "I want you. If we can't do it all, we can do other things." He cupped her chin and wrapped his fingers around the back of her neck, showing her the length of his fingers— they could be used for all kinds of exploring. "You might even get to take the lead."

"There's a deal I can't pass up." Because it rarely, if ever, was offered. Brock liked control. Control of his emotions. Control of his work. Control of their marriage. Control of those he loved. And most of all, he had to be in control of what happened in their bedroom.

"Go. Shower. I'll bring the dessert to bed."

* * *

A ten-minute shower changed everything.

She rushed through her shower, barely letting the hot water erase the day's woes. She quickly oiled herself with her finest, most intoxicating cream and wrapped herself in a towel only to find Brock in bed, reading. He lowered the paper, wearing a sheepish grin that instantaneously extinguished her lust.

He answered her unspoken question. "You were right. I'm not ready." He rubbed his palm over the dressing covering his incision, bringing unwanted attention to the real problem.

If Erika had a kink, it was the way her body responded to Brock's hard-ons. Her body softened, growing wet and warm, anxious for his touch. She wasn't turned on because he was long and wide and made whatever he was wearing pucker up in anticipation, but because it was physical proof of his aching for her. He wanted control over everything in the bedroom, but his disobedient erection triggered by her making him hot was her power trip.

He folded the paper and laid it on the bedside table. "Come to bed."

She nodded, a little disorientated by the abrupt change of mood. They had gone from steaming-hot-newlywed-couple mode to been-together-too-long-to-share-passion-couple mode in less than thirty minutes. She wandered, still confused, over to her dresser and slipped on a nightshirt.

Brock pulled back the bed covers for her. She slipped in and let him cover her, still bewildered. He cut the light, and they lay there silently, the mood intensified by the darkness.

"We have to talk about this," she said, staring up at the ceiling.

"There's nothing to talk about. You were right. My incision is bothering me."

She rolled over to watch him in the shadows of their bedroom, propping her chin up on her palm. "I promise I won't touch your incision." She couldn't make out his expression, so she lifted her hand to his groin.

He caught her wrist. "Don't."

"Why not?"

He didn't answer. He wrestled her away, maneuvering her hand until it rested on her own hip.

"Your scrotum was removed through your abdominal incision," she pointed out.

"I'm still a little swollen."

She shocked him when she said, "Let me see," and reached for his testicle before he could catch her.

Brock bolted upright, and the room blazed to life as he switched on the lamp. "Erika, no."

She sat up, wanting to see him clearly, searching for any sign of what was happening in his head. "You don't want me to touch you?"

He looked away, and for Brock, it was the greatest expression of his feelings she could have hoped for in this situation. He would not verbally admit to his shame. He'd pretend to be tough and undefeatable, blaming his change in libido on anything other than his own shortcomings.

"Now? Or ever again? The way I see it, things aren't going to be much different in two months or two years."

His eyes flashed wide, but he caught the indiscretion and fought for a neutral face. He hadn't considered the long term. He had lost one of his testicles—it wouldn't grow back. The change in his anatomy was permanent. Better to see how she dealt with it now than prolong the truth.

His reaction had other implications too. If he had been too busy to consider how his body had changed physically, what was he stressing about? Did he believe he would die from the cancer as his father had? Was his mind centered on living out his last days, righting his estate and ending his practice?

"Have you thought about us having sex again?" she asked, taking the most delicate route possible to try to get inside his mind.

"Of course I have, but obviously not as much as you have."

"If you're worried about how I'll react to you not having—"

"I'm not the one pushing this discussion."

She ignored his response because she knew it was related to his bruised ego. It had to be hard for a 35-year-old man to lose his testicle, as some believed it was a direct measure of manhood.

"Our relationship is about more than sex, and you know it, Brock. But sex is important too."

"If you want me to get you off, I will." There was no lust behind the offer, only anger.

"Then why didn't you?"

"I guess I didn't realize how important sex had become for you."

"It's about intimacy with my husband." She stretched across the bed to touch his arm, and he flinched, but she didn't pull away. "I enjoy having sex *and* making love with you. You have a very sexy body. I can't see that changing. Maybe you're sexy in a different way, but you're still sexy."

He watched her for a moment, his anger melting away. "I understand what you're doing." He exhaled hard. "I appreciate it. I do." He twisted to face her, gripping her upper arms. "Erika, I'm not ready."

She knew the confession had cost him a great deal of his pride. "It's okay."

"It's not about you."

"I know."

"You're sexy and hot and wonderful. I want you so bad, I . . . I can't. Not yet."

She placed her palm against his cheek. "It's too soon."

"You understand?"

She nodded. She would have to do a lot of understanding in the weeks ahead.

He moved in slowly, pressing his lips to hers for a lingering kiss. "Let me hold you."

She moved down in the bed, turning her back to him. He turned off the light and then fit behind her, draping his arm over her waist. He lifted her hair away from her neck and placed a kiss there. "I love you, Erika. I'm going to make this right. Just give me a little time."

CHAPTER 18

When Hassan entered the room, Brock violently realized he didn't want Erika there. They were sitting next to each other in twin chairs in Hassan's office. Whatever the biopsy showed, he wanted time to process it and present it to Erika in his own way. If she gave him one more look of pity or sympathy or understanding, he would scream. His guilt about coming home had already begun to return, starting the night he couldn't make love to her.

He had tried to get a hard-on the entire time she was in the shower. He relived his favorite moments with her in bed, and when that didn't work, he recalled especially dirty scenes from past-viewed XXX movies. Nothing worked. There had been a little stir of his permanently sleeping penis, but the more he tried to get it to harden, the more it resisted. If the sight of Erika coming out of the shower glowing and wrapped in only a towel, hungry for him, didn't do it, he worried nothing would.

"I won't make you wait in suspense," Hassan said, opening the envelope he'd insisted stayed sealed until Brock was in his office. He hadn't wanted the office staff to know his friend's fate before Brock did.

Erika reached over and took his hand, magnifying his guilt. This could be a death sentence—for him, and for her.

"Give us a minute alone," Brock told Erika.

Her jaw dropped. "Are you kidding?"

"I'll call you in after Hassan and I talk."

"No way." She blatantly ignored his request. "Hassan, tell us what the biopsy shows."

Hassan shrank a little under her potent stare down, but policy dictated Brock give him the okay before sharing the results with anyone—even his wife.

"Brock," Erika's voice was heady and laced with a hint of a threat, "tell Hassan to give us the results. Now."

Her tone made him want to shrink back, too, so he took back all the names he had just called his friend.

She leaned into him, and whispered harshly, "If I leave this office, I won't be outside in the waiting room when you come out."

He couldn't remember her ever being so forceful with him. This was not a challenge he wanted to take on. He cleared his throat and turned back to Hassan. "It's okay."

Hassan's eyes flashed between them as he ripped the envelope open. Brock would have to listen to his lecture about men and women having very specific places in the marriage later.

"Good specimen," Hassan announced, scanning the page.

Brock could feel Erika's eyes on him, but he couldn't look at her. Fear of letting her down made him keep his eyes trained on Hassan, but he could no longer hear what Hassan was saying. His thoughts had fast-forwarded to the possibility of being an invalid, dependent on Erika for everything he needed to live. He saw her smiling at him, trying to hide weary eyes and a tired spirit. He relived every moment of his mother's struggle with his father's death, and his chest tightened—he had trapped Erika into letting him come back home, using her commitment to him and their marriage as leverage. He felt low—lower than low—but he couldn't find the words to push her away. Not when he had once before and had almost lost her. He pressed his lashes together. He needed her. He loved her. He couldn't let her go.

"Brock?" Erika stroked his shoulder, bringing him out of his haze.

He shifted his body toward her.

"Did you hear what Hassan said?" She glanced across the desk at Hassan. "There's no evidence of the cancer spreading to any other organs. The report is clean for spread to the lymph nodes or vascular system. Brock, this is good news."

"No invasion? The cancer is localized?"

Hassan nodded. "To the right testicle. It looks as if we removed the cancer before it could spread."

"The other testicle?" Brock asked, uncomfortable discussing his future manhood in front of Erika. She'd made it clear: She wasn't leaving the office, and he couldn't wait until he got Hassan alone to find out.

"No developmental abnormalities. There were mature sperm in the epididymis, so the testicle was still producing sperm before we removed it—despite the tumor."

Brock's mind churned, allowing him to process the last few minutes. He jumped out of his chair and pulled Erika in his arms. If not for the sharp reminder of his abdominal incision, he would have swept her off her feet, swinging her in his arms. The best he could manage was a kiss, which was cut drastically short by Hassan's discomfort about public displays of affection.

"This is good news," Hassan said, also standing, "but it doesn't alter our plan. We have to proceed with radiation therapy."

* * *

Humiliation moved through Brock as he sat on the treatment couch, the radiologist manipulating parts of his anatomy he hadn't had the courage to touch yet. The swelling had gone down, and he wore the jock strap only if the fit of his slacks dictated its need, but after his failed attempt to make love to Erika, he couldn't touch the wrinkled skin, left sagging by the removal of his testicle.

"I'm aligning the radiation beam with the markings we made on your last visit," the radiologist announced. The squat man wore thick glasses, which almost made Brock run screaming down the corridor at their first meeting: He wanted the person aiming radiation at his crotch to have perfect 20/20 vision. When he'd ducked into the changing room, the first thing he did was whip out his cell phone and curse Hassan until his friend promised him this radiologist was the best in the state.

"Doctor?" Brock lifted his head to see down the line of his body. The protective gear draping the other parts of his anatomy was heavy and awkward, something he'd never noticed before when wearing a jacket into the room during his evaluation of a patient having a CT scan or X-ray.

"Yes?" The radiologist didn't glance at Brock. Good. He was focused and determined.

"No narrative." Knowing the details made him think of everything that could go wrong when all Brock wanted to do was imagine he was somewhere else. He knew too many details about the medical procedure already, which threatened to trigger another embarrassing anxiety attack.

"Yes, doctor," the radiologist answered, his expression never changing.

Thirty minutes of positioning later, the beam was aimed just right—Brock compared it to a defenseless country with nuclear weapons aimed at it. The radiologist and his assistants left the treatment room, closing the door tightly behind them and sealing Brock in with the radiation. The radiologist announced the beginning of the session seconds before the soft whir of the linear accelerator signaled the delivery of the radiation beams. Ten minutes tops and the procedure would be over.

Brock closed his eyes, mentally transporting himself into the waiting area where Erika sat. She had brought along a book to read while she waited for her husband's genitals to be fried. He'd thought the action strangely detached for her, who cried over any hardship one of her patients was experiencing. Somehow he felt entitled to more than a lift to the hospital, a peck on the cheek, and her wishes of "good luck."

He felt strangely detached himself as the quiet buzz was the only sign of the treatment he was receiving. There should be fanfare, maybe a little party before a man was asked to sit in the therapy chair and surrender his virility. Of course, Hassan kept telling him the radiation treatments affected every man in a different way. He thought about sterility—his body trembled, causing the radiologist to hop on the microphone and remind him to remain still. He had a fifty percent chance of becoming impotent. The thought of never making love to Erika or having kids with her was enough to make his breathing come in tiny bursts. He might be lucky enough to escape both those realities and become a victim of penile shrinkage.

He squeezed his eyes tighter, willing himself to think of other times. Happier times when he didn't worry if his wife would stop loving him because he had become half the man he once had been.

The side effects of the radiation therapy drove Brock to sleep in the spare bedroom.

"Brock, you don't have to sleep upstairs," Erika told him,

wearily pulling back the bedcovers. "I'm a doctor. I understand what your body's going through." She sounded supportive, but her days at the clinic were becoming longer and longer since the completion of his therapy.

"You're not my doctor. You're my wife." His pride would not allow him to admit the dribbling from his penis was the least of his worries. A week had gone by since the surgery and he still was not able to achieve an erection—no matter how much he tried.

"If it's what you want," she said crawling into bed. "I think you're being silly."

He grabbed the newspaper and headed upstairs, shutting off the lights as he left their bedroom.

The upper level of their home had three bedrooms. One was equipped for use as an office, but neither Brock nor Erika brought enough work home to put it to good use. His mother slept in the largest room with the single skylight above her bed. This bedroom was large and airy with a balcony and private bath. The elevator opened directly into her bedroom. She rarely used it, too stubborn to admit taking the stairs caused her pain, but Erika sometimes insisted she did, and his mother always listened when Erika put her foot down. The third bedroom was a spare bedroom for company, which had been used only twice when each of his brothers had come to visit.

Brock had been sleeping in the spare bedroom for three nights now. What he enjoyed most about their home was its coziness. It was large and spacious with skylights and the great room opening up to the second floor, but it was warm and felt like a real home. He credited Erika for achieving this with her endless hours of decorating. Every room reminded him of her. Her favorite colors. Her desire for style and comfort displayed in her selection of oversized designer furniture. The colors she'd selected for the paint and wallpaper flowed from room to room, neutral with a dramatic splash of color. As he climbed into bed, it saddened him to realize only their bedroom didn't seem to fit with the scheme of the house, and he wondered how it reflected on him and his commitment to his family.

After reading the paper, he shut off the lights but still couldn't sleep. His wedding day was heavy on his mind. It had been a day for girls with pretty flowers and extended family dressed in their finest. His smiles being scarce, posing for snapshot after snapshot was a bit trying, but Erika was so happy he would never ruin it for her.

He'd taken a backseat to the planning, like most men did, going along with Erika's selections without much debate. The planning of the wedding took longer than their actual dating history, but he pointed that fact out only once. When Erika tossed him a look of sheer exasperation, his glasses had fogged from embarrassment of his insensitivity, and he never spoke about it again.

The planning might have been a drag, but when Erika walked down the aisle on her father's arm, his chest had tightened and his throat constricted. Suddenly, he'd become afraid she would realize how much he didn't deserve her, stop midway, and go running from the church. But she didn't. She joined him, taking his hand and smiling up at him with so much love the church gave a collective sigh. To this day, he couldn't believe he had the power to make her happy.

When he concentrated, he could see her clearly, as if they were standing at the altar this minute. So beautiful. So happy. All his. Unbelievable.

Erika's sensitivity and upbeat outlook on life caused him to fall in love with her, but her classic beauty made him lust for her. He remembered holding her against his chest as they opened the reception with their private dance. She had looked up at him with stars in her eyes, and he promised himself right then he would never disappoint her. She made him want babies. She helped him define love. She gave him hope.

Brock was still reliving their wedding day, concentrating on Erika's beauty, when he felt his body stir. He slipped his hand beneath the sheets to find his penis semihard—more than he'd experienced in over a week. He stroked the shaft, slowly but firmly, thinking of the many ways he and Erika had experimented with sex in their early marriage. A familiar twinge moved through his scrotum as he grew long and rigid in his hand.

He wanted to bound down the stairs, wake Erika, and show her his hard-on, but he needed to see how far this would go. He couldn't slide into Erika's warmth unless his penis became solid; his entire length needed to touch her depths. He continued to stroke, his fingers venturing lower, but not brave enough to massage the skin of his testicles. He giggled like a teenage boy experiencing his first erection as the shaft of his penis stretched to resemble a column of steel.

CHAPTER 19

Erika had a full schedule of patients and she was late for work. She was never late for work. She rushed to the new van and hurried out of the driveway, enjoying the luxury of the burgundy-on-burgundy color scheme. This was the first vehicle she'd owned that wasn't standard black. Leather interior was luxurious, but the velvety velour tickling her thighs was nice.

It was early morning, around six, so there was very little traffic on the surface streets. The roads had been freshly paved and were ripe for driving sixty miles per hour in a forty-five-mile-per-hour zone. She noticed a hand-painted van parked outside the furniture store well before she pulled up next to it. Something seemed out of place about the raggedy van and army green car parked behind it. The store wouldn't open for hours, but there was a scraggly man with long blond hair running between the store and car with armloads of merchandise.

She didn't need a doctor's education to know the store was being robbed. The traffic light turned red and she stopped her van almost parallel to the green car. She glanced at the clock in the dashboard, trying to decide if being a Good Samaritan was worth being late for work. She would have kids one day, she reminded herself, and she'd want to set a good example for them. She used one hand to fish her cell phone from her purse.

The scraggly man jumped into the car and pulled out in front of her. She planned on reporting his license to the 9-1-1 operator, but the car moved too fast, and she wasn't able to see the numbers clearly.

Without much thought, she followed the car. The driver turned left at the first corner and then left again, bringing them onto a busy street with several cars. She maintained her distance but kept the car in sight. A third left brought the car back in front of the furniture store. The driver pulled up behind the van but didn't get out. Now she just felt foolish. The man was probably the manager or owner up early to organize the store.

She returned to her original route, discarding the idea of something amiss at the furniture store and again worrying about being late for clinic. She was driving too fast for the increased volume of traffic, but she didn't want to call on Ginnifer to cover her patients again. She'd been taking advantage of her friend lately with all the time she'd needed off to be with Brock.

Driving too fast, she told herself as she came up too quickly on the back of a car. The van was too large to drive at this speed, and it weaved as she tried to keep it inside the lane. The light changed to red and the car in front of her stopped. The brake pedal didn't seem to control the car's speed well, so she used her both of her feet, pressing down hard into the floorboard. She remembered thinking how it was awful a new luxury van didn't have a better braking system.

Two more close fender benders later, the traffic dropped off and she was alone on the road. She picked up her speed, glancing at the dashboard again to check the time. If she could maintain this speed and not be stopped by a cop, she'd make it on time.

She looked up from the dash, and to her horror the road was coming to an end. There had been no sign, no warning, yet the pavement in front of her took a sharp dip. She was so near the end of the cliff she could see the bottom had a landing of about five feet before it dropped off into the ocean.

If the economy-sized van toppled over the pavement, it would bounce and land in the water. She would never escape before the heavy vehicle sank, and she would drown. She took a fleeting moment to dream up other scenarios, including considering whether drowning was such a bad thing, before she stomped her feet against the floorboard, bringing the van to a screeching stop.

The front tires of the van were inches from dangling off the pavement. She remained calm, carefully throwing the van in reverse and flooring the accelerator. One good wind, or an unaware driver who couldn't stop in time, and she'd fall over the cement cliff.

"Erika!"

She jumped awake and almost fell out of her chair.

"What are you doing in here?" Ginnifer asked, stepping into the office and closing the door behind her. "Were you *asleep*?"

A headache banged at her temples. "What a bizarre dream."

"Must have been. You were mumbling something about being disgusted with the bad braking system. You said you might as well be Fred Flintstone."

"Do you have any Tylenol?"

"No, but you do. Top drawer." Ginnifer watched her closely as if she were a mental patient about to snap.

She ignored her friend and took two Tylenol, washing them down with her bottled water.

"Aren't you getting any sleep at home?"

"Very little."

"Are you going to tell me about this dream?"

She told Ginnifer the strange tale and awaited her reaction. "What do you think it means?"

"You're stressed out."

"It's weird, huh?"

Ginnifer nodded, still watching her carefully. "I hear themes of obligation, indecision, and panic—to name a few, but I'm not a trained psychiatrist."

"I don't need a psychiatrist. And stop looking at me like that!"

Ginnifer laughed a little. "It's kinda funny. Your feet went through the floorboards? Like on the Flintstones? Did you have a pink-speckled rhino-bird for your horn?"

"It's not funny."

"Okay." She struggled to get serious. "It's not funny. It's a sign of your guilt. Are you upset you took Brock back?"

"No, it was the right thing to do."

"*Right thing to do?* Don't you still love him?"

She rubbed her temples again. "He's been different since the operation." She shuffled the files on her desk, avoiding looking at Ginnifer. "I'm at work all day, nursing him at night, and at the doctor's office on my off days."

"The surgery is over. The radiation is finished. He'll be done with the treatment soon."

"Oh, the treatment phase is over, but now we have the physical exams, chest radiographs, and tumor marker labs every two months for the first year—every three months for the second year. He'll need CT scans every four months for the first two years, and every six months for at least five years." She mentally collapsed into a heap of tears. The weight of the world was on her shoulders, and she was struggling to balance her guilt on the bony processes of her spine. "This will never end."

Ginnifer was around the desk in an instant, hugging her

shoulders. "It seems bad right now because you've been through a lot. You're exhausted—mentally and physically."

Erika forced herself to stop sobbing. She took the tissue Ginnifer offered and wiped her eyes. "How unprofessional is this behavior?"

Ginnifer smiled forgivingly and perched her hip on the corner of the desk. "You know what you need? A day out. You've been taking care of Brock nonstop for weeks. You need a break—or you're going to break. Why don't you go out with me and Frick and Frack tonight?"

"I can't."

"Why not? It's Friday. Go casinoing with me and the guys."

"I don't like the casinos. I'm not much of a gambler."

"Me either, but you haven't seen the casinos until you go casinoing with Rhon. Professional gamblers are superstars in his world." She snatched up the phone and dialed home. "I'm telling the guys you'll be coming along. Go home and change into something fancy and meet me at my place. Will made dinner. You'll have good time."

Her temples throbbed again. "Brock made plans for dinner."

Ginnifer secured the phone with her shoulder. "I guess he told you about it one of the million times he called today."

"I'll talk to him." Since his second run-in with Mark, Brock had fallen into the habit of calling the office to chat with her during the day. She believed it was a combination of boredom and jealousy keeping him on edge.

"Have dinner with Brock. We'll swing by and pick you up after." Before Erika could make another excuse, Ginnifer was making plans for the evening.

Going out with Ginnifer and her men never came up during dinner. Brock was in a better mood than he had been lately, so

Erika didn't want to spoil his attempt at doing something nice for her. The restaurant he'd chosen served a chic menu of Italian food. The atmosphere was serene and elegant—the prices outrageous. Only a celebrity crowd could afford to patronize the place, and it was amazing Brock had secured a reservation. She didn't ask how he'd done it, only smiled when he stared across the table at her, proud of the evening he was providing.

Dinners like these were a welcomed treat in their early dating. Special things happened when Brock took her to places like these. If Erika hadn't been focused on watching the clock, she might have picked up some of his hints about this evening's surprise.

At home, Erika thanked him for dinner with a kiss on his cheek. He wrapped his arms around her waist, encouraging her to let the kiss linger. It seemed an awkward gesture in the middle of the kitchen, but she missed this clue too.

"I have to go," she announced, extricating herself from his hold.

"*Go?* Go where?" His voice was low, his version of shouting.

"I told Ginnifer I'd go casinoing with her tonight."

"You don't like casinos."

"It's hard to say no to Ginnifer." She kicked off her shoes and headed for the bedroom.

Brock followed her. "I thought we were going to spend the evening together."

She slipped out of the suit she'd worn to work, piling it neatly on the back of a chair in the sitting area. "You made dinner plans. You didn't mention anything else." She stopped undressing and turned to him. "Is there something else?"

The question was manipulative, challenging him to tell her she couldn't have a good time with her friend when they'd never been that type of couple. He played racquetball with his friends; she played golf with Ginnifer. There had never been a problem with them keeping separate friends, they just rarely had the chance to enjoy outside activities because of their hectic work schedules.

She was being bad and she knew it—craftily manipulating the situation—but she needed this. No matter how much she cared about Brock, she needed to be away from him and his sickness for one evening. She wanted to have a good time without feeling guilty about not focusing every thought on Brock's future. She had to breathe again.

"What time will you be home?" Brock asked, his shoulders slumping. She might as well have slapped him.

"I'm not sure. Don't wait up." Unable to watch his disappointment unfolding behind his eyes, she disappeared into her walk-in closet. She flipped the switch activating the motorized clothing rack. She concentrated on finding the perfect outfit to wear—anything to keep her guilt from rising up and choking her.

"Erika?" The timbre of his voice was so sweet she wanted to fold her arms around him and protect him from the things they couldn't control.

She couldn't look at him. "Yes?"

"Is everything okay? Are you all right?"

"Why do you ask?"

"Just checking on my wife."

She continued searching the clothing rack for something chic yet comfortable to wear, but she felt his eyes burring into her back. He sensed her apprehension with the new dynamics of their relationship. He wouldn't question her about it outright—it wasn't his way. He would study her, analyzing every move, every gesture, every word she spoke until finally she came to him . . . and he'd be ready with all the information he had gathered to confront her every argument. Controlling his emotions and effectively managing sticky situations were qualities that had attracted her to him before. Now, she resented him for being stoic when her heart and mind were having trouble digesting their future.

"It's only one night, Brock. I can't remember the last time I went out with friends."

"Your timing is strange." He stepped into her closet, standing closely at her back, but not touching her. "I wanted tonight to be special."

"Ginnifer invited me. I accepted, not knowing you had something special planned for us."

He was quiet for a long moment, watching her flip through her clothing. "It seems to be about more than a night with your friends . . . you're *different*."

Her head jerked in his direction, surprised by his uncanny ability to read her private thoughts.

"You *feel* . . . different." He turned and walked away.

Windfall erected forty stories of hotel rooms, restaurants, and shopping on the Detroit River and changed the downtown skyline forever. The casino on the fortieth floor catered exclusively to world-renowned professional gamblers invited to visit the tables. This was a casino where ESPN hosted world championship poker matches. Arab sheiks flew halfway around the world to play craps here. Being rich and famous didn't guarantee an invitation to Windfall, but being ranked in the top ten of professional blackjack players in the world assured Rhon a place at the high-stakes table.

The moment Erika slipped into the backseat of Rhon's gray Porsche Panamera she understood how lucrative playing blackjack could be. The Panamera was the German car company's first four-door, four-seater sports coupe, and first hit the market in 2009. Rhon had won the dream automobile in a big game sponsored by the automaker in France a year before mass production.

The engine purred when Rhon pulled away from the curb, and Erika could have sworn she saw Brock watching them through a slat in the blinds.

"Everything go okay?" Ginnifer asked.

She lifted a hand, shifting it back and forth in a so-so motion. She leaned in close to whisper, "They don't mind me coming along?"

"They don't mind sharing me," Ginnifer jokingly answered.

Erika raised her eyebrows, watching for a reaction from the men in the front seat.

It wasn't hard to understand why Ginnifer had found it impossible to choose between Will and Rhon. Still in his twenties, Will was a young, virile man. His poolside tanned skin glowed beneath his mop of shiny blond hair. His body was firm and muscular, still ripe for many years of future use. His demeanor was always cool in the my-good-looks-are-really-a-curse sort of way. He'd kept his cool when his parents threatened to disown him for living with a black woman. He'd upset the entire WASP upper crust when he traded Grosse Pointe living for his place as one of Ginnifer's two lovers. His parents eventually accepted his life. The trust fund remains intact. Ginnifer called him her "sweet devil."

Rhon was Will's opposite. In his early forties, his Mexican heritage graced him with dark skin and long, black locks bouncing against broad shoulders. His eyes were wide, large in his face. He rarely smiled, although Ginnifer insisted he had a wonderful sense of humor once he was comfortable with you. His accent was enough to make any woman melt, but when he dressed in an Italian suit and slipped behind the

wheel of a German prototype car, he was a wet dream waiting to happen. Erika found it hard to believe he was such a
good card player when he lost his cool in any mildly emer-
gent situation.

Ginnifer leaned over and whispered in Erika's ear, "Aren't
they beautiful?"

"They're gorgeous."

Will turned in his seat and winked at her.

Ginnifer was no slouch. Detroit born and raised, she had ac-
quired an education at a local university, making her a double
threat: She could hold her own on the street and in the business
world. Unlike Will, she never believed her beauty a curse, often
crediting her good genes for many of the breaks she'd gotten in
life. Her looks were unconventional: curvy when skinny was
the "in" thing, dark skin when honey brown was desired. She
embraced her flaws without any care of how others viewed her.
Erika wished she had a portion of her boldness.

This was a night of fun, so Rhon served as tour guide as he
ushered his entourage through the rooms of the casino. Some
were off-limits, reserved only for serious playing. Rhon
slipped into a cashmere chair at the poker table with Ginnifer
at his side. Erika couldn't believe how much money he placed
on each bet. Fifties and hundreds were flying fast and furious,
with Rhon fronting Ginnifer's bets too.

The excitement was palpable when Rhon built up a stack
of chips, drawing a nice crowd to the table to watch the out-
come. It seemed Rhon had a reputation for taking risks other
professionals would never consider—and always coming out
on top. Soon the other players at the table were out, leaving
the match between Rhon and a Texan with old oil money and
a long scar hidden beneath a cowboy hat.

"Erika," Will's soft voice tickled her ear, "why don't we try
a little action." His fingers wrapped around her hand and pulled

her away from the crowd. He walked her to a quiet blackjack table with a view of the Detroit River forty stories below.

The waitress appeared with drinks before Will could help her into a cashmere chair of her own. Will's hand pressed firmly into her back as he signaled the dealer to deal her into the next game.

"There's a thousand-dollar limit at this table, Will," Erika protested. "You play. I'll watch."

"You play. I'll be your good-luck charm." He kissed her cheek, lingering long enough for Erika to wonder if it was a friendly kiss or something more. "I have chips." He made two stacks in front of her. "Courtesy of Rhon."

A few drinks, and many wins later, Erika had loosened up and understood why so many people loved Las Vegas. Will remained at her side, cheering her on as she won hand after hand of blackjack. Ginnifer and Rhon joined them, delighted Erika was taking so well to the game. When she accumulated a six-figure winning total, the pit boss tapped her on the shoulder and offered her a room for the night.

"We aren't staying," she told him, barely giving him a glance over her shoulder.

"Maybe you'd like to try another game in our casino," the man persisted.

"She's hot," Ginnifer answered, "why would she leave now?"

Rhon stepped up, gathering Erika's chips. "It's been a long night. We should stop while we're ahead."

Erika and Ginnifer protested, but Rhon was already heading for the exit with the pit boss escorting him and their large winnings.

"They thought you were counting cards," Will explained as he slid into the back seat of the Panamera with Erika. "We weren't being asked to leave so much as being thrown out."

"Rhon," Erika apologized, "I'm sorry."

He smiled at her in the rearview. "Don't worry about it. If it were a big deal, management would have shown up. Just don't try to play blackjack at Windfall again."

Too excited to end the evening, they grabbed a pizza and made their way to Belle Isle. They sat on the grass, the headlights of Rhon's car shining over them, eating pizza while Erika and Ginnifer giddily relived the night. Will remained at Erika's side when Ginnifer and Rhon disappeared for an extra-long walk. When they returned, Ginnifer was a lot calmer and the shirt of Rhon's suit was buttoned incorrectly.

"Do you guys do this sort of thing all the time?" Erika asked.

"Only on Saturdays," Rhon answered.

"I love Saturdays." Ginnifer rolled her head, turning to grin at Erika.

"Me, too," Will added, leaning toward Erika.

"We're having too much fun to end the night now," Rhon said as they piled back into his car.

Ginnifer beamed. "Let's go to the driving range."

"The driving range?" Erika looked out the window, matching the time on the dashboard with the gray sky. They had been out all night.

Will reached between the bucket seats and squeezed her hand. "You can teach me how to play golf like I taught you to play blackjack."

"I should go home." The words were a gesture of doing the right thing, but she'd had so much fun tonight . . .

"You've stayed out all night," Ginnifer finished her thought. "You're already in trouble with Brock. Why not have the maximum amount of fun possible? You're going to pay for it anyway."

"If we were together, I would never keep you on a leash," Will added, being a little too helpful.

Ginnifer shared a knowing look with Erika, silently telling Erika their friendship wouldn't be damaged if she decided to walk on the wild side with Will. Erika mouthed an emphatic "no" to her friend.

"To the driving range it is," Ginnifer said, and Rhon accelerated the Porsche, making them all squeal.

CHAPTER 20

"I'll bring you a check first thing."

Brock narrowed his eyes at Ginnifer, making his disgust known without saying a word. He snatched up his wife by the arm and pulled her along after him, treating her like a wayward child and having no shame about it.

"Sorry, Erika," Ginnifer said as they left the police station.

"Bye, Erika."

Brock whirled around with such a fierce expression Will wouldn't dare flirt with his wife again. He was so angry it wouldn't take much to push him over the edge and act with uncharacteristic abandon.

They were inside the car before Erika tried to explain. "Brock, I—"

He raised a finger in her direction, stopping her cold. He pulled out of the parking lot with enough vigor to make several police officers watch them suspiciously. He recalled every tiny thing he loved about Erika on the drive home, hoping to cool his anger, but getting a call first thing Saturday morning from your wife asking you to bail her and her friends out of jail was enough to piss even him off.

After achieving his first erection since the surgery, he'd

planned a romantic evening with Erika. Instead, the candles in the guest bedroom remained unlit and the roses wilted while she jotted off to be with Ginnifer—and Ginnifer's two men friends. If he'd known Will and Rhon were going, he wouldn't have allowed Erika to go. He'd been stunned when she announced she was going out for the evening, ruining his plans. He didn't fail to notice she never mentioned the men tagging along, which raised another crop of questions in Brock's insecure mind. Staring down into Erika's innocent face now, he felt like a wicked stepparent ready to punish his charge . . . until she opened her mouth.

"I'm going to take a quick shower, and then I'm going to get some sleep. Don't even think about chastising me like I'm a child."

He blinked twice, shaking his head with the gusto of a cartoon character. "What did you just say to me?" His voice was so low he didn't think Erika had heard him when she turned her back and walked away.

"I went out with my friends. I had a good time. It got a little out of hand at the golf course, but we're going to use our winnings to pay for the repairs."

He followed her into the bathroom, having to raise his voice to be heard over the spray of the shower beating the tiles. "You don't talk to me this way. You never speak to me like this."

She began to disrobe. "Brock, I'm tired."

Was she dismissing him? "You stayed out all night—without calling. You never answered your cell. When I finally hear from you, it's a call to bail you out of jail. I deserve an explanation."

"And I gave you one." She stepped out of her skirt, momentarily distracting him with the firm shapeliness of her thighs.

"What is going on in your head? This isn't like you. None of it—staying out all night, the attitude—tell me what's going on. Are you mad at me?"

There was a slight hesitation as she pulled her sweater over her head, and Brock knew he had found the answer. He didn't know why, but his wife was angry with him, and she was displaying it in a passive-aggressive way.

"I just wanted to have fun, Brock. I needed a break. I'm sorry it got out of hand. You'll get every cent of your money back—"

"It's not about the money. It's about you."

"Then we don't have a problem, because I'm fine." She turned her back on him again, stepping into the shower and ending their argument.

Brock was so shocked by Erika's uncharacteristic flippant attitude, something in him became afraid to probe for an explanation. He dropped the subject, letting it go, and ignoring it ever happened. When Ginnifer dropped off a check to cover the bail, he accepted her apology and left her and Erika alone in the living room. As he snatched pieces of their conversation from the guestroom upstairs, he recognized Erika's new attitude. She reminded him of the sorority girls who lived in private dormitories and sought all kinds of mischief in the name of fun.

This was a side of Erika he'd never seen. He would have loved to blame it on Ginnifer, but Erika was too strong to fall under anyone's tutelage—unless she wanted to be there. It was almost as if she were trying to be the exact opposite of the woman she was—to spite him.

Is she trying to push me to leave? He hurriedly pushed the thought away, frightened by the possibility of it being the truth.

He would never say he was an easy man to please, and sometimes his demands were harsh, but Erika was the only woman who had realized those faults and still fallen in love with him. He had a problem spontaneously displaying his emotions, but he did the things a man did to let his woman know he loved her. He paid the bills, took her out to dinner on the weekends, and made love to her regularly—before the surgery and the separation. The woman chattering in the living room would say those things weren't enough.

The woman in the living room would realize she'd been shortchanged when she agreed to fall in love with him, and might even consider trading him in for someone more worthy. Or someone salivating for the chance to please her—enter Mark Garing.

If he questioned whether his worries were real, the following week would prove they were. Erika and Ginnifer became inseparable. There were dinners and golfing and museums. Erika worked all day, came home to change, and was out the door again. He lost account of her whereabouts.

Any time he made a move to be romantic with her, she would dart away, having some convenient excuse ready. It was hard enough for him to get up the courage to approach her, not knowing whether his equipment would work, and if it did, could he finish the act for both of them. After a while, he stopped trying to make love to Erika and focused on trying to keep her at home. Nothing could keep her home. She even started meeting him at the clinic for his appointments instead of going together.

It surprised him when she called from work a few weeks later and said she would be coming home early and wanted to have dinner together. Thinking maybe the sorority girl syndrome had passed, Brock planned another romantic evening where he would try to make love to his wife. He rushed to the store and brought flowers and candles, chocolates, oils, and creams. Being freaky would distract her from taking inventory of his missing equipment. He didn't want Erika to have to cook, so he stopped at their favorite take-out place and picked up dinner. After trimming his facial hair, he dressed in linen slacks and a matching shirt for the occasion. He was nervous as he readied the guest room, choosing not to use the master bedroom because he wanted her to be surprised. When she arrived home, he was waiting at the door.

"How was your day?" he asked, greeting her with a lingering kiss. He wanted to set the mood from the beginning.

"Interesting."

"Come sit down. Tell me about it." He added extra swagger to his stride as he escorted her into the dining room. He fought to keep his confidence high, forbidding himself to have any doubts about her acceptance of his body.

Erika sat next to him at the table, and he helped her dish out dinner. When their plates were full, he asked again, "Tell me why your day was so interesting."

She slipped the shiny silver fork between her lips, and Brock felt a stir below his waist. The movement was so erotic, and he was so hungry for her, he almost pushed the dishes off the table and took her right there.

"This is great," she said, watching him. Her eyes glittered. She knew what she was doing to him. "I haven't been the easiest to get along with lately." She shook her head, thoughtfully distracted. "Everything that has happened over the past few weeks . . . it's been a lot."

"It has," he agreed.

"I wasn't making things easier between us. I wanted to come home and start again."

He nodded, liking she'd come to her senses without him having to intervene.

"So I went by your apartment to pick up more of your things." She twisted around in her seat and rummaged through her purse as she spoke. "Kinda like a goodwill gesture to show you I wanted you back here one-hundred percent." She pulled out a nondescript envelope before facing the table again. "We forgot to have your mailing address changed back to here."

"I'll do it first thing in the morning."

She stacked his mail next to him on the table, the nondescript envelope on top. Her expression blazed with betrayal and rage. He glanced down to see what could have caused the sudden change in mood and found the envelope wasn't as innocent as it first appeared.

She was angry, but why? Because he hadn't told her about it? Or because of something else?

"I opened it," she informed him, her voice tight.

He still didn't understand the source of her anger, so he didn't speak.

"You went to a sperm bank?"

"I didn't know if the operation or the radiation would leave me sterile."

"Ah!" Her mouth dropped open in shock.

"We've always talked about having kids when both our careers were settled."

She still couldn't speak, her mouth hanging wide on its hinges.

"What? I was looking out for our future."

"When you went to the sperm bank, we didn't have a future. We were separated, and I had asked you to sign divorce papers."

"I told you that would never happen."

"So you made another decision for me. You decided to leave. You decided not to divorce me. You decided I would be up for being implanted with my children by a stranger."

"Listen, I have good sperm motility. If the sperm bank bothers you, I'll have the samples destroyed."

She visibly shivered.

"You do want to use the samples?"

She measured every word, struggling to remain calm as she spoke. "The night you came here and we had sex—" she swallowed hard, her eyes betraying the amount of control she needed not to explode. "You said you wanted to make a baby."

He shifted uneasily, seeing the trap before he stepped into it. "If we could have gotten pregnant before I became sterile—"

"You tried to get me pregnant on purpose? We weren't back together. How would we have raised a child with us being separated?"

"We were going to get back together. I told you that."

"You had planned everything—when was I going to be consulted?"

"You *do* want to use the sperm bank?" he asked dumbly, truly not seeing the purpose in arguing *what could have beens*.

"I want a choice!" she shouted, banging her fist on the tabletop. "You had this operation without talking to me first, but it affects me."

Now they were getting to the truth of the matter. "It's my body. I have the final say on what will be done to it."

"And you expect me to stand by and deal with whatever decision you make."

His insides coiled tight. Suddenly, everything was clear: the distance, the new attitude—it all made sense. "Say what you mean, Erika."

"The only decision you thought needed to be made was whether or not I stayed to see you die. You never considered I might not want to be here to watch you be sick."

The words stung, making the back of his neck tingle. He closed his eyes against the horrible images flooding him.

Deafening silence filled the room, and the only thing Brock wanted was not to be here. Erika had always been his rock. She loved unconditionally. She gave her emotions freely, standing strong when he couldn't. She was the light to his dark, the soft to his hard. To think she might resent being those things after all these years sickened him.

Erika spoke softly, her voice tranquil for the first time this evening. "You shoveled all this into my lap and expected me to deal with it without complaint. You expected me to be grateful you'd come back to me."

He opened his eyes and she was looking at him, earnestly, honestly.

"I saw a New Zealand travel ad on my computer at work today. It took everything in me not to walk out of the office and go straight to the airport. I felt trapped, like I needed to get away."

"Away from what?"

"Here. You. Cancer."

He hunched over slightly, an unexpected pain stabbing him in the gut.

"But I did what was expected of me. I pulled it together, ignored my feelings, and decided to take another one for the team." She fingered the envelope. "Then I found this. Another symbol of how little my feelings matter to you."

"I love you." He wasn't sure he said the words aloud.

"You didn't love me enough seven months ago to tell what was going on with you. You didn't trust me enough to be straight with me. Everything that has happened between us lately has been orchestrated by you, for your benefit. Because I can give you something you need, you came back. Not once have you considered me, or my feelings, or my needs."

"I was considering your feelings when I left. It was the wrong way to handle it—I've apologized—but I didn't want to hurt you."

"And what happens now? You're here. I'm here. We're in the same house, but nothing between us has been fixed."

"We work on it."

"Between doctor appointments, lab draws, and CT scans?"

"Being cruel doesn't suit you, Erika."

She inhaled. Exhaled. Pushed slowly away from the table. "I'm not trying to be cruel, but I am going to be selfish. For once in our relationship, I'm going to think about me."

"What do you mean?"

"I'm so stressed by all of this, I can't concentrate at work. I'm wound up tight, worried I'll say the wrong thing to you. I've had a headache for a week because all I can think about is losing myself in taking care of you. I'm trying to save what was, but you've changed."

"I've changed?"

"You have. You don't see it, but you have."

"We can work on it." He was pleading, but he felt Erika slipping away.

"There are things going on inside of me I have to deal with. I don't know how they'll affect our marriage, so instead of hurting you, I've decided we need to be apart." She shook her head. "This time *I'm* leaving."

He gripped the table to keep from toppling out of his chair. "What?"

"I care about you, Brock. I do. But I have to figure out what *I* want."

"And leaving this relationship will help you do it?"

She stood and walked around the chair, gripping the back. "I need to be able to breathe."

"I love you." He sounded desperate.

"I know."

"I want our marriage to work. I need you here."

"I know what you want. You've spent the last seven months manipulating me to get it."

His lashes beat frantically, hitting the lenses of his glasses. He didn't know how to handle the new Erika. Everything he'd tried to tell her had sounded trite or selfish. If she left, he might never get her back, but he didn't know what words to keep her there. "What can I say to make you stay?"

"This isn't about saying the right words."

"Have I done something?" Men were often clueless about these things, doing or saying the wrong thing without knowing it. He had tried to be on his best behavior since returning home, always remaining unobtrusive and refusing her help even on his sickest days, doing for himself instead. "Don't leave, Erika. Tell me what I did wrong and I'll fix it. Please."

"You haven't earned me back."

CLEAR!

CHAPTER 21

Titus Martin was a good man. He knew it. He believed it. He behaved that way. But when Virginia Johnson limped into the physical therapy suite almost a year ago, every lusty thought he'd had as a young man rushed at him, making him weave on his feet.

Everything Virginia did spelled class. The matching jogging suits she wore for her workouts were made of soft, thick material that felt good to his rough, calloused hands. Her hair was swept up and back, but Titus could tell it would fall into gray-speckled waves, flowing like cotton through his fingers. She had a firm little body made to be cuddled, but durable for a man like him who might hold her a little too tight.

He was drawn to her right away, but treaded carefully because her son—the doctor—walked protectively at her side with wary eyes prowling for anyone who might approach his mother the wrong way. It was weeks after Virginia's first visit before Titus found a way to maneuver the schedule so he was assisting in her therapy class. Two more weeks passed before her daughter-in-law—the doctor—began bringing her to therapy. The other Dr. Johnson was not as intimidating, and Titus found the nerve to work his way over to Virginia during her session.

He had lost a spouse, like Virginia, and used this fact to
become her friend. He still hadn't found the nerve to ask her
out to dinner. He was a good man, but he was a simple man.
He was part of America's working retired—working after retirement because his savings and retirement benefits weren't
enough to support him in a failing economy. He was healthy.
He'd raised two good kids who now had families of their own.
He was most proud of his kids, but his kids weren't on the
level of the doctors Johnson. He wasn't ashamed of himself
or his family, but every time he tried to ask Virginia out, a
pang of doubt about being good enough for her stopped him.

When Virginia missed a therapy session, his world turned
gray and overcast until the following session when she would
bounce in—she was walking much better now—and share
her stories with him. She was a little forgetful and often repeated the stories she told him about living in Memphis, but
he didn't care. He loved having all her attention. Missing a
session here and there because she was too stubborn to come
some days was one thing, not showing up for three weeks had
Titus an anxious mess.

Every day he looked for her, nervously watching the door and
waiting for her arrival. He inquired about her with the therapist,
but all he got was, "Dr. Johnson said she'd be away for a while."

"Missing so many days will set her back, won't it?" he
asked, genuinely concerned.

"I'm sure the doctor has made other arrangements."

Titus couldn't push the issue so he quietly walked away—
and waited. He moped for weeks and it didn't go unnoticed
among the staff. If his attraction to Virginia wasn't obvious to
her, it became obvious to every worker at the therapy clinic.
With Titus afraid she might never return, he didn't care how
obvious his attraction to Virginia became. He vowed more

than once, not caring who overheard him mumbling, he would ask Virginia out the very next time he saw her.

"Don't say her name too loud," the therapist practically giggled.

"Why not?" Mark leaned in, pressing his shoulder against hers in conspiracy.

"Titus, the assistant, is crazy about her. We all suspected it. Once Mrs. Johnson started coming, he started pressing his uniform, shaving every day, cutting his hair every week, and wearing cologne."

The therapist was free with information, as Mark had learned most of the employees of Mission Health were—residents of a tiny Peyton Place. It didn't take much to get people talking, but Brock had succeeded in keeping his private life private. Any time Mark inquired about Brock he was given Brock's statistics: how many residents he'd trained, how many papers he'd published, how many times he'd been the featured speaker at a conference, how many lives he'd saved. It sickened Mark. But never did anyone say anything about his personal life other than he was married to Erika and she was really sweet . . . until a particularly amorous woman working in housekeeping had mentioned his mother, Virginia Johnson.

"It's cute, don't you think?" the therapist asked. "Finding love late in life."

"I hope I'm still out there when I'm his age," Mark agreed.

"Look how scruffy he's become since Mrs. Johnson stopped coming to therapy. He kept up appearances for a while after she left, but now he seems depressed. A little surly."

Titus reminded Mark of the actor who played James on *Good Times,* John Amos. He was a good height and with a thick build, dark skin, and mostly gray hair.

"It's a shame," the therapist went on. "Even if she hadn't have left, I doubt Dr. Johnson would have let them date. He's protective of his mom. He picked up on the vibes right away and didn't seem to like the idea of his mother dating Titus."

Mark understood the power of the women in the Johnson family. Even if Erika was a Johnson by marriage and not by blood, she'd still found a way to inherit her mother-in-law's irresistible charm.

"I wonder why not? The old guy seems harmless enough."

"Titus is sweet." The therapist shrugged, moving away to greet her next client. "Some men are overprotective of their mothers."

Mark smiled as he backed out of the therapy suite. He'd gotten enough information from the therapist to redirect his efforts. He'd learned all about Virginia's fall, and her guilt over moving in with Brock. He wouldn't have suspected Brock to be overprotective of his mother—Mark thought his macho display over Erika was about pride and a broken ego. It was a good start. A new weakness to exploit. He felt as if he were holding defibrillator paddles over Brock's chest, charged and ready to fire. *Clear!*

Admittedly, Virginia's memory wasn't what it used to be, but she wasn't suffering from dementia. She was forgetful is all. There were days she forgot her husband had passed on, but then it would all come rushing back at her with painful clarity. Today was one of those days. She woke up with him on her mind, only to be jolted into reality by one of her grand-daughters when she hopped up on the bed gleefully squeal-ing about their visit to the airport this morning.

Sadness drowned Virginia, but the tide quickly receded when she thought about going home to her daughter-in-law, only to rise again when she remembered Erika's melancholy brought on by Brock's leaving. Before Virginia could adjust her emotions to this reality, she remembered her oldest son telling her Brock was sick. "Very sick," he'd said.

Watching a man filled with vitality waste away had been hard on her. She couldn't bare it happening again to the son who was a replica her husband. Sure enough, Junior had his father's identical rugged good looks, but Brock had his father's mannerisms. Sometimes, when Virginia's memories played tricks on her, she caught herself mistaking Brock for her husband. And now he'd inherited his father's disease.

"What's wrong, Grandma?" Her granddaughter climbed into bed next to her, swiping at her tears with a tiny but pudgy finger.

"It's time for Grandma to go home."

She pulled herself from bed, slowly, fighting a bum hip to begin her morning ritual. The daughters-in-law had helped her pack the night before after a huge family dinner that took two days to prepare.

From all Brock's reports, he was doing well. The biopsy showed the cancer was localized. He'd still have to be careful, following up with the doctor for the next few years, but he was expected to fully recover. But two years was a long time, and anything could happen. When she thought about the possibility of losing her son, two years suddenly shortened, not nearly being long enough.

"If you don't want to go home, Grandma, Daddy will let you live with us. He said so." The tiny munchkin followed her across the room, even at such a young age trying to fix the problems of grown-ups.

"I want to go home, but I want to stay too." She took the baby's hand. "I love you, but there are people at home who need me too."

"Uncle Brock."

Virginia nodded. "But I promise to come back to see you soon."

"In the winter," the child answered, clearly not understanding when that time period could be.

"And I'll stay past Christmas."

The girl brightened, now forming an idea of time. "Good!" She ran off squealing, "When Grandma comes back, it'll be time for Christmas. I can't wait until Grandma comes back because . . ."

Virginia smiled, truly enjoying the enthusiasm of her grandkids. Except for the death of her husband, Memphis signified only the best things about her life. Now it was time to return to the city. As she contemplated Brock's future, she vowed to enjoy the time she had with her family.

She also needed to enjoy the time she had left on this earth. Brock and Erika were always encouraging her to make friends and stay active. They were willing to drive her where she needed to go without much advance notice. They never let her contribute a cent to the household, frowning when she paid for her personal purchases. They indulged her whims, stepping in to support whatever choices she made—even when they didn't quite agree with her decision.

There was something else she needed in her life, and she wondered how charitable Brock would be about her getting it. She needed the comfort of a friend—a special friend. One she could make a home for, doing the things a wife does for her husband. Even at her age, she had the need to be comforted. And she had a man in mind for the job. If she were honest with herself, she had to admit she was a little anxious about returning to her therapy sessions.

CHAPTER 22

Brock hadn't moved from the dining room table since Erika walked out the door. He sat unblinkingly in the dark, trying to create the will to rise and clear the table. As the evening fell, casting shadows on the room, the household noises were amplified: the ticking of the grandfather clock he'd given Erika for her first birthday after they were married, water making its way through the plumbing toward the showerhead he used to spray Erika's body after they made love their first night in their new home, and the tools hanging in the garage he used to assemble the headboard of their bed were moved by a gentle wind. Every loving moment he'd ever shared with Erika scratched at his brain, torturing him with memories he wanted to forget right now.

He was a man who held his emotions close, not being as verbal about his feelings for his wife as Erika would like. She never commented on his shortcoming, instead always accepting him for the man he was, but Erika was a romantic at heart. He showed Erika how much he loved her by providing for her. He insisted she save her earnings and picked up extra shifts when they needed the down payment on their home. He refused to let her contribute a cent when they went on the lavish shopping spree at Mitchell's dealership and purchased the Zephyr and the Navigator. Erika's engagement ring had cost him a fortune, but he needed her to know how much he loved her and felt it was reflected in direct proportion to the rock on her left hand.

As Brock sat in the dark, in a home wrapped in luxurious things, he wondered what gift he could buy Erika to make her come back home.

Their courtship had been fairly easy, a smooth ride down the road to the altar. They made eyes at each other over a mutual patient, he lingered with her in the corridor afterward until he raised the nerve to ask her for coffee, they fell into an easy routine of dating; then he was at his father's graveside proposing. Erika wore her feelings on her sleeve, no matter what advice her friends offered to play the dating game, she was too open and honest to be successful at it. He'd known with their first shared look she had a thing for him and she wasn't going anywhere— ever—until they played out their romance.

He was so hard. She was so soft. The perfect fit. He had no intentions of going anywhere either, because they were meant to be together.

Maybe he was a little arrogant in his pursuit of Erika.

Maybe he'd taken her for granted when he'd walked out on her.

And now that she was gone, he had no idea what to do.

Everything changed the day she stepped into his office waving a divorce decree. She changed. He changed. Life changed. Soft, overly emotional Erika, who never challenged his decisions transformed into a woman of independence who shouted at him over his own dinner table—a woman who would leave her husband because she didn't feel she had enough "choices." His life had taken a sharp turn and he hadn't even noticed the shift in the pavement of the road . . . until he hit a pothole.

Erika asking for a divorce had to have been masterminded by Mark. How had he gotten into her head? How was he able to step into the middle of their perfect fit and rip it apart?

Brock gripped the edges of the table, willing the sturdy wood to crumble between his fingers as he imagined Mark having his "firsts" with Erika. Their first date, first hug, first kiss, *first time making love*.

"Erika."

Brock's attention perked up at the sound of Erika's name coming from the answering machine.

"Erika, this is Junior. I've been calling Brock and can't reach him on the phone. Remind him Ma is flying in first thing in the morning. Somebody call me back and let me know you got this message."

Brock let his brother hang up without attempting to get to the phone. He missed his mother, but he didn't feel like explaining why he never told her he had testicular cancer. He didn't want a million questions about why Erika had left, because he didn't really understand it himself.

Thirty minutes later, Brock was still sitting at the dinner table, the smell of cold food threatening to make him sick, when his brother called again.

"Erika, I'm getting worried now. It's Junior again. Brock's not answering. You're not answering. Did something happen to my brother? Is he back in the hospital? Call me as soon as you get in."

This time Brock raced to the nearest phone extension. He had worried his mother enough. He didn't want her getting upset about him again. As he talked to his older brother, he realized he had responsibilities, no matter if his personal life was going downhill fast. He had to get his mother home and settled, back into her routine. He would be returning to the office on Monday—his patients were depending on him to be on top of his game.

He needed to find his wife and bring her back home. There were unlimited places a woman of her means could go—hotels anywhere in the city, state, or world—but somehow he sensed Erika would remain close. She'd want to be in driving distance to the clinic. This, and the fact she'd done little preparation before leaving, limited her options.

Trying to dissect his wife's reasoning motivated him, and he finally left his seat and began to clear the dinner dishes. By the time the kitchen was cleaned, he had narrowed Erika's choices down to three. She might have gone to her friend Ginnifer. Her parents would gladly take in their favorite daughter, although he doubted she'd want them to know she'd walked out on their marriage.

Erika's third option was enough to stifle the return of familiar stirrings in his groin. Was she angry enough at him to go to Mark? Would she give up on their marriage in a fit of rage and sleep with another man? Mark would gladly have her. Brock didn't doubt his encouragement resulted in her decision to pack and go.

He'd have to work quickly, getting Erika back before she made an irreparable mistake. He planned into the night, searching for any available leverage to persuade her to come home. He was a smart man, able to decipher riddles and complete the *New York Times* crossword puzzle in record time. Finding a way to bring his wife home wouldn't stump him. He concentrated, working his mind with the focused attention of a computer, searching for the answer to a riddle: How do you bring an unhappy woman home?

By morning, he had several ideas, but it wasn't until he was in the car driving his mother home that he tripped upon a workable solution. It was heavy-handed and unfair, but he had to use what was available to him. He was working out the details—presentation would mean everything—when his cell phone chirped signaling waiting voicemail messages. Before he could punch in the retrieval code, it rang.

"Where you been, doc? I've been calling you for an hour." Mitchell sounded frantic.

"I'm picking my mother up from the airport."

"How is she? Tell her I said hello." He rushed on, hardly pausing between his sentences. "Listen, the wife is in labor. I have the kids here and they're climbing the walls. The hospital staff is sick of them, and I am too."

Before Mitchell could ask, Brock remembered the promise he'd made to his friend with each of his wife's pregnancies.

"I need you to swing by and get my kids."

Dr. Brock Johnson had returned to his old self by Monday morning after a weekend that had been tumultuous at best.

Friday—Wife walks out on marriage.
Saturday—Mother returns home; grills for three hours about Friday's activities. Mitchell's wife goes into labor, and six messy kids move into his pristine home.
Sunday—"Uncle Rock" takes wily kids to a carnival for an adventure he'd never speak of during daylight hours.

Come Monday morning, Brock's nerves were a little frayed, but he remained focused on putting his marriage back together. He chose the tailor-made suit Erika gave him last Christmas for his return debut at the office. After showering and shaving, he splashed on her favorite designer aftershave and slipped into the silky wool material. The shirt was Mui Fina—custom-made, 100 percent Egyptian cotton in cherry. The jacket and slacks were a J. C. King original, contemporary styling made from fine Italian wool, light enough for the summer weather. The blue-black color of the suit set off the cherry shirt perfectly, making his dark skin radiate with a vigorous glow. A handmade silk tie finished the look, sending the message he was trying to convey today: *I'm strong, intelligent, determined, and most of all, healthy.* Compliments on his appearance, along with a few lingering stares from the nurses, gave him the confidence he needed to summon his wife to his office at the end of the day.

Erika stepped into his office wearing a respectable black tunic dress beneath a three-button single-breasted jacket with a clover leaf lapel the color of sin—a blazing *Scarlet Letter* red—and for a brief moment, Brock lost a measure of his confidence. The way she wore the suit over the flare of her hips and the full curvature of her breasts put him in mind of a dominatrix with a respectable day job. Her hair was slicked back, shiny and black, into a bouncy flip that bobbed on her shoulders. The severe style paid complement to the soft planes of her face, the compassionate brown of her eyes, and the sumptuous upturn of her lips.

Beautiful as ever, she looked different today, but he wouldn't figure out the change until she took a seat across from his desk, boldly looked him in the eye, and asked, "Did you ask to see me?" Her tone was harsh and intolerant. She sounded like a woman who had finally discovered she was too good for her no-good husband.

Again, he felt a measure of his confidence slip away.

"It's getting late," she said. "I've had a long day." There was no hint of her emotions in her words, and Brock found it most disconcerting. She had always been easy to read. Even when she tilted her chin up with determination, he knew if she was feeling scared or apprehensive inside. Today, he found it impossible to get a lock on what her heart was saying.

A picture of her lying in Mark's arms flickered before him, and his poise quickly returned. She wanted it straight, no small talk, and he would give it to her that way.

He tilted back in his chair, just a hair, enough to slide open the drawer situated at his waist. He ignored the clumsiness of his long fingers and pulled out a dusky gray portfolio professionally prepared by his attorney three years ago. He caught the narrowing of Erika's eyes when she saw the packet, even though she quickly recovered, trying to hide the show of emotion.

He drew out the moment, needing to have her off guard for the delivery of his power move. He placed the folder in front of him on the desktop, closed the drawer, and readjusted his seat. He gazed at her intensely, knowing the gesture would either turn her on or unnerve her. She was the first to break eye contact, drawn to the document underneath his elbows. He thought she might recognize it, but she gave no indication she did. He used the tips of his fingers to slide the portfolio across the desk toward her.

He saw her chest lift as she took in a deep breath before flipping the document open. She glanced at the package, skimming all the parts of the legal document neatly tucked away in its own slot. Confused recognition filled her eyes when her dark lashes lifted to look at him.

"This is our prenuptial agreement," she said softly, in a questioning tone.

"What did you think it was?" he asked coldly. "Divorce papers?"

She pulled the corner of her lip into her mouth. "Yes," she breathed.

"Is that what you were hoping for?" He caught the first flash of her emotions. "Or afraid of?"

She took a second to recover. "Why do I need to see our prenup? Now?"

"You needed a reminder of what's in those papers."

"What?" She was truly baffled.

"Have you forgotten how in love we were when we had those documents made up? We were in it for the long haul. Divorce would never be on our agenda."

Slow recognition began to twist her brow. Her composure began to fade with the slumping of her shoulders.

He pressed. "Do you need a minute to look them over?"

"What are you up to?"

"Look at the papers, Erika!" His cool was shattered in an instant, exploding in a shout that made his wife jump. He had never raised his voice to her and could only justify it now with his desperation to get her back home. Love had twisted him, making him crazy, impulsive, and reckless. He was losing his wife, who cared about propriety?

"You opened this Pandora's box; you tell me what you're trying to say."

"I want you back home tonight, or we start living by the rules of the prenuptial agreement."

A myriad of emotions played over Erika's face, but when the show was over, she leaned back in her seat and stared at him with something he didn't want to name. "You—are—such—an—ass," she ground out.

Her response was so unexpected, so un-Erika-like, he whipped off his glasses and pinned her with his glare. "What did you say to me?"

"You are such an—"

"Don't you dare speak to me—"

"Stop it. Please. Did you really think this would work?

You're so . . . puffed up over yourself. Everything can't be about you. My life can't only be about you." She pushed out her chair and stood to leave.

"Don't take another step." This was quickly escalating to a place he'd never imagined it would go. He figured she'd be a little mad, but she'd comply. She always went along with his decisions. If this heavy-handed display of his love didn't work, what could he do?

"You're doing it again, making my decisions for me. Do you think you'll get me to come back home if you do the one thing that made me leave in the first place? This is supposed to be a partnership."

"It was a partnership the day we sat down with my lawyer and made this agreement."

"You want to force me to come home?" she asked incredulously.

He wanted her there any way he could get her there. "If you don't come home tonight, I call the attorney in the morning and we start marriage counseling this week. You don't show up for the counseling sessions, we get a legal separation—and then I start playing dirty. In order to get your legal separation, we have to undergo six additional months of marriage counseling. If after six months you want a divorce, I'll honor the prenup and give you your divorce, but there will be consequences. You won't have to worry about keeping my name so you don't lose your patients. By the time I finish telling the medical director about your affair with Mark Garing, you'll both be looking for new practices."

CHAPTER 23

"You have to admit, it's romantic."

"It's controlling, deceptive, and manipulative." Erika hiked up her shades so she could see Ginnifer clearly. They were sitting by the pool of Ginnifer, Rhon, and Will's mansion home, soaking up the early evening sun, drinking fruity blended drinks while waiting for the timer to signal dinner being ready.

As always, Will was sitting at her elbow watching her with puppy-dog eyes. Cute in a rich-boy-gone-bad way, he never left her side, supplying her with endless innuendos. His eager eyes and sly touches were proof of his intentions.

Rhon was off to Vegas to earn his share of the exorbitant rent. During her brief stay with Ginnifer, Erika noticed Rhon was in-and-out of the house, always traveling to a "big game" or tournament. When practicing his craft, he was cool and unreadable, a master of skill at playing his cards right. At home, he bent easily to Ginnifer's will, often skittish and unsure of his actions toward her. The three of them together made the perfect group, building confidence off the others' strengths.

Erika envied Ginnifer's ability to live to be happy, regardless of what others thought—or expected from her. She didn't flaunt her personal life at work, always remaining professional at the office, but she was living a wild lifestyle. Last night, Erika had made the mistake of getting lost on her way to the kitchen for a late-night snack when she stumbled into a room with a large bed and three entangled bodies sharing it. She apologized her way out of the bedroom, unable to take her eyes off the threesome's ridiculously wild display of passion. They barely noticed her entrance or exit, not pausing at the height of their activity.

Ginnifer had found a way to have everything: two gorgeous men, a fun and fulfilling lifestyle, a beautiful mansion, and pricey cars. Erika had lived a safe, boring life, and now she wondered if she had missed out on too much.

"You're kidding, right?" Erika asked her friend. "You think what Brock is doing is romantic?"

"It's not the stuff of date movies, but, yes, it's romantic." She leaned forward and her hair fell in a dark sheet across her eyes. Will reached out instinctively and tucked it behind her ears; then he caressed Erika's arm reassuringly. "Listen, Brock wants you back so bad he's dying inside. He just doesn't know what to do to get you. He's desperate, trying any trick he can come up with." She relaxed back against her seat. "It's cute."

"It's controlling."

"That too." Ginnifer laughed, taking a sip from her drink.

Realizing their glasses were low, Will rose from his chair and went inside. Erika had no doubt he'd return with a fresh pitcher of the fruit smoothie.

"He's very flirty," Erika observed, carefully broaching the subject.

"He's very determined for a man his age, don't you think? Very self-assured. He knows what he wants and he goes after it with the quiet prowess of a killer lion."

A perfect description, and right now Erika felt like his prey. "It doesn't bother you when he flirts with me?"

She shook her head. "Not at all. Will, Rhon, and I are true to each other. We split the bills, we each have our responsibilities around the house, and we're a happy threesome. We agreed a long time ago not to try to conform to traditional relationship rules."

"So you see other people?"

"I try not to think about it, but I suppose the guys do. I have enough with these two, but it would be hypocritical to tell them they can only date me."

"You've set up a home here. If one of you were to leave, wouldn't things get messy?"

"We've made arrangements. Nothing as elaborate as your prenup, but we realize this relationship could have emotional consequences, and we've seen to it our hearts never get tangled with our finances."

"You're happy living this way?"

"I am. For now."

Erika imagined herself in the middle of a simultaneous relationship with Brock and Mark. The excessive sex definitely wouldn't be a hardship, but loving multiple men seemed impossible to her when she couldn't handle the one she had.

Ginnifer picked up the conversation. "Sometimes I examine my life and try to tell myself it's time to settle down if I want kids before I'm too old to have them. But then I come home to Will and Rhon, and it's so wonderful I can't imagine not having them around every day."

She thought about Brock and how wonderful their marriage used to be. No matter how bad her day at the office, she could always come home to his strength and support. She lapsed into memories about the special times she'd shared with Brock, reexamining what her marriage vows meant to her. She honestly sorted out her feelings about the testicular cancer and what it might mean to their relationship, and became confused all over again.

"Have you decided what to do?" Ginnifer asked.

"He didn't give me much time to think about it."

"If you don't go back, you have to warn Mark. He's been a good boy and left you alone just like you wanted, but his job is still on the line."

"Why do I feel like we're all attending a code blue and I have the paddles in my hands, charged, and everyone's screaming at me to fire?"

"Because you're a doctor, and only a doctor would use that metaphor." Ginnifer tried not to laugh too hard. "Brock, clear! Mark, clear! Everybody, clear!"

"Nobody's moving."

"They're all waiting for you to make the first move."

It did all rest on her shoulders: her marriage, Brock's happiness, and Mark's career. Everyone was waiting for her to make a decision, and she was in too much turmoil to honestly examine her feelings about her life.

"Are you going home tonight?"

She looked up as Will placed dinner in front of her. Ginnifer had disappeared some time during her internal musings.

"I'm not sure I have much choice. Besides, it's the grown-up thing to do."

Will slipped into his chair, somehow moving it a fraction closer without her noticing. "Being a prisoner is being grown-up?"

"Marriage isn't like being in a prison."

He cut off the tip of his steak and made a show out of placing it between his lips. He was cute enough—sexy enough— to be a temptation, but one she wouldn't touch and complicate her life further. "You were so tight the night we went to Windfall. You aren't that way now. Now you laugh. And smile. You can't wait to get out of your suit when you come home from work. At first you were shy about wearing a bathing suit. Now you're lounging by the pool without a wrap. Seems like you were in prison to me, because now you're free."

Was she really? Did being away from the man you love to uphold a principle make you free? Or just stupid? "You're too young to be so observant."

"I'm not too young for a lot of things. Things you need to try to help you enjoy life more."

"The arrangement you have with Ginnifer and Rhon is probably most women's fantasy, but it's not for me. I need commitment, and security."

"You've been there. Tried that. And now you're here having fun with us."

"Yes, but I can't stay here forever."

"Actually, you could." He looked up at her with so much earnestness in his young, naïve face, he made her feel protective of his innocence. When his fingers crept up her thigh, she quickly remembered he was sin wrapped in a golden body waiting to strike.

She stopped the travel of his fingers with her hand. "I've never been unfaithful to my husband, and I never will be."

He reluctantly pulled away. "Sex with me doesn't wipe out your marriage vows."

"You're wrong there. If Brock ever found out I slept with another man, my marriage would end."

"Isn't that what you want? Your marriage over?"

Her brain felt scrambled. "No."

"But you were pissed off when he told you to come home tonight or else." He calmly fired his observations, taking her right where he wanted her to go.

"I don't like being controlled. There are other issues too."

He offered a wicked grin. "What are the other issues,

because until you try it, you won't know how good being controlled can be."

She skated around the comment, not wanting to delve into his sexual appetite. She'd witnessed a flash last night, and it had been much too hot for her. "Testicular cancer is serious," she stumbled.

"No shit." He grinned again.

"It takes a lot out of the patient, and the family."

"So you really don't want to go home because you don't want to take care of Brock."

And there it was, laid out on the patio table in the setting sun for everyone to see. Her shame had been rightly determined and easily dissected. She loved Brock. Still. She always would. But watch him die? Taking care of him when he transitioned from her rock to a helpless invalid? She wasn't that strong. She couldn't live through it and come out whole.

He'd already started to change, leaving the management of the household to her while he moped around the house all day. Moving to the guest room so she wouldn't be witness to the side effects of his radiation treatment. Sending his mother away instead of holding her closer when she was worried about him.

She needed him to be stronger. Instead, he was more dependent on her, watching her closely with narrowed eyes capable of reading every one of her emotions.

"It's not that I don't want to take care of him," she lamely defended herself.

"What is it?"

She was afraid. Afraid to watch the love of her life shrivel into some unrecognizable mass of helplessness. She was furious when he threatened her with the prenuptial agreement, but she was glad to see a glimpse of his old fight resurface.

Brock was bigger than life, strong and intelligent. He was

the man everyone turned to for strength and support. He was reliable, dependable, and protective. He made her feel safe. There were many reasons she'd fallen in love with him, but these were her favorites. These qualities made him a man to be reckoned with. Without them, was he still the man she'd married? Did she want this new man in her life?

Could she be strong enough for him? Did she have enough resolve to hold him when he was sick? To help him settle his estate if the cancer reappeared in a vital organ? Could she forgo having a family to support him through the unknown? Would she be able to raise their children alone if she were widowed?

The more she debated the issues, the more clear it became that the problem wasn't with Brock—it was inside her.

"You don't have to tell me," Will said when she didn't answer. "You have to live your life. Do what you need to do to be happy, but you have to deal with whatever it is. If you don't, it's not going to work out if you decide to go back to him."

Erika keyed Brock's number into her cellular. She didn't expect him to answer at this late hour—Mitchell's kids were staying with him and he had an early morning ahead of him. A heartbreaking smile lifted the corner of her mouth. She wondered how he was getting along with six kids. His mother would be a big help, but this would be a good test of his character.

She disconnected before the line could ring, amusement over picturing a frazzled Brock with the kids making her doubt her decision. She tapped the phone against her forehead. She'd thought it through and made her decision—Brock should be the first to know. She dialed his number again, relieved when voicemail picked up. She pressed the phone against her ear, liking the rumble of his deep timbre. The sound vibrated against her ear, doing things to her body, reminding her she missed him in other ways.

Since the operation, he guarded his body, keeping her at a safe distance. She knew there were issues, but he refused to discuss them with her. If he had, he would know cosmetics meant nothing to her. She just wanted him to love her. To assure her he still desired her after their long separation by the way he dominated her body.

The message beep came before she began rethinking her decision, considering sex and sperm bank deposits into the equation. She took a deep breath, then spoke slowly and concisely, "Brock, it's Erika. I'm not coming home."

CHAPTER 24

Erika didn't come home.

But she left him a damned voicemail message. "It's not what I want," she'd said. "If you want to push the prenup, go ahead. But I know you won't. You don't want me back if I don't want to be there."

She was so wrong.

Brock cursed, throwing the phone across the room.

He found with shocking clarity he wasn't beyond stooping to acts of pettiness to get his wife back. So the evening after his ultimatum, he called a nanny service to sit with Mitchell's kids, dropped his mother off for therapy, and drove across town to where Erika's parents lived.

The neighborhood was quiet with huge homes whose architecture clarified the date of construction. The blocks of homes were neatly made and well cared for, deceiving unfamiliar visitors into believing the area as safe as it was pristine. As the years had passed, the sturdy homes had survived, but the character of the neighborhood crumbled. Brock and Erika had offered to buy her parents another home in the suburbs, but her father had declined, saying this was his first home, the only piece of property he owned, and he planned to stay there until he died. No amount of bargaining would change his mind, so they lived on in the neighborhood, sometimes worrying Erika when a piece of terrible news struck too close to their street address.

Brock didn't know James and Susan Hendrix well, learning about them through Erika's childhood stories more than social settings. As a couple they lived a separate life away from their families, happily showing up for social events, which weren't frequent enough to establish a strong bond. Since his mother had moved in, most of their communication was with his side of the family. Erika supported this shortly after her older sister, Corrine, made a pass at Brock at a holiday dinner.

Brock drove past the house several times before finally recognizing some obscured object in the front yard. He parked his car and boldly stepped up to the door, ringing the bell.

"Brock," Susan answered the door, instantly alarmed when Erika was nowhere in sight. "Is everything okay?"

James stepped up behind her, raising his voice over a chorus of screaming kids and the blaring television volume. "I'll handle this." He didn't wait for his wife to acknowledge his decision. He stepped in front of her, pulling the door behind him as he joined Brock on the porch. He grunted something, indicating with a wave of his hand Brock should follow him.

As they crossed into the backyard heading to the garage, Brock understood Erika had told her father—but probably not her mother—she had left her husband. Knowing little about James, only that Erika had told him he was bigger than life—although most women felt this way about their fathers—Brock changed his approach, readying himself to talk man-to-man with James.

They stepped into the dank, darkened garage. James turned in the direction of the light switch, but instead curled his fist and hit Brock in his jaw. The surprise blow was shockingly hard, deceptive of the man's age, and sent Brock staggering back. Before he could regain his balance, James came at him, solidly landing a combination that sent Brock sprawling against the car. He couldn't beat up his wife's father—his strength would overpower the man, but he had to consider the long-term ramifications, as well as the potential injury to his still-healing body. He remembered the story Erika told him about Ali's mysterious accident and stayed down, blocking the man's punches as best he could until James tired out.

James staggered back, panting as he bent over, placing his hands on his knees. "Why'd you come here? You think you're going to win over Susan and have her help you get Erika back?" With some effort, he slowed his breathing. "Let me tell you something. I love my girls. Corrine hasn't turned out the way we hoped, but I don't love her none the less for it. Erika has been our shining light. She's my baby. I don't take kindly to anybody hurting her. I'm an old man, but I can still protect my family—like you should be doing." James straightened up, standing tall, proud of what he'd done. "You hurt my little girl, I'll kill you."

Brock tried to slip into his bedroom before Mitchell's kids realized he was home, but the oldest was standing in the kitchen drinking milk from the carton.

"Damn, Uncle Rock, what happened to your face?"

"Does your father know you talk like this?"

"My father knows I'm a man," Conrad answered.

Fourteen was hardly a man, but Brock didn't have time to argue. He snatched the milk carton. "Use a glass."

Conrad followed him into his bedroom, a string of nonstop

chatter accompanying them. "I'm insulted, Uncle Rock. Why'd you get a babysitter?"

Brock rolled his eyes and rummaged in the medicine cabinet for something to patch up his wounds. After washing away the dried blood, the injuries didn't look as bad as they felt, but he still needed to cover them before seeing patients in the morning.

"Who did it?" Conrad asked, sitting on top of the closed toilet seat. He looked like the typical teenager wearing jeans low on his waist with earplugs for an iPod draped around his neck.

"This is grown-up business, kid," he grumbled.

"Where's Auntie?"

"Why don't you go pay the service?" He dug into his wallet, then handed Conrad enough to pay the bill. "And don't try to keep the tip," he called after the boy.

Before he could finish dressing his scrapes and bruises, Conrad was back eating a bowl of cereal. "So where's Auntie?"

"Food stays in the kitchen. Can you watch the kids while I go get Ma from therapy?"

"No problem. She called."

"Who called?" he asked, studying his wounds in the mirror.

"Auntie."

This got his attention. "Erika called?"

He nodded, scooping up a huge spoonful of soggy flakes.

"When?"

"Early this morning."

Before he'd gone to see her parents. "And you're just now telling me?"

"Forgot."

"What did she say?"

"She wanted to know how it was going staying here. I told her Mom had the baby, but Dad wanted us to stay here a little longer. She said seven kids is a lot to handle. How does she know that, Uncle Rock? You don't have any kids."

He grimaced, hating the perception of teenagers. "What did she want?"

"She wanted to talk to you. I asked her if I should take a message and she said no, she'd call again later."

He hated this, but he asked, "Did she tell you where she was calling from?"

Conrad stared at him, sadly triumphant. "Are you guys getting a divorce? Dad said you left because you needed to handle your business, but now you're back and Auntie is gone."

"We're not getting a divorce." He wouldn't allow it. *Never.* "We're going through some—Just give me the rest of the message."

He shrugged. "That's all she said. Except she'd stop by and see us before we went back home." The boy dropped his shoulders and loped out of the bathroom in that annoying way teenage boys have of walking, as if time is of no consequence and everything in the world should wait on them.

He stopped mending his wounds and dialed Erika's cellular, not receiving an answer. He didn't leave a message. Imagining what she might be doing was enough to ignite his jealous anger. He'd never really considered himself a jealous man before, but Mark's egotism had the power to enflame him. Before he could start another reverie about the Mark situation, he noticed the time. He called to Conrad as he left, hurrying to pick his mother up from physical therapy.

Having Mitchell's six kids around kept his mother too busy to hound him about his failing marriage. There were still times her memory failed her and she'd ask what was keeping Erika from dinner. Every time one of the kids would squawk and the subject would be lost. The kids renewed her spirit, making the transition back home a little easier. She was always a little melancholy after visiting the grandkids in Memphis. The visits sparked her loneliness and she would speak about her memories of his father for days. This time having the kids gave her something new to focus on: "When are you and Sugar going to give me a grandbaby?"

The question made him cringe. His plan to store his sperm with their future in mind had gone drastically wrong, sending Erika out the door with her bags packed. He was still trying to understand what had set her off about his initiative when he arrived at the therapy clinic.

"Good evening, Dr. Johnson." A young, bouncy therapist greeted him. Her overenthusiasm had been the thing to push Erika to suggest she would transport his mother to and from her appointments.

He returned the greeting, being cordial but professional in his dealings with her. "How'd my mother do today?"

"Great. Going to therapy while on vacation helped. A lot of the time it's like starting from the beginning, but Mrs. Johnson didn't miss a beat." She went on about the Memphis therapist's remarks she had received via his mom's medical records. He stopped listening when he saw his mother laughing with an older man.

He vaguely recognized the man from before, having asked Erika if she knew anything about him. He'd had a bad feeling then, but his stomach was ready to erupt now. The older man, still fit and obviously active enough to flirt, focused all his attention on Brock's mother, and he wasn't too happy about it.

"Who's that with my mother?"

The therapist didn't need to look to answer. "Titus Martin. He's been moping around here since the day Mrs. Johnson left. He was all smiles today." She turned to watch the couple. "Aren't they cute together?"

Brock raised an eyebrow at the familiar touch Titus laid on

his mother's shoulder as she moved across the room. Titus
was there, grabbing up her jacket before she could reach for
it. Brock didn't like the way the man's fingers lingered at his
mother's neck after the jacket was securely over her arms. His
mother turned to Titus, and Brock saw an expression he
wasn't familiar with in relation to his mother. She was batting
her eyes, smiling broadly, and fidgeting with her hands.

The mask dropped and she returned to her old self when
she saw Brock approaching. He rushed her through introductions, already thinking of ways to break the news to her: she
would be going to a new therapy place by the end of the week.

"What is wrong with the women in my life?" he mumbled,
rushing her out the door.

"Where's the fire?" She shuffled along beside him, her
jagged stride reminding him of her bad hip. He placed his
hand in the small of her back and escorted her outside.

"Ma, be careful of that man."

"What man?"

"Titus. He seemed overly friendly. Not very professional."

The corners of her lips eased up into a smile but quickly
faded when he turned his attention to it. "Titus is harmless."

"He didn't look harmless." Brock was a man and knew
what the gleam in Titus's eyes meant. "Men in Michigan are
much different than men in Memphis."

"Really?" The idea interested her.

"You're a grandmother. You're my *mother*. He might not respect what that means."

"Hmm."

The way she said it made him look closer at his mother. He
tried to see her as another man might, erasing motherhood
and grandchildren from the picture. She was lovely, classy,
and vibrant with a loving touch that everyone who met her
commented on. For a man her own age, she was a good catch.

"I have to find you another therapy center by Monday," he grumbled.

"Hey! What happened to your face? Were you in a fight?"

He hurried her along, moving her away from watchful eyes and curious listeners. "It's nothing." He'd done his best to hide the scrapes and bruises, but his mother wasn't fooled.

"Don't tell me nothing happened when I can clearly see *something* happened." She shuffled along beside him, demanding answers he wasn't interested in giving. Once they were inside the SUV, she used her best chastising tone on him. "I want an answer right now, Brock Johnson. What happened to your face?"

He exhaled loudly. "I had a run-in with Erika's father."

"Erika's fa—" She made the sign of the cross over her chest, which would have been funny if she wasn't truly horrified. "You had a fight with Erika's father? About what?"

He kept his eyes trained to the road. "He's not particularly happy about the way things are between Erika and me."

She crossed her arms over her chest, pulling the lap belt tight. "I'm not particularly happy about it either. Since you're bringing it up."

"I *didn't* bring it up. You've been hounding me with questions since we left the clinic."

"It's all the same. So what are you going to do about it?"

"I'm going to let him cool off. When the time is right, I'll talk to him—over the phone."

"I mean about your marriage."

He strummed his fingers on the steering wheel, willing the light to turn green.

"I've never interfered in your marriage—"

"And I appreciate it so much," he said with a bit of sarcasm.

"—but this has gone on too long. You need Erika. She's miserable without you. When are you going to fix it?"

"Me? Erika walked out—"

"You walked out last time, but she never stopped trying to get your marriage back together."

He glanced at her inquisitively. Her mind was sharp today. He thought to question her about Erika's involvement with Mark but doubted she knew much, if anything. He couldn't imagine Erika bringing Mark around to meet her husband's mother.

"She doesn't want to be together right now, Ma. I've tried everything. She doesn't want to come home."

"What? What have you done to get her back?"

Just yesterday I tried to blackmail her with our prenuptial agreement.

"I miss Sugar," she added her special brand of mother's guilt to the conversation. Her voice even quivered during the delivery.

"I don't even know where Erika is."

"What do you mean you don't know where she is?" she shrilled. "She's your *wife*."

He scrunched down in his seat a little, feeling like a royal ass.

"I thought you'd make it right once you were feeling better. I didn't realize your father's death had been so hard on you until you got sick. But you caught the cancer in time. You're doing better. You learned something from his mistake, now learn something from the things he did right."

"What do you mean?"

"He waited too long. Ignored the signs. He was afraid he knew the diagnosis, so he figured if he did nothing he wouldn't get sick. By the time he went for help it was too late. He regretted it, but he couldn't take it back. He suffered—we all suffered. Now we have to live our lives the best we can. You know it's what he would have wanted."

Brock remembered how strong his father was in all things. He strived to be as good a man, but lately he was falling short.

"You learned from that mistake. Now remember how good a man he was. The way he always took care of his family. The way he loved us and supported us—always. Think about what he would have done if I walked out on our marriage."

His father would have turned the entire city of Memphis upside down until he found her. He would have had every lawman, friend, and relative out searching. He wouldn't have slept or ate or went to work until his wife was back at home where she should be. Because he loved her too much to be apart.

"If you love Erika and want your marriage back together, you'd better find that woman and make it right . . . before someone else figures out how to do it for you."

CHAPTER 25

Avoiding Brock while at the clinic wasn't as hard as Erika had expected. She'd prepared herself for him to come stomping into her office with a pair of handcuffs, demanding she return home with him. It never happened. He never even called to badger her about her decision. His silence became maddening and she worried he might have had a setback. Or more likely, he was sitting in his office, steaming hot mad as he conjured up new ways to force her to do what he wanted.

"I need you to back me up with the Palmers," Ginnifer announced, catching her as she left an exam room.

"What's the issue today?" She finished scribbling orders on the chart and placed it in the slot outside the door, pulling out the appropriate flags to signal the nursing staff.

"Drugs. Always drugs. I need to present a united front."

Erika nodded and headed toward the exam room Ginnifer had just exited. Mr. Palmer was a retired school teacher who suffered from a back injury, which started him on a nightmarish journey. As Erika had seen before, the back injury was so severe pain medicines had been prescribed by his previous doctor. Mr. Palmer became dependent on the drugs, and Mrs.

Palmer became dependent on the peace in the home provided by keeping her husband drugged.

"Ginnifer won't give me my medicine," Mr. Palmer blurted out before Erika was all the way in the room.

"He needs his medicine," Mrs. Palmer added, sounding more desperate than her husband.

Erika sat on the stool and positioned herself between the couple. She spoke in a low, soothing tone. "Mr. Palmer, we explained to you on your last visit we would no longer be prescribing you narcotics. Ginnifer gave you a referral to the Pain Clinic. They will manage your pain. It's important one doctor has a handle on this, with all the medication you need being prescribed by one central person."

"The clinic didn't help—" Mrs. Palmer started but was cut off by her husband.

"They wouldn't give me anything for my pain either. The doctor over there wanted me to check into rehab. *Drug rehab.* I'm not a dope fiend."

Erika watched the fine tremors causing his body to quake. She took in the grayish appearance of his skin, covered by find droplets of perspiration. "This isn't your fault. Let me be clear on that. Sometimes, as physicians, we want to make things better for our patients and we can get caught up in a cycle of prescribing drugs. I think that has happened to you, Mr. Palmer."

"You think I'm a junkie?" he shouted.

"I think you need the narcotics to function, and it isn't a good thing. You need to clean your system of the drugs and find another way to manage your pain. To do that safely, you need to be monitored, and that happens in rehab."

Erika's declaration prompted a string of curse words from Mr. Palmer while his wife broke down into tears. She settled in, prepared to spend a great deal of time with the couple, because she would not let them leave her office like this, hopeless and ashamed.

The Palmers were an older couple, but not many years away from where she and Brock would be some day—if they could overcome their problems. The wife was an enabler, but she wasn't a deserter. Shame attacked Erika so violently she toddled on the tiny stool.

What am I doing?

Her marriage had become such a mess her entire life was off-kilter. She'd become a different person, and she wasn't certain it was the person she wanted to be. She ducked out of the exam room long enough to tell the staff to shift her patients to Ginnifer's schedule. The patients Ginnifer couldn't see were to be rescheduled. She had an obligation to Mr. Palmer. She had an obligation to herself. She'd lost hold of her morals and values as her marriage disintegrated—running around with Ginnifer and her men—but Mr. Palmer was in crisis, and right now she needed to help him.

She spent the balance of the day getting the Palmers situated, which included convincing Mr. Palmer to enter a treatment center. To lessen the chance he'd back out, she'd kept him in the office until everything could be arranged and placement found, even escorting them to the locked unit in the main hospital building.

Helping the Palmers relieved some of her guilt, but at the end of the day, she still had to return home to an empty house without her husband waiting to share her day. She wanted to call Brock up and tell him she loved him and wanted to be with him. Every time she thought about their reunion, the scene was destroyed by her fear. She was afraid to love him as much as she did, because if he left her, she'd die right along with him.

* * *

"This is the last place I thought I'd find you."

Erika shrieked, instinctively covering her nude body when she stepped from the shower to find Brock sitting on top of the closed toilet seat. The candlelight shower and soft jazz was meant to relax her and help clear her mind. It had acted as a shield for Brock's stealth entrance. She wondered how long he had been there. Watching her and waiting for her to step from beneath the hot spray.

Presumed ownership made him grip her wrists and pull her hands to her sides, leaving her totally exposed and fully open to his hungry inspection. Even in the darkened room she could see the brimming need and angry possessiveness in his expression. As much as he wanted to be in control, he wasn't. He wanted her. He was ravenous for what he had been missing these last long months.

She fought her nervousness by playing on his desire, seizing control of their interaction by slightly arching her back as she slowly, tantalizingly slipped a towel around her body. "Were you looking for me?"

"Of course. Don't play coy." He stood up, and the steam in the small bathroom dissipated, trying to escape his wrath.

"I left you a message."

He grumbled something about Conrad not getting it right. "You should have answered when I called. I gave you a hundred opportunities."

"I've been busy," she quickly added, "with work." To avoid his questioning glare, she twisted her hair, wringing out the water over the sink. "The staff has been complaining about the number of personal phone calls I get each day."

"Screw the staff. You're the boss. I'm the boss's husband. When I can't find you anywhere but work, I have to call there over and over until I get in touch with you."

"What was so important?"

"You're staying in my apartment?"

"I used the key you gave me when I came to pick up some of your things."

His nostrils flared, but to his credit, he didn't comment on her craftiness at pulling off the switch of residency. "The last time I saw you, we talked about our prenup."

"You *threatened* me with our prenup."

"You left me a voicemail telling me you were ending our marriage."

Ending the marriage! She needed space to breathe and time to clear her head. His words were too permanent. Did he really believe she didn't love him anymore? Did he think she could live without him—forever? "I didn't say our marriage was over."

"You should have told me face-to-face. What did you mean when you said you weren't coming home?"

"I didn't like you pressuring me and giving me ultimatums."

He moved swiftly, one stride taking him across the cramped space to press against her back, shifting control of the situation back to his favor. She liked him this way—dark and on the edge of uncontrollable desire. He was in charge, and not wimpy with indecision or submissiveness as he had been lately. This was when his facial features darkened into a feral handsomeness she couldn't put into words. His body radiated power, highlighting the perfection of his sleek musculature. "When are you planning on coming home?" he growled, but it wasn't from anger.

To regain the advantage, she reached over and cut on the lights, taking away the heightened prowess of his presence. Shocked by what she saw in the mirror, she swung around. "What happened to your face?"

His eyes briefly narrowed in confusion, but for Brock, it was as if he shouted his surprise.

She cupped his chin, being careful not to touch his cuts and bruises. "Brock, what happened to you?" Her voice shivered when she asked the question, her first thought being he had paid Mark another visit and this time they'd done more than argue.

"Your father," he answered with a rough exhalation.

Shock moved quickly through her body, but never disbelief. She'd seen what he'd done to Ali when she was in college. A number of scenarios flashed through her brain, but none adequately answered why her father had assaulted her husband . . . and why no one had told her. This was the sort of thing Corrine would love to rub her face in.

"My father . . ."

"Apparently, he's on your side in all of this."

"Are you okay?"

He nodded and she realized she was still holding his chin. "I'm fine. Your father's fine." She moved to pull away, but Brock seized her wrists again, trapping her touch. "You . . . are . . . beautiful."

Before she could sort out what was happening, Brock pressed his lips to hers and began a ravage assault of his own. He moved into her mouth urgently, quickly, before she could stop the madness. He was hot and knew how to use his tongue as a preview of what other parts of his body could do. He probed her, never gently but with care as he plundered her mouth, destroying her resistance.

A barrier broke and she didn't try to fight any longer. She began her own assault, wanting his naked skin next to hers, needing his hard muscles to cradle her. Fresh from the shower, her skin was blazing, fueled by his touch. She fought with the buttons of his shirt, tore at the belt surrounding his waist, and grabbed at the zipper of his pants until he was half-dressed, pressing his body against hers.

The rim of the sink bit into her ass cheeks. She pressed her palm between his solid pecks, forcing him back a few inches. She ran a manicured finger over the roughened scar on his abdomen. The minor flaw made his body perfect. He was ripped, his stomach muscles taut and flexing with every move. His long arms felt like cotton over stone, soft but unbreakable. His legs were tall pillars with a fine sheen of dark hair.

Brock ignored any limitations on his health and hoisted her into his arms, moving through the darkened apartment by memory until reaching the bedroom. He dropped her on the bed with a bounce, snatching the towel away before the mattress settled. He yanked off his shirt and kicked off his pants, coaxing Erika beneath the sheets.

She waited anxiously for him to join her. Her eyes moved low on his body, wanting to see how much he wanted her. She had felt the beginning of his erection when he had her pressed into the sink. She wanted to see every inch that would move into her, claiming her as his again.

"Right here," Brock said, cupping her chin and bringing her mouth up to his. He slipped out of his boxers and climbed into bed beside her while he kept her focus on his pillaging tongue. The sheets instantly warmed from his heat, helping her forget how badly she'd wanted to see his body and the changes that had been made to his manhood.

She wiggled until her arms were around his torso and she was pressing her body to his. She broke away from his mouth long enough to whisper, "It feels so good to hold you."

He mumbled something she couldn't make out just before he flipped her body around. He pressed his front to her back, wedging his erection between the globes of her ass. They had never tried this before, and Erika questioned Brock's timing now. He humped against her, fitting his penis into the cushion of her cheeks. While she fought the twinges of desire trickling between her thighs, Brock changed her focus. He pressed a kiss against her neck. He used his tongue to paint her spine, stopping only to swirl the tip in tiny circles. When he reached her behind, he nibbled the flesh, soothing his bites with kneading fingers.

Her body began to simmer, heating with desire. She bucked, flipping over onto her back. Brock was immediately there, his fingers dancing across the tiny ringlets of her mound. She was soft and pliable, welcoming his long fingers as he reacquainted himself with her body.

"Damn," he said, taking her leg and throwing it over his thigh. Before she could whimper her delight, his fingers were slipping into the heat of her cavern. He fit two fingers inside the channel, moving in and out with a twisting motion.

She had just found her rhythm, gyrating her hips to match his pistoning strokes, when he swirled his thumb around her tiny, erect bud. She felt a bead of moisture escape. He swiped at it, catching the droplet. She moaned in protest when he removed his fingers from her hot canal. He slipped his thumb between his lips and sucked . . . hard . . . on and on, watching her reaction to his seductive display.

When his hand returned to the slit between her thighs, it took one stroke to send her over the edge. She bucked against him, enjoying the spasms he had set off, but wanting more.

"Come inside me," she said, her teeth clenched against the pleasure-pain moving through her body. Her orgasm hadn't ended, but she was already wanting more.

She felt a shiver move through his body, but he retained his composure, allowing her to rock against him until the very last shiver moved over her bones. He stroked her wet hair until her breathing returned to normal. He held her in his arms, his fingers trailing down her arm as her body settled.

"You're still hard," she told him, wiggling her bottom against the pole jabbing her back.

"Hmmm." He slipped from behind, laying her flat on her back.

Missionary position might be boring to some, but the way Brock fit between her legs, filling her completely and pressing the weight of his muscles down into her, was heaven for Erika. She raised her knees, digging her heels into the mattress and preparing for his entrance.

He moved between her legs, leaning down to give her another mind-stirring kiss. His teeth nibbled her lips. His tongue lapped at the seam of her lips until she opened for him, accepting whatever he wanted to do to her. His hands gripped her thighs, his blunt nails biting into her flesh. She trembled beneath him, anxious to have him buried deeply inside her. *Home.*

He pulled his mouth away, leaving her with a devastating feeling of loss. He hovered over her for a long moment. She didn't speak, afraid words might push his indecision in the wrong direction. She wanted him. She needed him. She wanted to tell him, "Damn all our issues, just do it!" But she didn't. She waited. Inhaled sharply when he gripped his penis, adjusting the direction of his erection, pointing it at the bulls-eye between her thighs.

"Erika," he breathed. Desire was there, but something else was too . . . regret?

"Brock," she assured him.

He dipped his head, his tongue touching her clit before his mouth met her engorged lips. The movement was so sudden, so unexpected, it sent tiny shocks through her body and she arched off the bed. His hands gripped her thighs, pushing her down and steadying her for the work he was about to do.

He trapped her weeping bud between his lips, applying enough pressure to send chills up through her belly. His tongue never stopped working, darting between her slick folds, searching for the heat marking her entry. His tongue marked the spot, and his thumb moved into her cavern, pressing deeply. He increased the suction on her erect bud, sending tremors down her legs. He moaned, letting her hear how hungry he was for her. His thumb began to stroke while his moans sent harsh vibrations across her folds and deep inside her body.

Delicious tension began to build in her belly, currents of lightning moving across her nerve endings and gathering at the juncture of her thighs. Her body wound tighter. Her muscles locked, aching for relief. She stopped breathing. Her heart thudded. She reached for Brock's shoulders, scrambling to pull him up to her.

"I want you inside me when I cum," she told him, but he didn't move.

He increased his efforts, working his thumb feverishly while flicking the rigid tip of his tongue over her clit. A flash of light went off behind her lids and she screamed out, jerking upward off the bed.

Brock let her ride the wave of pleasure, gently lapping at her until she was too sensitive to stand it. Then he rested his head on her thigh and stroked her slit top to bottom with one well-lubricated finger.

"Bro—"

"Shh. Go to sleep."

"You have a full house."

Enjoying the sultry sound of Erika's voice, he trailed his fingers across her belly. "Surprisingly, it's not as crazy as it should be."

"When are the kids going back home?"

"This weekend." He kissed her shoulder, not able to take his hands off of her.

"Hmmm." She turned to him in the early morning glow, pressing her nose to his. "We fell asleep before we could finish."

Her hand reached beneath the sheets, but he caught it, bringing her wrist to his lips for a kiss. "I have to go soon." He stretched around, reading the time on the clock next to the bed.

"We have time."

He'd managed to keep her satisfied without the use of his penis. If he could duck out of bed fast enough, she wouldn't realize his penis was bursting, straining to get inside her, but his scrotum was flat, deformed by the absence of one of his balls. His pride could not stand it if she found the extra skin a turn-off. He'd struggled all night to keep Mark's words out of his head, but as the sun came up, so did his doubts.

"I want you home," he said, returning to their original argument.

She shifted uneasily.

"What?" He tempered his tone, but his jaw jumped in frustration. It was easy. He wanted her home. She wanted him—if her body's response to his touch was any indication. "Why can't we do this?"

She rolled onto her back, the few inches separating them becoming an overwhelming chasm of distance. "I'm not ready."

"Why?" he asked carefully.

"We have things to work out, Brock."

"Last night—"

"We fooled around. I've never stopped wanting you."

"Have you stopped loving me?"

The question caught her off guard and it took a moment for her to answer. "Never. There's so much . . ."

"What?" he pressed, unable to let it go.

She grasped the sheet, pressing it to her breasts as she moved to sit up against the headboard.

He moved up, too, keeping them on even ground. "We've been needing to talk for months. Let's talk. Everything out in the open."

She watched him, wary of his intent.

"Ask me anything," he offered.

"Why did you run out on me?"

He tried to convey his sincerity with a warm expression. "I wasn't running out on you. I didn't want you to go through what my mother went through. I didn't want to hurt you. I thought I was doing the best for you."

"You did hurt me—leaving me without any explanation. I had to find out what was going with you through Ginnifer. If Will hadn't cut off his finger, I still wouldn't know."

This he couldn't deny. If he could have kept it from her until the end of time, he would have.

"You should have told me everything right away."

"Would it have made a difference in how you feel about me now?"

Her emotion closed down with the efficiency of an automatic shutter system. Suddenly, everything became clear to him. "It would have made a difference," he squeezed out in an agonizing whisper. "It *does* make a difference."

"Let me try to explain."

"I think I finally understand." A fist tightened around his heart. This level of pain was so unfamiliar to him it took a moment for him to catch his breath and stop the room from spinning. "My wife, who loves everyone, and cares about each of her patients as if they were her family, has no compassion for me." He scrubbed his face, closing his eyes against the burning acid in his stomach. "You aren't upset I didn't tell you because you wanted to be there to support me. You're upset you didn't have the chance to *leave* me. Finding out after the operation obligated you to stay. You're pissed off because if you leave me now, people will think less of you—you'll think less of yourself." He threw back the sheets and jumped from the bed, not able to be this close to Erika without hurting her body as much as she had broken his heart.

"Brock, wait."

He fumbled around on the floor, searching for his clothes. "I was trying to protect you from having to live the nightmare of watching me get sick and possibly die from this thing. You don't care that I'm beating it. You're only interested in being left with half a man."

"'This thing,'" she repeated. "'It.' You have cancer. *You* can't even say it. You expect me to deal with it? Without any warning, you told me you were sick and made it my responsibility to care for you. You gave me no choice, Brock."

"What choice did you want?" he shouted, his composure shredded.

She looked away and he attacked.

"Did you want me to die? Do you wish I had? Your life would have been a lot easier if I had. Then you could have been with your perfect boyfriend."

"I never said—"

"The only thing you're saying is you can't deal with me because me with cancer isn't what you signed up for when you married me." He jerked on his pants.

"Yes, I want the man I married," she shouted, her anger flaring for the first time. "I need you to be strong again. That's why we fit—you're hard and I'm soft. You deal in logistics and I manage the emotions. I can't stand you being half a man, wallowing in self-pity. You wouldn't even sleep in the same bed with me after your radiation treatment."

He stood stunned, his arm half in his shirt. "This isn't my caring, compassionate wife."

"I'm standing up for myself."

"Really?"

"Yes, looking out for me. I don't want to learn anything else about my marriage from an outsider."

"You know everything."

"There's more you're keeping from me. What is it, Brock?"

"Nothing." He was unnerved by her revelation.

"You don't want me to touch you." Her voice quivered and her eyes became shiny, her emotions threatening to erupt. "You don't want me to look at you." Her eyes fixed on the crouch of his pants, leaving no questions about her meaning. "You won't make love to me." The first tear fell. "You took my choice away, and then you took your love away. I'm standing on an island, not knowing if it's safe to love you, or if I should keep my distance because you're so unstable I don't know what will come next." She delivered the final blow. "Do you think I want to spend the rest of my life like this?"

CHAPTER 26

Mark could hear Erika and Brock's raised voices in the hallway. He had come by to surprise Erika and take her to breakfast. By chance, he'd stumbled into one hell of a fight. He lingered outside the door, ducking into the stairwell whenever a harried medical resident raced down the hall. He couldn't make out the entire conversation, but he heard Erika saying things like "half a man," and it was good enough for him. He smiled, knowing his lips turned up sinisterly but not caring. He was elated. Finally, Erika had gathered the courage to dump her loser husband.

As the voices drew closer, he made a hasty exit, just getting inside the stairwell before Brock stormed out. He took the stairs by two, wanting to pull his car out of the garage before Brock could see it. He didn't want the man to have any leverage to ignite Erika's guilt, and accusing her of having an affair would be just what he needed to guilt her into coming back to him.

He scrapped the idea about breakfast, choosing to use this information for a more thought-out attack. If he'd pieced together the argument correctly, Erika had rejected Brock thoroughly enough to squash any hopes of them getting back together. This was the perfect opportunity for Mark to renew their relationship. She would go through a vulnerable phase and he would be her rock, ready to help her pick up the pieces and start all over again with him.

Why is Brock at Erika's place so early in the morning?

The menacing voice popped into his head from nowhere, bringing doubts too painful to consider.

Maybe he stayed the night with her.

"She was breaking up with him," he argued. He hadn't heard the nagging voice in over a year. It was one of the reasons he loved Erika—her quiet nature kept the voices quiet.

Are you going to let this one get away too?

"No." Mark gripped the steering wheel, a small flame of rage beginning in the pit of his stomach. No, Erika was his. She just hadn't realized it yet. "I'm working on it."

The sinister voice laughed. *I hope you're not too late. You know what happened the last time with Sarah, and before that with Anne.*

"Sarah and Anne are different from Erika."

His relationship with Sarah had been a one-of-a-kind romance. They'd met at a coffee beanery when he literally bumped into her, spilling her beans. It was a particularly hard time in his life—he had just received his diagnosis from the psychiatrist and was trying to find a medical regimen that didn't kill his libido or leave him a slobbering vegetable— so meeting Sarah with her endless ability to make light of anything was just what he needed.

She didn't push him away when he told her about the bor-derline personality disorder, saying only, "Everybody's got problems," when she found out. She wasn't so forgiving when he accidentally blackened her eye. And she didn't offer the emotional support she should have when he experimented with the coke and it got a little out of control. She started pulling away when their relationship hit a series of ups and downs, leaving him feeling unloved and unworthy.

When he announced his acceptance in a local residency program, Sarah used the opportunity to pull away. She wouldn't relocate with him, instead suggesting they give up the apartment they were sharing and "get some space" from each other. No matter what he said or did, she wouldn't change her mind. The residency was grueling—his mentor suspected his mental imbalance from the very beginning and went on a mission to prove it. He needed Sarah more than ever, but she started avoiding him altogether.

It wasn't until he took the bottle of pills that she came around, but once he was released from the hospital, she withdrew again. This time when she moved, she didn't give him her address or phone number. He'd used a big chunk of his savings to hire people to find her. His suicidal threats didn't work to bring her back. The emptiness grew inside him, smothering him until the only relief he found was in watching her.

He spent every free moment of his life following her. He knew her routines. He had the people she worked with checked out. And when she started dating, he protected her from herself by scaring the men off. Then one night she spotted him and they argued. The next thing he knew, she had gotten a restraining order against him.

It was crazy—Sarah loved him, she had told him so a million times. He couldn't just let her go. She couldn't just walk away when what they had together was stronger than any love ever known. So he did what he needed to do to keep her—he never thought it would get out of hand, but when he ended up in jail, and her latest boyfriend ended up in the intensive care, his father had to step in and save him. If it wasn't for his father's lawyer getting Sarah to admit on the witness stand that she'd instigated her boyfriend into starting the fight, he'd be in prison today.

With intense therapy and redirection of his life goals, Mark finished his training and began working as an ophthalmologist. He never told anyone about the mysterious voice that appeared at the most inappropriate times to encourage him to do wrong. The voice could be suppressed with the right medications, so he took his pills and channeled all his energy into his work, finally finding something in life he was good at. His mother encouraged him, calling him handsome and charming with the ability to win over the most difficult people. His father was relieved: finally, his problem-child was settling into reality and making a living. After a few mishaps at several clinics, his father had been forced to fund a small independent practice. Mark worked in his clinic without incident until the chronic feelings of emptiness became unbearable and he introduced himself to Anne, the owner of the flower shop next door to his clinic.

Anne was the luscious beauty he'd been forced to leave behind when he relocated to Michigan. Their relationship was intense, moving faster than she had wanted. Not wanting to be abandoned again, he held tight to Anne. Her backing away from him, and her constant cheating—although she denied it—prompted the reckless driving incidents. Soon he was on a downward slide, his emotions uncontrollable, and the circle of events escalated until Anne was packing with a broken arm to leave the state.

When the police detective rang his father's doorbell, his father quickly put everything in motion, jetting him away for a little R & R. Mark quickly learned R & R meant an exclusive retreat in Saratoga Springs, New York, with penthouse-like accommodations, gourmet chefs, lush grounds, and a Who's Who roster of guests. Despite the niceties, there were also sealed windows, locked exit doors, and patrolling guards at the resort. Mark followed all the rules, meeting with the psychiatrist, taking his meds, and attending group until his father came for him. They took the limo directly to the airport, and a few hours later he arrived in Detroit at his new downtown apartment—medical credentials in hand.

He'd been able to control his behavior—exhibiting his quirky moods only at home when no one else was around. The voice was gone, thanks to his meds. It wasn't until the last month things started to go wrong again. When Erika announced she was abandoning him, too, he became desperate, thinking he could keep her if he could show her he loved her. He stopped taking his pills, because the pills decreased his libido. A month later, the evil voice appeared, and he was driving toward the hospital having a full discussion in an empty car about his future with Erika.

"Erika has feelings for me," Mark said aloud.

She doesn't know the truth about you!

"Erika knows more about me than any woman ever has. We've spent a lot of time together."

She's been too distracted by her crumbling marriage to notice who you really are.

"I'm not sick anymore. I'm treating patients again. Everything is fine."

What if your patients knew the truth? If the medical director ever finds out your parents paid off members of the state medical board to clear your license to practice, you're finished. Not to mention what your father will do if he has to save your ass again.

"It's not going to happen." He was so absorbed in his conversation, he missed his turn and had to circle the block around the hospital to get to the parking garage.

Not unless Brock makes good on his threat and exposes you.

Erika had warned him about Brock's threat to go to the medical director about their affair if she didn't honor their prenup and go home. Mark had encouraged her to stand her ground and stay true to her heart. No way would a private man like Brock put his business on display for the medical director to dissect. So far their gamble had paid off, but Erika didn't know about his stint in the mental hospital in New York, or about the little voice that encouraged him to do outrageous things when he was boxed into a corner.

If you're going to steal Erika and you don't want to lose everything, you better take care of Brock Johnson.

Brock relived his argument with Erika over and over again during his drive home. Her words sliced through his heart with the precision of a surgeon's knife, but the reality was, she was absolutely right. He didn't know what to do. He was angry at her harsh confession, but he still loved her.

You took my choice away, and then you took your love away.

I'm standing on an island, not knowing if it's safe to love you, or if I should keep my distance because you're so unstable I don't know what will come next.

Do you think I want to spend the rest of my life like this?

He dialed Erika's number, but she didn't pick up. He glanced at the clock noticing he was dangerously close to being late for work.

You don't want me to look at you.

You won't make love to me.

He wanted to make love to her so badly his entire body ached, but he was apprehensive. If she rejected him . . . if she found his body disgusting . . . if his anatomy turned her off . . . he wouldn't withstand her rejection. He had managed to hold it together through the cancer scare and the crises in their marriage, but his emotional state would disintegrate if she found him repulsive.

If he could just explain his fears and make her understand he wasn't pushing her away. He tried Erika again, this time dialing her office and cell. He was scared he wasn't enough of a man for her. He realized he had taken her choice away again, but he would apologize and try to work it out. She didn't pick up. He called several more times before he reached his house, becoming so angry he tossed his cell out the window, leaving a pile of parts on the highway.

She would go to Mark Garing—and he would be happily waiting. The man was a nut-job with his falsely cool exterior and sudden flashes of aggression. Brock understood he had been the one to drive Erika to another man, but it still caused his chest to burn with rage. It wouldn't be hard for Mark to fool Erika because she got along with everyone, liked everybody, and saw only the best in people. He'd had to scold her plenty of times for accepting dangerous patients other doctors had tossed out of their offices—the mental patient pulling a scalpel on her a few weeks back being a great example. She'd never sense the underlying deception in Mark, but Brock had picked up on it during their first conversation. If he couldn't save their marriage, he would still do everything possible to keep her away from Mark.

Picturing Erika in Mark's arms ignited his jealousy. If she wouldn't speak to him over the phone, he'd see her at the clinic. He zoomed up into his driveway, tires screeching like a madman.

"Ma!" Finding the kitchen empty, Brock jogged up the stairs to his mother's bedroom. "Ma!"

"What's up, Uncle Rock?" Conrad appeared beside him, still fighting sleep.

"I'm running late for work. Where's your grandmother?"

"I dunno. I just woke up. What happened to your clothes?"

He cringed. They were rumpled from lying in a pile on Erika's floor all night.

"Call your dad and tell him I need him to come pick you up. My mother too," he added, stopping the boy's protests.

"Did we do something wrong?" The angry teenager scowl melted away into a look of contrition.

"No." He tried to calm his voice, but he kept punching away at the numbers on the keypad of the phone. "No, I need time alone with Erika."

"What happened?"

I've been acting like an ass and now Erika is about to leave me for good. "Please, go call Mitchell."

Conrad slinked away with his head hanging. Brock found his mother in her bathroom. He spoke through the door, assuring her the service would be there by ten to watch the kids.

"Okay," she called back.

"Is Erika taking you to therapy today?"

"No therapy today. Tuesday and Thursday only now. It's Friday."

"Oh, okay. I've got to dress and go. I'm late. Conrad's up." He hurried downstairs and changed into a new suit. He paused only long enough to dial Erika's clinic. The receptionist answered in a lazy voice on the tenth ring, obviously trying to decide if she should start work before the clinic officially opened.

"This is Dr. Johnson. Is my wife in?"

"She's in a staff meeting."

"Tell her I need to see her today. She shouldn't leave the clinic until I come by."

"I'll tell her, Dr. Johnson." Did he hear sarcasm?

He disconnected and dialed Erika's cell phone, leaving the same message.

Virginia Johnson hadn't done anything so impulsive, so wicked since she was a teenager sneaking behind the ice house to experience her first kiss. He called, and she dressed in the cute little skirt and jacket suit Erika had spent too much on during their last shopping trip. She dabbed tea-rose–scented perfume behind her ears and said good-bye to her six adopted grandkids. Conrad didn't mind being left with the babysitter service today because the beautiful young woman who arrived captured his attention.

Titus was a gentleman, helping her into the front seat of his car. "I hope a lunch date is okay," he apologized, "but I have to work most days, and I didn't want to wait another day to take you out."

She smiled, girlishly enjoying his nervousness.

"I thought we could have lunch at a restaurant not far from here. One of the doctors suggested it—Mark Garing. He said he takes his girlfriend there all the time." He paused as he slowly pulled away from the curb. "I thought I'd take my best girl there too. Maybe we can make it our special place."

Mark knew only one place where he could buy a drink this early in the afternoon. He needed something to relax his frayed nerves. He'd been trying to see Erika all morning, but the receptionist kept telling him Erika had a hectic schedule and couldn't come to the phone. He had to know if Brock had spent the night at her apartment, and if he did, did it mean they were back together.

He moderated his speed and drove to his and Erika's favorite restaurant. He'd spent hours there, weaving himself into her life and fighting for a place in her heart. He told the valet to leave the car up front—he had time for only a quick drink before he returned to the clinic. He went straight for the bar, not bothering to engage himself in his surroundings until he'd downed his first drink. With his tremors under control, he relaxed and watched the people in the restaurant.

He had to keep Brock away from Erika until he could convince her they needed to be together. He had no idea how he would do it . . . until he spotted Virginia Johnson huddled up with Titus, the therapist assistant from the physical therapy clinic. He finished another drink, forming a vague plan, before he walked over to them. He'd work out the details later. Right now, he needed alone time with Erika so he could express his feelings for her without Brock's interruptions.

"Well, look who's here." He smiled brightly, keeping his mind focused on his mission.

"Doctor." Titus stood and shook his hand, then acquainted him with Virginia. "Would you like to join us?" he asked, his expression wary with the thought Mark just might.

"No." He checked his watch. "I'm late for a meeting. With your son, as a matter of fact, Virginia. Do you mind giving him a call and telling him I'm running a little late?"

"Brock wasn't home when I left. He's probably at the office. It seems he's always working."

Brock did stay the night with Erika! Or he got up mighty early this morning to talk to her, the detached voice mocked him, knowing he wasn't in a position to argue.

He sucked his teeth in feigned distress. "No, I already tried there. Do you have a cell number for him?"

His patience threatened to crumble as he waited for the old lady to search her purse for her phone; then she fumbled with how to operate it.

Smiling, she explained, "I never use it. It's a gift from Brock to use in case there's an emergency."

Titus moved closer, trying to help her figure it out. "Dr. Johnson has programmed numbers in here, but by name, doctor. She won't be able to give you the number outright."

"Do you mind calling him?" He smiled graciously, checking his watch again and prancing as if in a hurry to leave.

"Sure," Virginia answered.

Titus helped her figure out how to make the call.

"Brock? Brock? It's your mother—Brock?" She held the phone away from her. "I can't hear anything on this tiny thing."

Titus took the phone from her, letting his weathered fingers linger longer than necessary when he touched her. "Dr. Johnson?" he shouted into the phone. After several attempts to complete a conversation, the other patrons in the restaurant were becoming annoyed, drawing too much attention.

"It's okay," Mark said. "The reception in here is bad. Can I see the phone? Maybe I can get the number and call him from outside."

Mark retrieved the number from Virginia's phone and left the restaurant, stopping by the bar to gulp the last of his drink and settle the bill. The valet pulled his car up right away, and he jumped inside, rushing away from the scene.

The old lady hadn't seen Brock all day, but Mark knew where he was before heading to the clinic. This fight was heating up. If he could keep Brock down, and scare him enough to stay away from Erika, he'd only have to convince her they belonged together. He needed only to move Brock out of the way so he could cultivate her feelings.

At the next light, he whipped out his cell and dialed Brock's number. The connection was bad, the line popping and crackling, but it was clear enough for Mark to get his message across while providing a shield against Brock recognizing his voice.

He gripped the phone, waiting for the static to clear enough for Brock to hear him ask, "Do you know where your mother is?"

CHAPTER 27

Shame ate away at Erika; then the remorse set in. She hadn't meant to crush Brock with the sad reality of her fears. She had been overwhelmed by his refusal to make love to her after bringing her body and her emotions to a fevered pitch. She sat at her desk, leafing through the twenty messages he'd left her this morning. He wanted to talk, but she couldn't. She'd made her decision, no matter how wrong it might be, and now she had to honor herself. She had to test her love for him. She needed to know if she loved him enough to endure anything and everything. Or were her feelings for him intense but fleeting, coming to an end now that they were going through a rocky episode in their marriage.

Her father had always accused her of being too naïve and overemotional. He worried she would be taken advantage of out in the mean, mean world, and when Ali attacked her, his concern had only intensified. She couldn't believe he had beaten Brock! Her earlier conversation with her mother had confirmed it. She had to admire Brock's resolve in taking the beating without fighting back.

"I've been calling you all day."

Erika looked up to find Brock looming over her desk. She'd been so preoccupied she hadn't heard him come in.

"I got your messages." She held up the slips of paper she had been reading.

"You didn't call me back." He eased into a chair, his outward appearance cool and collected, but his nails bit into the armrest, betraying his anger.

"I've been busy this morning."

"I want to talk to you about this morning."

"Brock," she said softly, prepared to let him down gently, "we talked this morning. What I need from you now is space."

"Space?" he whispered, his face suddenly looking haggard and worn.

"Yes, I did some thinking after you left. We've both made monumental mistakes lately. I need time alone to sort through everything."

"Alone? Or with Mark?"

She closed her eyes and exhaled before going on. "I want time to think. There are things I need to work out within myself. If I don't feel it'll work out between us, I'll be honest with you."

He shot out of the chair, and for a second, she thought he would come over the desk, but he quickly regained his composure and stalked away. When he finally spoke, his voice was a whisper. "Are you leaving me for Mark?"

She shook her head. "This is about us."

"I came to tell you I'm sorry. I finally understand what you mean about taking your choices away. I was worried about hurting you, and I didn't trust you enough to be up-front with you."

She knew his confession cost his pride, but she had finally made a decision and she had to see it through. "Thank you," she told him sincerely.

"We can work through this together."

"No, we can't." She went to him. "Brock, you have to know

I love you. I'll always love you, but what I'm feeling now is terrifying. I shouldn't hesitate to support you. Instead, I'm having selfish thoughts about how your illness affects me."

"It's understandable. We've both seen it a million times with our patients."

"I don't understand where these doubts are coming from. That's why I need time to work things out. I need to be sure."

"Sure of what?"

"Sure of my feelings for you."

She couldn't have struck a harder blow. Brock weaved as if he had been punched, his six feet threatening to go down like a big brick. He pressed his fingers to the corners of his eyes, lifting his glasses so they framed his forehead.

"Brock?"

When she reached for him, he turned away. He didn't speak, but she noticed his shoulders trembling. She wished she had become a psychiatrist so she could better deal with raw emotions. A lump formed in her throat and she couldn't speak. She was hurting as much as he was—she really did love him. She just didn't know if she could sacrifice having a normal life for him. She touched his shoulder and he pulled away.

"Brock, I'm not trying to hurt you. I'm trying to be honest with you—with myself."

He turned to her, his eyes piercing her soul. "Erika, I know I messed up our marriage." He shocked her with his next words. "If you need time, take time." He wasn't a man who surrendered without a fight or renounced his needs when he knew it was best for them both.

"Are you okay?"

He nodded once. "If you decide you want to come home, I want you there. I love you," he said, swiftly leaving her office.

* * *

Erika should have felt relieved, but instead she felt like crap. She had wounded Brock twice in one day, and all he was trying to do was get her to come home. He hadn't done it with a card and flowers and pretty words like some women would have preferred, but he wasn't that type of man, and he'd done it in his own special way. They'd been married three years, she wasn't going to change him now. Still, his confession of love and the hurt distorting his handsome features were enough to break her heart. She was still rehashing her actions of late when she bumped into Mark in the corridor outside her office.

"Hello." He smiled down at her, steadying her. "Where are you? You ran right into me." His hands lingered on her arms, pulling away slowly.

"Long day. How have you been?"

"Better than you from the look of it." He held out his arm, letting her lead the way. He easily fell into step with her. "You have a deer in the headlights look on your face. What's wrong?"

This was how their friendship had grown into more than casual acquaintances. It would be easy—and comfortable—to fall back into rhythm with him again, but she didn't need more complications in her life. Despite what Brock thought, her indecision didn't have anything to do with her friendship with Mark.

"Erika," he admonished. "We're still friends. If you're upset about something, you can talk to me." He looked around, contemplating his options. "Look, do you have plans tonight?"

She shook her head, suddenly feeling emotionally exhausted.

"Grab your things. We'll go talk." He held up his hands. "I'm only offering friendship."

She watched him, a little skeptical, but his expression was innocent, and she needed a friend. He was a great listener, always remaining nonjudgmental, although he was quick to offer his negative opinion of Brock. She couldn't go home to Ginnifer's place right now with Will's constant flirting and the ruckus coming from the bedroom the three shared.

"We'll sit on my balcony," Mark offered "I'll throw steaks on the grill and we'll talk."

She'd always enjoyed sitting on Mark's balcony, looking out over the city across the river into Canada on warm nights. Tonight couldn't have been a better evening for it. The International Firework Show was scheduled to illuminate the sky at 10:30.

"Friends?"

"Always." He smiled, reminding her how handsome she had found him on those lonely nights not long ago.

At his apartment, Mark grilled steaks and Erika felt strangely contented in his kitchen cooking the sides. Being with him was easy—no long emotional discussions, no arguments, no obligation or illness to manage. She pushed away her guilt and decided for this one night she would relax and not worry about her obligations.

The conversation was light, with Mark remaining a gentleman and never pushing the limits of their friendship. They were lounging on the balcony sipping smoothies and watching the fireworks when he finally asked about her mood earlier. "Everything come crashing in on you?"

Her eyes were on the red, white, and blue explosions lighting the sky when she answered. "My life's out of control."

"How so?"

She turned to him. "I'm doing things that are out of character for me." She watched his reaction closely.

"You're being too hard on yourself," he said after she'd told him about being arrested. "The police dropped the charges. Your permanent record remains clean." He laughed, soft but masculine. "You had one wild evening. With everything you've been through lately, you deserved one."

"I left Brock."

He shifted in his lounger to face her. His voice dropped to a hypnotic low, and his dark eyes focused on her, making her feel as if the only thing that mattered in the world was her feelings. She needed to feel this important. "You're not okay with your decision."

"It was the right thing to do until I figure everything out."

"Where are you staying?"

"At his old apartment."

"Let me guess. Brock's trying to pressure you into coming back to him."

"Not pressure, but I hurt him."

"And he hurt you," he shouted, but quickly caught himself and apologized. "I hate to see the way he treats you. Any other man would be thrilled to be with you. I wouldn't take you for granted."

Something about the way he looked at her made her uneasy. "Maybe I should go."

"I didn't mean anything by it . . . He keeps coming to see me when he doesn't know what to say to you."

"I'll talk to him."

"It's fine. We're men. We'll work it out."

"It's not fair to talk about Brock with you. I'm sorry."

"Don't apologize. This is what friends are for." He shifted, watching her in the settling darkness. "You said you needed time to work some things out. What are you trying to figure out?" When she didn't answer right away, he went on, "If you should end your marriage?"

She nodded, growing uncomfortable with the conversation when she saw the grin lift his lips.

"Most women would have left a long time ago. You've

been trying to do the right thing. Maybe you should do what your first mind tells you to do. You're not happy like this. Anyone who knows you can see it. Do what you need to do to be happy and all the rest will fall into place. People will be hurt, but in the long run, it's better to hurt a little now than for the rest of your life."

She settled back to watch the fireworks, the silence between them not as comfortable as it was earlier. Coming to his apartment hadn't been the best idea. No matter how platonic he claimed their friendship could be, he always found a way to subtly hint about renewing their relationship. She suddenly wanted the firework show to end so she could go home. Mark must have sensed her apprehension, because he mixed up a fresh pitcher of smoothies and insisted she have one. After her first sip, she felt a little woozy.

"I added a shot of gin," he announced proudly.

"I probably shouldn't drink anymore. I have to drive home."

"Don't worry. You can always stay here tonight." He smiled at her, looming over her for a moment before he returned to the lounger next to hers.

After the show ended, Erika stood on wobbly legs and helped Mark bring the dishes inside to the kitchen. If she didn't know better, she'd wonder if there was something other than a shot of gin in the smoothies. She'd consumed half the drink because Mark kept a watchful eye on her, insisting she "drink up" almost to the point of intimidating her.

"Whoa," he said, catching her when she weaved. He wedged her between his body and the countertop. "Are you okay?"

She didn't like the smile crossing his lips. "I need to lie down."

"Sure, I'll take you into my bedroom and you can—"

"At home," she managed, although her head was beginning to swim.

"Look at you," he laughed. "There's no way you can drive."

"You take me."

"I'd rather you stayed here tonight."

"Can't." She couldn't even speak in complete sentences. She knew what she wanted to say, the words just wouldn't come out.

"Sure you will." He lifted her up and carried her through the apartment to his bedroom. In all the months they'd dated, she'd carefully avoided going into his bedroom. Tonight, she had no control of what he might do to her.

"Drugs. In. The. Drink?"

He dropped her on the bed and her body bounced limply. She felt as if her brain were knocking around inside her skull. "I gave you a little something to help you relax." He sat next to her. "You've been so wound up the past few weeks. Tonight I'm going to take care of you." He snagged the neckline of her shirt with his finger. "I'm going to take all your tension away."

She focused on gathering her energy, using every ounce to move away from him to the opposite side of the bed. He didn't notice her struggle as he began unbuttoning his shirt. She watched as he stood and pulled off his pants.

"I know where I messed up with Sarah and Anne. You can't give a woman too many choices. I tried to wait until you figured out what you wanted to do, but it was a big mistake. Look at this mess."

His words slithered down her spine, and the very theory of choice she'd used against Brock came back to haunt her. How could she have gotten herself in this position again? Hadn't she learned anything with the Ali incident? Here she was all these years later about to be forced to give her body to man.

"Who the hell is Ali?" Mark raged, jumping on the bed and almost pouncing on her.

She couldn't answer through the tears.

"Stop crying! I'm doing this for us." He snatched her up and then pushed her away, leaving the bed as he rambled nonsensically. "Or would you rather see me dead? Because that's what'll happen if you leave." He scrambled back to the bed, seemingly unaware of his nudity when he petted her. "Don't you see how much I need you. I love you. My life is nothing without you."

She fought a muddled brain to process what was happening. She didn't know this stranger who had drugged her and trapped her in his apartment. The look in his eyes was wild and lost. His words were strings of sentences she didn't understand. It was as if Dr. Mark Garing had been replaced by an evil twin.

"If we make love," he kissed her temple, sidling his naked body up to hers, "you'll understand. You'll feel what I feel."

She bucked wildly, refusing to be a victim again. She wouldn't be forced to sleep with Mark because he felt it was time and had drugged her into submission.

"Settle down!" he shouted. He held her down by crossing his body over hers. He fished through the bedside table, looking for something.

She fought the drugs in her system, determined her will was stronger than anything he could give her. At her most desperate moment, Brock's face—wearing his perfect smile the day they stood at the altar—appeared before her. If she was hallucinating, it was enough to energize her. She had to see his smile again—when she returned to their home, announcing she loved him and never wanted to be apart again. She had been stupid, leaving the love of her life because she was afraid their time together would be too short. All the selfish reasons she'd used to justify her behavior seemed gaudy and insignificant as she fought the aggressive moves of a rabid man.

Mark produced a syringe he promptly notified her contained Dilaudid, a pain killer potent enough to sedate a narcotic virgin like her for hours. Hours Mark could do whatever he wanted to do to her. She would not go back to Brock as damaged goods.

She stopped struggling, catching Mark off guard enough to make him juggle the syringe. Her energy coiled into a tight ball and she harnessed the power and used it to strike. She snatched the syringe, tipped her hips, and stuck the needle into Mark's chest near his shoulder. He yelped from the force. She pushed the plunger hard and fast. When he rolled over to dislodge the syringe, she scurried off the bed, bumping into the walls as she ran from the apartment.

Mark threw the syringe across the room and ran after her. She didn't run from him. She ran to Brock, and it was enough to get her to the door. She screamed at the top of her lungs, easily making enough noise to make the neighbors across the hall believe a murder was being committed.

Mark tackled her, calling her "Sarah" as he tried to cover her mouth. She bit down hard, sinking her teeth into a chunk of flesh. He screamed.

A man's voice came from the other side of the door. "Is everything all right in there?"

"Help!" She still couldn't form complete sentences, but she could shout the essentials. "Police!" she screamed, drawing out the word until she was breathless. "Police!" she chanted until Mark's fist connected with her temple and she was no longer able to speak.

BEGINNINGS

CHAPTER 28

Do you know where your mother is?

"What the hell?" Brock dropped the newly purchased cell phone into his lap. He scrambled for it, keeping his eyes on the road as he moved toward home at a nice clip.

After Erika's announcement, his day had only gotten worse. He couldn't keep his emotions under control, and his thoughts kept wandering to her during rounds with his residents. The junior doctors were frustrated; he grew impatient, then his temper flared. The doctors were shocked by the uncharacteristic display. Embarrassed by his lack of restraint, he turned over rounds to the senior resident and retreated to his office until the end of the day, which came quickly when he remembered he'd thrown his cell out the window that morning when he couldn't reach Erika on the phone. Frantic Erika might try to call him when he wasn't at home, he rushed to the cell phone store and purchased a replacement.

He was on the way home from the cellular store when he decided to check his messages, hoping for a call from Erika telling him she had changed her mind about needing "space."

Do you know where your mother is?

He pulled over to the side of the road, listening to the

message over and over until he placed the man's voice. Was Mark *threatening* his mother? Could he be so twisted? How did Mark know his mother? Had Erika been bold enough to bring him by the house for dinner?

It took a minute to clear his muddled mind; then the panic set in. He jabbed at the keypad, practically shouting when Conrad picked up. "Is your grandmother there?"

"She's gone."

Brock pulled out into traffic, the back wheels of the Navigator spitting gravel as he darted out in front of a compact car. He ignored the blaring horn and punched the gas, heading home at top speed. "Gone where?"

"She went to lunch with this old guy."

He cursed, accelerating. He had a thousand questions for Conrad, grilling him without allowing a chance for the boy to answer. *When did she leave? Where did they go? Did she say when she'd be back? What did the old guy look like?*

"What's going on, Uncle Rock?" Conrad's voice squeaked.

"I'll be there to pick you up in five minutes—have the babies ready." With Mark threatening his mother, he'd feel better if Mitchell's kids were with him instead of a babysitting service. He disconnected and dialed his mother's cell, not really expecting her to answer. He'd given her the phone to use in case of an emergency, but she never took the time to learn how to use it, and she rarely turned it on. He received no answer.

He took the next turn on two wheels, dialing with one hand and gripping the steering wheel with the other. He dialed Erika, hoping she could give him answers. Maybe she'd told Mark she needed "space," too, and out of spite he'd left the scary message for Brock—just to rattle his cage. She might be able to explain Mark's thinking—threatening an old woman to make a point. His mind was racing, fright dictating his every move, because he wasn't in any position to make decisions.

Erika didn't answer. His body went cold—what if . . . ? He pushed the thought away. Erika was fine. Mark cared about her, he wouldn't hurt her. Brock pulled into his driveway, jumping out the car with the motor still running. He would find his mother, check in on Erika, beat the crap out of Mark, and everything would be fine in the morning. He kept repeating the mantra as he ran into the house and ushered Mitchell's kids into the SUV.

"Uncle Rock," Conrad said, scooping up one of the baby girls, "I found a note." He held the crumpled paper up. "Grandma left a note saying where she was going for lunch."

"She hasn't been home since lunch?" He had a baby in each arm, pushing another ahead of him to the door with his knee.

"No."

"Why didn't you call me?"

"I did. I left a message on your cell like you said."

Seeing the hurt on Conrad's face, he tempered his tone. "My phone was broken. You did the right thing."

When all this was over, he'd have a man-to-man with Conrad. Despite his complaining, he enjoyed Conrad looking up at him. For a teenager, he wasn't all bad. He managed to keep his eye on his five little brothers and sisters while his mother was in the hospital adding another to the family. He never complained about the kids, and actually he had a good way with them, sometimes able to stop the crying when Brock and his mother couldn't. He didn't hang out in the streets or do drugs. No, Conrad wasn't that bad at all.

"I need your help, Conrad."

Conrad perked up, happy to be needed.

"Let's get the kids in the car and go find your grandmother. Read the note to me while we walk."

* * *

"Brock, what are you doing here with these babies?" His mother slipped out of the booth to take the youngest boy in her arms.

"What are *you* doing here?" He didn't attempt to hide his displeasure with her companion. "There was this crazy message on my cell . . . Are you all right?" He glared in Titus's direction.

"I'm fine. What are you going on about?"

"We can talk about it later—at home. I need to take you and the kids back to Mitchell's place until I can explain."

"Uncle Rock," Conrad interjected sheepishly.

Brock waved off his interruption with a flip of the hand. "I hate to rush you, Ma, but I'm pressed for time here."

Virginia whispered so as not to awaken the sleeping baby boy snuggled against her chest. "You may be pressed for time, but I'm not."

"What?" He was distracted, his mind on Erika and what might be transpiring at the clinic with Mark down the hall watching her. He had to get to her. His stomach was twisting in nervous knots, tightening until he could see with his own eyes she was okay.

"I'm not leaving. I'm on a date."

"A date?" Brock and Conrad asked simultaneously.

Brock threw the boy a displeased look before addressing his mother. "Ma, we don't know this man, and you shouldn't have gone off with him alone." He told her about the message from Mark. "How do you know Titus and Mark didn't plan this together?"

"Plan what?" Titus asked, offended by the accusation.

"Whatever Mark is trying to do! I don't know you, and neither does my mother. You sneak her off to lunch and here it is near dinnertime and she still isn't home. Meanwhile, I get a weird message from Mark that has me worried half to death something's happening to my mother."

"I'm on a date," his mother added softly.

"This can't be a date. You're not ready to date. Dad has only been gone—"

"Too long," Virginia interrupted. "I love living with you and Sugar, and I know you've worked hard to give me anything I need or want, but there are some things a child can't do for his mother." She rested her hand on Titus's arm. "Titus is a good man. You don't know him, but I do, and you'll have to trust my judgment on it."

Titus looked away shyly, his chest puffing out with pride.

"Whatever Dr. Garing is up to doesn't concern him or me." She told Brock about Mark stopping by their table earlier. Afterward, they'd finished their lunch and ended up at the movies, taken a walk in the park, and now were back to the restaurant for an early dinner.

Titus spoke up. "Son, I care about your mother, and as long as she's with me, nobody is going to put a hand on her. You can count on it. If Dr. Garing comes back around, I'll let you know."

"Now," Virginia said, "I'm having a good time, and I want to finish my dinner. These children are your responsibility— you need to get them home to Mitchell. I'm not leaving."

"Uncle Rock—" Conrad started, but Brock interrupted.

"Ma, I really don't have time to do this now. I have to get to Erika—"

"You obviously don't understand what I'm telling you. I'm out on a date with Titus, and I won't be returning home until it's over. If you have business, you should get it in gear and get these kids back to their parents. I won't be babysitting today."

Brock opened his mouth to protest, but his mother wasn't finished.

"You messed up your marriage. You need to do whatever you

have to do to get it back together. Go fight for Sugar, but do it on your own. I have my own relationship to worry about now." She kissed the baby and gestured for Brock to lift him up.

"Uncle Rock," Conrad said as Brock settled the baby in his arms.

"What is it, Conrad?"

"Mom and Dad don't know we're coming home today."

"What? Why not?"

"Well, we didn't want to go home. I figured we could stay with Grandma for the weekend. Mom and Dad went to take the baby to see our grandparents."

"What?" Brock's raised voice drew unwanted attention to the pack of people standing over the table.

"I didn't know Grandma would be getting her groove on."

"Where do your grandparents live?"

"Flint."

Two hours away! Brock needed a target to unleash his growing anger on—immediately, Mark came to mind. He'd told Conrad exactly what to do, but he'd done the opposite. His mother was making goo-goo eyes with a dirty old man. Erika had decided to distance herself from their marriage and was now ignoring his calls. All this, and he stood in the middle of a restaurant dragging six kids along who didn't belong to him.

"Sir, is there a problem?" The manager appeared at his side.

"No, no problem," he snapped.

"Ma'am?" the manager asked his mother.

"Actually, we'd like to enjoy a quiet dinner," Virginia said, avoiding Brock's glare.

Titus coughed into his hand, hiding his smile.

"Sir, I'm going to have to ask you and your children to leave."

"Ma! You'd let him thrown us out?"

"I'm on a date, son, and you have business to take care of."

* * *

"Uncle Rock, we've been sitting here for twenty minutes."

Brock glanced up into the rearview mirror and was suddenly overcome by the innocence of the kids sleeping in the back of the car. Each baby was strapped into his or her individual safety contraption, comfortable enough with him to have fallen asleep while he made all the decisions. With all his grousing about suddenly having a houseful of kids, he had to admit they really were little angels. The girls were soft and cuddly, rushing to snuggle into his lap the moment he returned from the hospital. The boys were rough and tumble, always in some sort of mischief while Conrad, the oldest, was oblivious, absorbed in music or video games.

He and Erika had dreamt of making their own family—where was the dream now? Completely obliterated by his foolish actions. The crushing sorrow of what he'd destroyed rushed at him, flooding him with emotions his pride never wanted to admit he possessed. He'd stripped Erika from her right to choose, hidden the truth from her as if she were too weak to handle it, and then tried to bully her back into his life. Her love for him was in question, her being angry with him at best. His mother had just told him to get a life and had moved on with her own. Had he lost everything important to him?

"I'm sorry, Uncle Rock. I didn't mean to cause trouble." Conrad's raw pleas drug him from his reflective haze. "Don't be mad at me."

Brock looked at Conrad, confused about his level of distress until he realized the source. He pulled down the visor, seeking visual conformation. He was crying. Releasing his emotions this way had never seemed manly—until he met Erika. He'd cried the first time they'd made love. And now he was crying again—afraid he may have lost the best thing to ever happen to him.

"It's not you," he told Conrad, wiping away the tears with the back of his hand.

"What's up, Uncle Rock?"

"I miss Erika," he admitted.

"Why don't you go get her?"

"What did you say?"

"Why don't you go get her?"

The question was so simple it was profound, striking a cord with Brock and opening a floodgate of ideas. He turned the key of Erika's Navigator, the engine purring with the same subtle softness she possessed.

This is what Erika had been trying to tell him. She wanted him to know exactly what he wanted, and to come strong when claiming it. She wanted him to stand up and fight the cancer, never doubting the power of his determination. She wanted him to be open and honest, giving her the facts and allowing her to make her own choices about how she would receive it. She wanted everything he had to offer, but she didn't want to lose herself in supplying his needs. It was complicated, but weren't all women?

He understood now the only way to win Erika back was to come to her ready to share his deepest emotions. He would have to open himself up to her scrutiny and allow her to do what she felt best for her. He would have to rely on the strength of her love for him to bring her home to him.

He had to believe Erika still loved him as much as he loved her. Mark was inconsequential—a symptom of their problems and nothing more. Mark was messing with him by leaving a message suggesting his mother was in danger. Why would he do something so low-down and immature? *To distract you.* The thought popped into Brock's head suddenly, striking his temples with a sharp snap. *To distract me while he makes his move on Erika,* he corrected, but it wouldn't happen. He wouldn't lose the love of his life.

"Where are we going?" Conrad asked as he pulled out of the restaurant parking lot.

"I'm taking you guys to Mitchell, and then I'm going to bring my wife home."

CHAPTER 29

The drive up to Flint took longer than it should have because of the summertime road construction. The kids had done well, sleeping most of the way. Being stuck in the car gave Brock time to have a heart-to-heart with Conrad, and it had gone better than he'd expected. Once you got past the layers of teenage rebellion of adult ideas, Brock found Conrad was smart and had big plans for his future—just like Mitchell, and if he was anything like his father, Conrad would achieve every goal and more.

Brock couldn't help but imagine making a family with Erika. One son, one daughter had been their dream. He'd want his son to go into medicine but would support him in whatever he chose. He wanted his daughter to pursue a career path more cerebral—maybe engineering or accounting. Erika would punch him if she ever heard him say it aloud, but he wanted his daughter to be pampered.

The solo ride home gave Brock time to formulate his plan to get Erika back. He had handled the entire situation wrong, and it would take nothing less than admitting his mistake and begging forgiveness to get his wife back—he had no illusions about it. But she still wasn't taking his calls. He'd dialed her office, apartment, and cell every ten minutes during the last leg of the drive, but she hadn't answered. Finally, he resorted to leaving voicemails and trying to be patient enough to wait for her call. She needed time and ⸱⸱⸱ ⸱⸱ to figure out what she wanted for her future, he understood that, but he wouldn't be too far out of her mind while she contemplated her life. He wanted to remind her of the good times, and how they'd gotten past the bad times before. He wanted her to know he wouldn't let go without one hell of a fight.

If he had any questions about his body's sexual capabilities, his subconscious tried to answer them that night. Thinking about being with Erika again made his body achingly hard when he fell asleep, and it was still that way in the morning. The first thing he did was check the caller ID on the phone—Erika hadn't returned his calls. He tried her apartment and cell, but got no answer. He even tried her office, although it was too early for her to have arrived.

Frustrated, he rolled over onto his back and studied the welcomed lump in the bedcovers. Having an erection didn't mean he'd be able to complete the sexual act, and if he wanted to have babies, he needed to do more than just get a hard-on. He closed his eyes and burrowed his hand beneath the sheets, placing himself in Erika's position, imaging what she would feel.

He would have to explain his intentions of having a scrotal implant. He shuddered at the thought of having that conversation, but he wouldn't make the same mistakes. She wanted to know everything; then she wanted to make her own choices. His hand moved over his scrotum to his penis, and even the gentlest touch made him flinch. There was no pain, only the unbearable need to have Erika's hands—lips— tongue—mouth—touch him.

He rolled out of bed in the morning with purpose, happier than he'd been in months, because today he would hear Erika tell him she loved him and she was coming back home. He would do whatever it took to make it happen.

By the time he was ready to go into the office, his mother was up humming her way through the house as she completed her morning routine, but Erika still had not returned his messages. He gave up on calling her and went in to work early to see her.

"Hi, Brock," Ginnifer said when she turned around from the receptionist's desk and saw him entering the clinic.

After greeting everyone, he asked, "Is Erika in her office?"

The guilty look on Ginnifer's face answered questions he hoped he wouldn't have to ask. "She's not coming in today."

"She's not?" Erika never missed work. "Why not?"

She studied the bouquet of flowers he was carrying and gestured for him to follow her. They were behind the closed door of her office before she answered. "She called in sick."

"What's wrong?" His heart was beating double-time while his grip tightened on the flowers.

Ginnifer shrugged. "She was a little worn-out mentally with everything you guys are going through, but the last time I saw her she was fine physically."

He felt his own guilt weighing on him. He had been putting her through a lot of stress the past months. "I'll go to her apartment to check on her."

"I'm not sure it would be a good idea."

"What? Why not? What are you keeping from me?" He wished he hadn't had to ask.

"Dr. Garing called in for her."

He was a smart man, and he was proud of that fact, but his intelligence took him on a roller-coaster ride he wished he didn't have the mental capacity to understand. "Mark called in for her, and she hasn't been sick *physically,* so you think . . . she and Mark . . . they're together . . . and she's not coming to work . . . because . . . they're . . . together." Every word spoken aloud made it more of a reality. He felt as if his emotions were being squashed and it became hard to breathe.

"I'm only telling you because I like you. Really. I want to see you two back together."

"It won't happen if she won't return my calls, but she's playing hooky with Mark."

"She needs time." Ginnifer tried to comfort him by rubbing his arm.

"Time to do what?"

She pried the flowers from his grip and laid them atop her desk. "To get her head together. She loves you, and she wants to be with you."

He made a sound that could have been interpreted as anger, disbelief, or pain.

"She never had a conversation while staying at the house that didn't have something to do with you. You're on her mind all the time. She wants to be with you. She's just trying to work out some things that are in opposition, so when she comes back she's there forever."

He read her eyes for sincerity, finding comfort in Ginnifer—a person he'd never had believed was his ally in all this. "Do you want us back together enough to help me make it happen?"

She watched him, clearly torn between her role as coworker and friend. "I don't know if I should get involved."

"You know me well enough to know I don't ask for help often. And I never like to bring my personal life to the office, but, Ginnifer, I love Erika and I want her back. Today. I need your help to make it happen."

Her wary expression lifted and she smiled a gorgeous smile that helped Brock understand why two men would rather share her than not have her at all.

* * *

"Brock, I tried."

"Did you really call her?" he accused Ginnifer. He understood their new friendship was fragile, still in the developing stage, but he was anxious to be with his wife again. As the minutes passed throughout the day, he realized just how much he needed her to make his life whole. He had been looking to his penis to make him complete when it was really Erika who made him a man.

"Of course I called. I wouldn't have said I was going to if I wasn't."

"She didn't answer?" he asked, his voice reflecting his contrition.

Ginnifer shook her head, her top lip bunching together in a frown. "I called her twice on her cell, but she didn't call back."

"Page her." He didn't mean to demand it with such bite, but he was beginning to have a bad feeling. Erika didn't go missing, especially if she felt one of her patients might need her.

"I did."

"And she didn't answer?"

Ginnifer shook her head again.

Brock planted his elbows on top of his desk and rubbed his temples. "Why wouldn't she answer you? I understand she's probably avoiding me, but why isn't she talking to you?" When Ginnifer didn't say anything, he looked up, reading her true emotions for the first time. He cursed, jumping up from his chair ready to do something, but he didn't know what. "Something's wrong. Erika is always assessable to her patients."

"We don't know anything's wrong for sure." Ginnifer's words were reassuring, but her voice trembled a little, adding doubt.

He snatched up the phone and dialed Erika's parents.

Remembering his last confrontation with her father, he handed the phone over to Ginnifer and told her what to say.

"They haven't heard from her." She placed the phone back in its cradle. "Now I'm starting to get worried."

Brock paced his office, his stomach twisting with a familiarity he associated with dealing with Mark. "Call Mark."

Her eyes widened a bit. She realized it was only logical and came around his desk to dial the phone. After a quick conversation, she told him, "Mark's finishing up at the office."

"I thought he called in for her today."

"He did. He said they spent the morning together, but she went home earlier this afternoon. He was on campus, so he stopped by his office to do some work."

Mark was lying. Erika wouldn't take an unscheduled day off from work, and if she did, she would do it because she needed only a few hours. She would have come to the clinic after she finished . . . *whatever* she needed to do. "Do you believe him?"

"I don't think he would lie."

"Erika wouldn't have stuck you with her entire patient load." He swore again. "I knew it didn't sound right when you told me this morning. If they were together and Mark could come to the office, Erika would have too. She'd feel guilty about overworking you."

"Where are you going?"

He shoved his arms into his suit jacket. "I'm going to her apartment. If she calls you, let me know."

"You too."

"Thank you," he told her before he bolted out the door.

Brock searched the apartment in record time and found no evidence of Erika having been there this morning. The damp towel he had peeled from her body a day before was still pooled at the foot of her bed. He went through her closet but found nothing useful. He was pacing in circles in the living room when he realized her purse and keys were gone. He raced down the stairs to the parking garage. The Zephyr was gone.

Erika's behavior had been erratic lately—for her—but disappearing and running from her problems wasn't her style. A tinge of regret moved through him—it had become his way of handling his illness, which is why he was standing in a vacant apartment trying to figure out where his wife had gone.

"Mark, that bastard."

He was out the door and running across the hospital campus to the medical building where the clinics were housed before he could logically think through what he was doing. He was uneasy, but his bad feeling was growing. He needed to know where Erika was and that she was okay. His body reminded him he wasn't completely healed, his abdominal scar coming alive with a blazing heat, but nothing would stop him from getting to Mark.

"Where the hell is my wife?" he asked, bursting into the clinic.

Mark turned his back to him, crossing the empty waiting room to lean against the receptionist's counter. "If she doesn't want you to know, I—"

"Stop playing games. If you know where she is, you damn well better speak up." His fingers were balled into tight fists and he realized that he would pummel Mark the second he got the information he needed from him. Jealousy made him furious, but there was more. It wasn't just Mark's arrogance or his meddling in their marriage. It wasn't even the smug set of jaw. Brock didn't like the fact that Mark had deceived Erika, making her think he was a good man when he was a crazy bastard.

"I left her this morning." He smiled wickedly while running

his palms down his thighs, suggesting what had taken place between them.

"You better not have touched her."

"What if she touched me?"

Brock crossed the room in two leaping bounds, but Mark ducked behind the door leading to the exam rooms before he could reach him. He pulled at the knob, but it was locked.

"Don't think I'm afraid of you," Mark taunted as Brock contemplated jumping over the counter onto the receptionist's desk. "I'm doing this for Erika. If I were to beat the crap out of you, she'd probably feel sorry for you . . . and I just can't have her feeling sorry for you when I'm inside of her."

Brock tried the door again, kicking it while calculating if Mark would have enough time to run away before he jumped over the counter.

"Go home, Brock. You and Erika are over. I'll tell her you stopped by the next time I see her."

CHAPTER 30

Ginnifer snuggled her naked body up to Rhon, burying her nose in the freefall of his black locks. It gave her comfort to press against him, his body heat radiating beneath the sheets to warm her. Will sensed her movement, automatically pressing his nude body against her back. The boys hadn't checked the schedule when she'd climbed into bed behind Rhon, with Will joining them minutes later. They were as worried about her as she was about Erika. They had grown fond of Erika—even Will who hadn't found a way to convince her to share his bed for a night—and they were worried about no one being able to find her for two days.

Will peeled off his pajama pants and pulled Ginnifer over onto her back. His hands were soft, unlabored, as he stroked her temple. He was going to occupational therapy, but he never let anyone treat him as if he were handicapped. She knew from intimate experience he'd fully recovered and was capable of using the reattached pinky finger just fine. "You're worried about Erika," he said, whispering so not to wake Rhon.

"This isn't like her."

Rhon turned to face them. "We're worried too. What can we do to help Brock find her?"

"I don't know," she admitted. She held out hope Erika would call, telling them she'd only gone away to get her head together. She wouldn't be able to face opening the clinic Monday morning without Erika there.

"We'll think of something," Rhon said, pressing a kiss to her temple in rhythm with Will's stroking finger.

"Erika is a fighter. She's just fine," Will offered, glancing at Rhon and silently asking permission, the way he always did when he wanted to make love to her in Rhon's bed.

Rhon gave a tiny nod and let his fingertips dance down the side of her body until they rested on her thigh. "We'll do whatever we can to help. Do you think Brock is on to something? About the eye doctor?"

"That would be too weird," Will answered, letting his fingers follow the same path as Rhon's, only stopping to caress her hardening nipple. "He's a doctor. Doctor's don't hold women against their will."

"What about the dentist a few years ago who drugged his patient, got her hooked on drugs and kept her as a sex slave?" Rhon asked, a small shiver moving through his body.

"Dentists don't count," Will explained.

"Why?"

Will shrugged, not bothering to elaborate.

"Can we change the subject?" Ginnifer shivered from their combined touches. "I don't want to think about my friend being a sex slave right now."

"We were just talking," Rhon apologized, kissing her navel. "Erika is probably at Club Med sipping drinks on a beach."

She ran her fingers through his long locks. His hair was her Kryptonite. When he let it hang loose, dripping like liquid pearls onto her belly, she could focus only on how badly she wanted him.

"In the morning," Will said, licking her breast, "we'll brainstorm." He was always the most submissive one-on-one, but the most aggressive two-on-one. "Tonight, we'll get your mind on something else."

Susan lay next to her husband in the darkness, her eyes locked on the ceiling. "James, you shouldn't have hit the boy."

"He deserved it," he grumbled, rolling onto his side, ashamed to face her.

"You can't keep fighting Erika's battles by beating up anyone who hurts her. What if he had fought back?" She knew it wounded his pride to suggest Brock had let him win the fight in the garage, but Susan knew the truth, and it was time he faced it. "You're not a young man anymore. What in the world got into you, hitting Erika's *husband?* We love Brock like he's our own son."

"He hurt my little girl," he defended. "But he won't do it again."

"James! You don't know what goes on in someone else's marriage."

He whipped his body around, facing his wife. "You don't think it's Erika's fault their marriage is in trouble."

"She left him."

"He left her first."

Susan sighed. James refused to believe Erika could ever do wrong. "So two wrongs make a right?"

"Doing my baby wrong makes anything she does in return right."

"I want you to stay out of this. Brock has been good to Erika. They're going through a rough time right now, but I'm hoping they work it out . . . and they will if we stay out of it."

"If—"

"No, 'ifs.' We stay out of it. Let them work out whatever the problem is." He started to protest, but she placed her finger against his lips. "Promise me."

He grumbled, but agreed.

"One more thing. When they get back together, I want you to apologize to Brock for hitting him."

James sputtered in disbelief.

"*James,* promise."

His wife didn't ask for much, but whatever she wanted, he delivered. "I'll apologize, but I won't like it."

"Thank you." She kissed the tip of his nose before turning her back to the wall to go to sleep.

"What'd you think those calls were about? Brock looking for Erika? Did she tell you she was going away for a while?"

"No, she didn't mention it. Maybe she left a message with Corrine. We'll ask her in the morning."

James loved both of his daughters, but Corrine was irresponsible, and she and Erika weren't as close as he wished they were. Erika wouldn't tell Corrine she was going away and not mention it to him. Matter of fact, she would have come to her father first.

"I'll go see Brock tomorrow, first thing. Apologize and let him know we still think of him as one of our own," he told his wife. In his head he was thinking, *I'll take my .45 along in case there's something to Brock's fretting.*

He laid quietly as he replayed Brock's messages in his head. The boy had sounded downright beside himself the last time they talked. A foreign uneasiness crept up James's spine. Brock was a lot of things, but irrational and hysterical weren't two of them. If he was worried about Erika, there was a reason. He slipped out of bed when Susan fell asleep, taking the cordless phone into the kitchen and dialing Brock.

"You heard from my daughter?"

"No, sir. I've been to every place I could think of she might go. No one has heard from her. She hasn't gone to the clinic. She's not answering her phones. If you know of anyplace she might go to think . . ."

"I'll check with Susan, but the only place I know Erika would run to is here—to me."

"You're calling so I guess it means you haven't heard from her either. It would be cruel for her to be there and you not tell me." There was a biting quality to Brock's accusation, but James couldn't tell if it was from nerves, attitude, fear, or tiredness because the boy sounded as if he hadn't slept in the last two days.

"What do you think is going on?"

"She wouldn't leave without telling someone. She wouldn't abandon her patients." He exhaled across the phone line. "She wouldn't ignore me like this. No matter what our differences are."

"Did something happen between you?"

"We were still trying to work it out. She was confused. Sir, I know what you're thinking, but I'm telling you I understand Erika and her emotions and the way she thinks better than I understand myself. Something's wrong. I feel it in the pit of my stomach." He exhaled again, trying to remove the quiver from his voice. "I've gone to the police."

The police wouldn't start looking for a grown woman because her estranged husband requested it. There were protocols and waiting periods. James would have a hard time maneuvering around the system, and he was an insider—Brock wouldn't have a chance. The fact that he had gone to the police meant he believed Erika was in real danger.

"I'll start looking for her in the morning."

* * *

James was at Brock and Erika's home before sunrise, but Brock was already out looking for her. Virginia let him in, served him coffee, and gave him access to the home office. He used all the skills he knew to pull data off of Erika's hard drive, but there was nothing incriminating to be found. The more nothingness he encountered, the more he began to buy into Brock's theory: His daughter had been taken.

He called Brock's cell. The boy wouldn't have come up with the theory out of the blue. Something had gone on between them to suggest someone would kidnap a 30-year-old woman. When Brock finally answered, the connection was so bad James couldn't understand a word he was saying other than "golfing buddy."

Let him follow that lead. He went downstairs to find another. Virginia had lived with Erika for seven months after her son left. She hadn't shared a home with his daughter and not seen something useful. He had been told Virginia was a little forgetful, but he'd never have known it the way she chattered on over lunch.

"Did Brock tell you he thinks Erika is missing?"

"He did." She didn't look up from her sandwich.

"You don't seem worried."

She hesitated, but James told her to place herself in his position. After an earnest moment of silence, she opened up. "Brock and Sugar are having problems. They try to keep the details from me, but you can't live in the same house and not know what's going on."

"If you know anything to help me find Erika, I'd appreciate you telling me."

Virginia hesitated, staring down into her cup of tea as she slowly mixed the three sugar cubes. "Sugar was seeing someone. She tried to keep it from me, but I overheard her a time or two."

James sat in disbelief, ready to defend his daughter against the woman's accusations. This was why their marriage wasn't working: Brock's mother was instigating trouble.

"Brock found out about it, and he wasn't happy. But he knew he pushed her to it, so he forgave her." She finally looked up from her cup. "I've been listening to Brock the last few days and he's set on believing Dr. Garing has something to do with why Erika won't come home."

James stopped at three gas stations to get directions before finding his way to Brock's-now-Erika's apartment. It took a lot of nagging—and pretending to be Erika's senile old father—before the manager would let him in to wait for her. He found evidence of Brock tossing the place, searching for any clue. He went over the place again. This was his forte, he could find trace evidence after the place had been gone over twice by the world's best forensic team. His wife and daughters had no idea what work he had "retired" from, and they never would. Although their suspicion had been raised with the Ali incident.

With all James's skills, he couldn't find anything to lead him to Erika's whereabouts. There were oddities—the missing purse and keys, but none of her clothes seemed to be gone—but nothing solid. The only lead he had to go on was Brock's suspicion. He pulled out his notepad and reviewed the information he'd gotten from the boy. He used his cell to dial a number that would force him to destroy the phone after the call, and made his inquiry.

"I need you to get me everything you can on Dr. Mark Garing. Yes. Yes. Yes, I want everything—on the record and off. How fast? Yesterday! My baby daughter's missing."

He took one more look around the apartment before leaving. When he opened the door, a dark skinned beauty was standing there.

"I'm Ginnifer. Is Erika here?"

He knew by her worried expression, Erika was a friend. "I'm her father."

"She's my best friend, and I'm worried about her."

"I am too." And he was getting more and more worried as her friends came forward, distressed about the situation. "I've put some things in motion. Brock is out checking with anyone who knows her. I'm going to make another trip to the police station."

"The police?"

He nodded. "It's gotten serious."

"Will they do anything? Brock said they pretty much showed him the door—after questioning him like he was a suspect in her disappearance."

"I have some old contacts."

Her face brightened. "I have a connection too."

"Gawd, I love this woman." Bradley stared at the collection of video screens with the dreamy enthusiasm of a teenage girl mooning over a rock star. It was silly really, his crush on Ginnifer. She was involved with two young pups. Although he'd had his chance before she'd even met those punks. He should have made a move, but he knew she was too good for him. . . . He thought it would never last. He was an ex-cop, the head of security at the hospital. She was a nurse-practitioner, her career on the rise. He was a middle-aged white guy. She was a young, Nubian beauty. He could have spit when she took up with the college student and the gambler. It sounded like the title to an old western movie: *The Nurse, the Gambler, and the Gigolo.*

Of course her taking up with the two porn stars didn't lessen his feelings for her at all. The exact opposite happened. He realized there was a freaky side beneath the professional he'd fallen in love with. The things that excited him and got his blood boiling would be welcomed. She wouldn't make him feel like a deviant just because unconventional sex was his turn-on.

Bradley watched footage of Ginnifer leaving the clinic yesterday evening. He wasn't being a voyeur—it was his responsibility to review the security footage. With the state of the world, he had to be extra vigilant with the employees' safety. He watched her lithe body walk away from the camera as her flared hips switched back and forth with a hypnotic rhythm. He groaned, adjusting the front of his pants when his package began to press into the zipper.

Erika exited the clinic minutes after Ginnifer. Nice woman. Very kind. She'd taken care of his father until his death two years ago. Pretty too. Bradley hated seeing her apart from Brock. Brock was a good man, just misunderstood.

Bradley was about to cue up videotape of Friday morning's "Arrival of Ginnifer" when a shadow caught his eye. He rewound the footage several times only able to make out someone in the corner watching the women leave the clinic. After the disturbance with the psycho psych patient a few weeks ago, Bradley wanted to check it out.

His curiosity took him down a mysterious trail. In reviewing film, he found sneaky little shadows dating back weeks. It wasn't a coincidence the shadow hung around waiting for Erika to leave the clinic every weeknight. And it was no surprise when the shadow finally revealed himself, stepping out and "accidentally" bumping into her as she left a few nights ago.

Bradley was an observant man by way of career hazard. He'd noticed Dr. Garing's fondness for Erika a long time ago. He even suspected something was going on between the two. But Erika had gone back to Brock, so Mark slumping around in the shadows, avoiding the security cameras, was enough for Bradley to launch his own mini-investigation.

He spent most of his day pulling file footage and reviewing the tapes. His findings made him dig deeper, searching the security film outside Brock's office and then the apartment where he had been staying. An entire story unfolded and Bradley learned the intimate details of the Johnson's failing marriage. He worked through lunch, fascinated by how easily it was to intrude into a stranger's life.

"Ginnifer." His heart stuttered when she stepped into the security office.

"You haven't been around much lately."

He couldn't stand to be around her, watching her but not able to have her. It took him a moment to move past his damaged heart and process what she'd said. She'd noticed he hadn't been around. It had to mean something, right?

"Are you okay?" Ginnifer asked, concern creasing her smile.

"I'm fine." He cleared his throat, nervous he might mess up and alienate her. "Thank you for your concern, though. Did you need something?" His horny body assigned double meaning to the question, but he reigned himself in.

"Are you looking at tapes of our clinic?" She moved to the screens, leaning over him to get a better view. He itched to reach out and touch her.

"I really need to see Erika about this. It's important."

Ginnifer studied the determined lines in his face before saying, "I have a feeling I came to see you about the same thing you want to see Erika about."

"Tell me." He offered Ginnifer a seat. He crossed his shin over the opposite knee. Having little patience for waiting, he strummed his fingers across his thigh as she unfolded the story of Brock and Erika's problems. He nodded, fighting to keep his mind on what she was saying and not on the tight brown slacks hugging her legs. When she was around, he stammered, hardly able to think straight enough to form a sentence. If he had his way, no words would be necessary between them.

"Bradley, you look funny," she said, ending her story, "and it's upsetting me."

He sat forward, immediately alert and apologetic. "I surely don't mean to upset you."

"Did you hear anything I said?"

"You were telling me about the Johnson's marital problems." He hesitated, but only for a moment, seizing the opportunity to verify the vibes heating the room. "Erika has two men in her life fighting over her, and you're worried the fight might have clicked up a notch and gotten pretty dirty."

"There's more."

"Yes." He moved to the edge of his chair, and when he placed his hands on his knees his fingertips brushed the soft fabric of Ginnifer's pant leg. "She's juggling two men, and I caught disturbing incidents on the security cameras today." He dropped his voice, staring in Ginnifer's eyes with unmistakable intent. "Having two men rarely works out—no matter how in control the woman feels she is."

Ginnifer's eyes narrowed in understanding, and he could swear she stopped breathing.

"A woman should strive to find everything she needs in one man. It makes life less complicated."

She was not the ordinary woman, and after she overcame her surprise, she fired back at his banter. "Maybe it takes two men to make one good one. Or maybe having one man is boring."

He dared touch her knee. "I'm one man—a good man— and life would never be boring with me. If you'd give me one day, you would never go back to the Gambler and the Gigolo."

Her bottom lip dipped in shock, making him bolder, but she recovered quickly, crossing her arms over her breasts in defiance. "You couldn't handle a black woman."

She didn't remove his hand from her knee, which gave him hope, empowering him to do what he should have done a long time ago—go after his woman. "I've heard the stereotyping, but don't you believe it. You aren't a screaming banshee who'll turn me into a cowering simpleton, and I'm too much of a man to let you if you tried. Or do you mean I couldn't handle you in bed?" His hand crept up her leg, squeezing tightly into the plush flesh of her thigh. "Those kids you're messing around with have opened the door for you, but until you try what I've got—experienced what I want to do to you—you don't really know what good sex is all about."

She pursed her lips, ready with a quick comeback, but his next words stumped her. "Has it ever been so painfully good to you that you cried, begging for more?"

Her proud shoulders slouched a tad, showcasing her surprise at his brazen words.

"How about it, Ginnifer? Will you give me twenty-four hours to show you what a real relationship is like?"

Ginnifer watched him reflectively, a curious gleam in her eyes. She was torn, trying to rationalize an already outrageous situation.

"I didn't come here for this. There's a favor I need to ask—"

"I know. You came here because you're worried about your friend's marriage. I understand you have something important to talk to me about, but right now there's a question on the table for you, Ginnifer. And I don't think I'll be able to process anything you have to say until you answer me. Afterward—no matter what your answer—I'll concentrate on whatever problem has your eyes looking so sad today, but I can't go on until I have an answer from you."

Ginnifer's lashes batted wildly, clearly confused by his bold attitude. She considered his proposal for so long he thought she wouldn't answer until she whispered, "Twenty-four hours."

A slow—and he hoped seductive—smile widened his lips. "It's all I'll need."

CHAPTER 31

Brock.

His eyes were narrowed, focusing on their target. His lashes beat against the lenses of his glasses as he peered down at the jagged skin. His concentration was intense, drawing her gaze to the scar weeping with blood. The man was flinching while the nurses tried to calm him with reassuring words. She ignored the chaos, tuning in to the doctor with perfect brown hands and manicured fingers suturing the open wound. His center of attention remained on his work, keeping a steady hand when the world around him seemed to be exploding. She stood near the door, afraid to flinch and distract his attention. He was breathtaking, with manly good looks, a tight body, and unwavering intensity. His tension made her body tighten in places inappropriate to think about at work.

When he finished, he took his gloves off, carefully turning them inside out before tossing them in the trash. He turned to her, slowly, as if he had known she was watching him and didn't want to frighten her away. She was glued to the floor, her heart pounding as he approached.

"Dr. Erika Hendrix?" His deep timbre made her knees

buckle. "I've heard you meet each of your patients at the hospital if they're admitted."

"It fosters trust," she managed.

He nodded, considering her. His lashes dropped behind his glasses, lingering on the parts of her body left exposed by the business skirt. "I'm Dr. Johnson. Brock."

She couldn't reply. What do you say when you meet the man you know you want to spend the rest of your life with?

He turned, watching the staff comfort the patient as they dressed his wound. Her eyes moved over his back, taking in the terrain before he turned to face her again. "This may be totally inappropriate, but would you like to have a cup of coffee with me?"

She didn't drink coffee. "Yes."

"Brock," she whimpered.

Her eyes came open and the first thing she saw was the bottom of the white porcelain toilet bowl. She rolled over onto her back—very slowly because her body ached, and she was cold. She laid there, staring at the ceiling, trying to figure out where she was and how she had gotten here. Confused snatches of conversations, quick memories of pain, and the unrelenting feeling of fear swirled around her until she remembered everything.

Mark had her.

She was with him against her will.

He had injected her with drugs. Dilaudid, by the way the drug made her feel high and confused, sweaty, and hot—completely helpless, but not hopeless.

I have to get out of here.

She listened, but there were no sounds.

Brock. She only needed to get to Brock and everything would be okay again. Days ago—or weeks?—she had no concept of time—she had thrown her love for Brock away, foolishly wanting to explore other worlds. Now she would give anything to have one more moment with him. She didn't care if he were sick, or if their time together was limited. She loved him. She needed him. She wanted him . . . and she would give herself the chance to tell him all those things.

She concentrated, pulling Brock's energy into her body, focusing as he was the first time she saw him. He was strong, she was vulnerable. He was hard to her soft. She needed those characteristics now if she was going to survive. Gathering all her strength and channeling it at her goal, she found the strength to sit up. The moment she went upright, something jerked her back down.

She lifted her hand to her neck. A collar. A red leather collar with silver ringlets connected to a chain attached to the piping of the sink. She untangled the chain from beneath her and measured the length. There was enough to walk around the small bathroom, and maybe enough to get halfway into the next room, but not much more.

She shivered from the cold and realized she was dressed in only her bra and panties. None of her other clothes was in sight. She examined her body, trying to find proof of Mark's violation. She found two tiny, tiny pinpoints—probably where he had injected her with the drugs.

What about the man who had come to the door? The man she begged to call the police and send help? She didn't know what had happened, but she was still with Mark, a prisoner leashed to the bathroom sink. What did he do to her? Had he forced her to . . . Her stomach turned and she hugged the toilet, heaving, but not able to bring anything up. When the nausea passed, she realized she was sick with hunger. Or withdrawing from the drugs?

How long had she been here? Chained to the bathroom sink

like a household pet? The days and nights were crammed together in her mind, and no matter how much she concentrated, she couldn't get the story straight. She remembered fighting and stabbing Mark with the syringe, crawling to the door, and screaming for help. Then there was a black pit of emptiness—no, she was in the blackness, locked in . . . a closet. Next, she remembered being carried, unable to do more than lift one arm at a time. And now she was awake, chained to the toilet. Pieces of her memory were gone, and the unknown events jostled her security, pushing her to freak out.

Whatever Mark had done to her body couldn't be reversed. Better to concentrate on not letting him have a chance to do anything else.

"Brock," she tried to speak, but it came out a croaking sound made inaudible by her tears. She allowed herself a moment of self-pity, crying so hard her upper body shook. Brock always lectured her about her soft feelings and allowing strangers to command her emotions. He warned her one day it would all be too much—sympathizing with every patient's heartaches—and it would break her down. He told her to feel it for a moment, inhale, and then let it go, because a sick patient didn't want a crying doctor—they wanted to be healed. She cried hard, inhaled, exhaled, and then let it go because she wanted to be with Brock again, and he wasn't there to save her, so she'd have to save herself.

Mission Hospital's chief and director of the medical clinics was a man you'd rather not encounter. Every physician asked to join the hospital's staff was required to meet him some time during the interview process, but all hoped their encounters with the man stopped there. Dr. Adelman was a serious man with an authoritative demeanor. In his early sixties, he held a great deal of power in his grasp with several more years of service in front of him. He was a well-respected physician who had been assigned to four medical task forces in Washington by three presidents, including the present one. If you did your job well, he was generous with the rewards, but make a mistake, and he had the power to end your career.

Brock had decided it was best for his future career plans to stay out of Dr. Adelman's radar . . . until Erika went missing and he was sure Dr. Mark Garing had something to do with it. He didn't care if his friends felt he was overreacting. Or if his mother watched him with pity in her eyes. He ignored the police detective's advice to "wait until she comes home." Erika was in trouble; he could feel it, and he wouldn't wait around doing nothing until it was too late.

"You've been with us since your residency, right?" Dr. Adelman asked, infamous for remembering some little detail about each of the physicians he employed.

Brock nodded, not pushing, but very anxious to get on with his purpose in coming.

"This is the first time you've come to see me. Ready for a move? Aren't we treating you right? I hear only good reports about you."

The comment made his mind stutter, but he shoved the knowledge of the director watching him aside for the moment. "I'm very happy here, Dr. Adelman. This is personal."

The director's eyes narrowed with concern. "This is unusual." Obviously he was aware of Brock's reputation of never bringing his personal business to work.

"It is, and I wouldn't come to you with it unless I believed it to be a serious matter."

The man gestured for Brock to continue, his sleeve lifting just enough to flash the gold of his Rolex.

Brock's mouth went dry and he found it hard to speak. All

these years he had strived to be a certain type of doctor. This one meeting would destroy his professional image and possibly ruin three medical careers. He might regret it, but Erika might never forgive him.

"Dr. Johnson, get on with it."

This was the most powerful man at Mission Hospital, and Brock had his ear. He couldn't go back. Careers were one thing. Erika's life was another. "My wife is missing, and I believe Dr. Garing has something to do with it."

The man's face paled, leaving his cheeks a ghostly white. "You're married to Erika Hendrix."

The man knew too much about his personal life—he would investigate how much and why later. "Dr. Erika Johnson now. Internal Medicine."

"Garing?"

"Mark Garing, ophthalmology."

Dr. Adelman's eyes dropped, as if he were trying to recall some insignificant fact about Mark. "The new ophthalmologist," he repeated, sounding unsure. He scratched the back of his neck. "A doctor is missing, and I didn't know about it?" His tone was harsh, angry about being out of the loop. "Start at the beginning and tell me what's going on in my hospital."

Brock poured his soul out for this stranger's inspection. He told Adelman about his separation and his cancer—the director didn't seem surprised to learn any of this. He explained how he had jeopardized his marriage for self-preservation and how badly he wanted to get Erika back. "She started seeing Mark Garing," he confessed, wounding his pride for the sake of love. He told Adelman everything, including how smug Mark had been acting since Erika's disappearance.

"These are serious accusations, Dr. Johnson."

"I know, and I—"

"Do you have any evidence Dr. Garing knows where your wife is? Or that she is anywhere against her will?"

He told Adelman about her missing work. "She would never leave her patients unattended—no matter what was going on in her personal life."

He scratched his neck again. "I've heard that about her. She's a very dedicated woman."

"Even to me, even though I screwed up our marriage. She wouldn't go off and not let anyone know where she is. I know her. She wouldn't do it."

"You may be right to be concerned, but you have not given me any evidence Dr. Garing has done anything wrong. According to you, he's been at work every day, and other than being a little cocky, nothing's out of the ordinary. I think you're right to have gone to the police, but until you have something solid, there's really nothing more I can do."

"Dr. Adelman—"

"I feel sorry for your situation. I do, but I run a medical center here. I can't accuse doctors of kidnapping on the word of a scorned husband. I'm sorry to be so callous, but it's the truth."

Brock stood up, his anger and frustration ready to spill out between his lips. He was fed up with no one believing him. He knew Erika, and her disappearance was about more than a petty fight between them.

"Dr. Johnson," Adelman said, stopping him before he could say or do something stupid, "take some time off. Find your wife. If you come across anything, bring it to me." He tried to convey a message with his eyes. "I'll keep closer tabs on things around here." It was as good as Adelman authorizing a complete investigation—off the record—and Brock took him up on the offer.

* * *

Three days missing and the police still weren't seriously investigating. Brock knew because he'd been down to the police station all morning yelling at the detectives to do something to find Erika. James, Erika's father, was calling in contacts from his mysterious secret life. Brock humored the man—anything to keep him out of the way—and feigned interest in his covert references at living a double life. The Ali incident did make you wonder, but it was something Brock put on his list for later scrutiny. Ginnifer and the men she lived with were worried, but there wasn't much they could do. Hassan and Mitchell thought he was crazy with grief, although Mitchell did offer considerable financial resources to the cause.

The third day seemed to be the hardest for Brock. He hadn't slept, had hardly eaten, and was sick to his stomach with grief. His illness wasn't important. His frozen sperm didn't matter. The minor disfigurement of his body was inconsequential. Eating, drinking, showering—it all seemed petty without Erika in his life. When he found her, he would spend every single day showing her she was loved.

He put only positive thoughts out into the atmosphere, and knowing Erika believed in the power of the mind, he felt assured she would know he was doing all he could to find her—which was why he had taken Adelman up on his offer and taken a leave from work and was using the time to follow Mark. The day was almost over, and he had spent every minute watching the entrance to the ophthalmology clinic. The one time he took a break to go to the bathroom he'd had Hassan sit in his place. Mark never left the clinic, but now the day had ended. The receptionist left an hour ago. Mark would be leaving soon, so Brock made his way to the physician's parking lot and angled his car to see Mark pull out.

It couldn't have surprised him more when he followed Mark to the resident's apartment building. As bold as he pleased, Mark sauntered up to Erika's apartment. Twenty minutes passed before he returned to the parking garage. Hoping Erika had returned, Brock waited for him to leave before he made his way to her apartment. His emotions were crushed—right along with his hope—when he entered the apartment to find she was not there.

He collapsed on the sofa, his head resting in his hands. Maybe Hassan and Mitchell and the police were right: Erika just didn't want to see him. He was so fixated on saving their marriage he was projecting his feelings onto her. Her telling him he needed space might have been her version of ending their marriage. After all, she had served him with divorce papers—how much clearer could her message be? He had been the one to put them through the shredder. He had walked away from their marriage to save her, and the move had given her time to clarify what she really wanted out of life.

Before he was swallowed up by a vat of despair, he decided to take one more look around. He cursed violently as he stood at the bedroom closet. Some of her clothes were gone. He dove to the floor and rummaged around, finding a pair of shoes and an overnight bag missing. He pulled out his cell and dialed her father.

"James, did you take anything from the apartment?"

"Nothing. What's going on?"

"I'm back at Erika's and some of her things are gone— clothes and shoes." His emotions teetered. He didn't know whether to be happy she was alive, knowing she was hiding from him because she didn't want to see him, or scared something bad had happened wherever she had gone to find her answers about their marriage and she was no longer able to contact him.

James grilled him with questions, demanding, "Don't

touch anything. I can have someone there within the hour to dust for fingerprints."

For the first time Brock believed James did have secret contracts from some sort of double life. He left James to his business and rushed to the parking garage, hoping Mark's trail hadn't gone cold.

Mark fought the urge to run through the parking garage, casually strolling instead as he tried to maintain a cool exterior. He couldn't afford to draw attention to himself. Brock was doing enough of that, skulking around the clinic asking questions about his involvement with Erika. He tossed the gym bag with Erika's things onto the passenger's seat and stood outside the door, taking inventory of what he had gotten from her apartment.

What are you planning to do with her? Keep her chained up in the bathroom for the rest of her life?

"Once she realizes how devoted I am to her, she'll come around."

And you'll live happily ever after?

"Erika isn't like Sarah or Anne. When she loves, she loves forever. Think about how many times she told me about how important her marriage vows were. No matter how much of an ass Brock is, she insists on honoring her vows."

Exactly, so what makes you think she'll dump him for you?

The question startled him. He believed if he could prove how much he loved her, Erika would see Brock wasn't a good man and turn to him. She wasn't a woman who abandoned her lover. She would stick it out with him, and not run like Sarah, or tell him he was obsessive like Anne had. He only needed to make her love him.

When Brock comes running in like some possessed fairy-

*tale knight in shining armor, she'll go back to him like she
always does.*

"Brock doesn't need to save her from me."

Really? The annoying voice cackled. *You have her collared
and chained to the sink, idiot!*

Mark's rage flared, and he shouted, "I won't let Brock get
in the way!"

How are you going to stop him?

The ding of the arriving elevator caught Mark's attention
moments before the door opened. Looking to see who was
joining him in the garage, he noticed Erika's Navigator
parked behind a huge white column. How could he have
missed the gigantic SUV? Brock had switched cars with her
because he needed the space to haul around a bunch of kids.

His vision swung back to the elevator, and out stepped
Brock. He watched as Brock crossed the parking garage. He
stooped low, hiding his body as he waited to see what Brock
would do next. Brock's head swiveled in his direction, and he
ducked down inside the door, but the light was on and it drew
Brock's attention. His heart jumped erratically when the sound
of Brock's angry footsteps changed directions and headed his
way. He wedged himself between the door and the seat.

The alarm on Erika's SUV chirped, signaling Brock had
disarmed it. Mark bent lower, pressing himself into the floorboard, careful to stay out of sight. The Navigator's engine
roared to life, making his heartbeat decrease to an almost
normal rhythm.

Suddenly, a door slammed and quick footsteps beat against
the pavement, heading in his direction. Before Mark could
stand, Brock was barreling down on him.

"What the hell are you doing here?" Brock's anger was
enough to rattle him—if he didn't have the prize they were
fighting for at home. "I told you to stay away from my wife."

He stood slowly, mustering as much dignity as possible seeing he had just been caught crouching, hiding next to his car. "What are you doing here?"

"What are you doing here?"

"I stopped by to check on Erika."

"Where is my wife?"

Brock insisted on calling Erika his wife. Well, Brock could have the title because he had the real thing. "Erika will contact you when she's ready."

"Do you know where she is? Have you done something to her?"

"I wouldn't hurt Erika—physically or emotionally—unlike you."

Brock's fists closed slowly, his jaw tightening. "I've had enough of you. I've tried to handle this the right way, but you just don't get it."

"So now you want to handle it the wrong way?" He wouldn't back down to Brock. He had won Erika, and he wasn't above fighting to keep her. He'd compromised his principles so much already—spying on her and her mother-in-law, drugging her to keep her quiet when he had to leave her alone—a brawl in the parking garage would be right in line with the rest.

"What's in the bag?" Brock inclined his head to indicate the gym bag.

"My workout clothes."

Brock watched him with discriminating eyes. The stare was meant to be intimidating while he searched for the truth behind the words. It wouldn't work on Mark. He'd spent years in various therapy chairs learning to say the right thing, show the perfect amount of remorse while facially displaying his regret for his wrongful actions. He knew how to wear a blank face—the face society wanted to see on a man who had been labeled "crazy"—and he gave Brock the full effect of his skills now.

"You keep getting in the way," Brock said. "I know you've done something to her. Erika wouldn't disappear from her family, her friends, her clinic—me—unless something was wrong."

"Maybe you have it reversed. Maybe *you're* in *my* way. I'm coming. You're going."

Something in Brock snapped, and before he had enough time to move, Brock snatched him up by his collar. They scuffled, but Brock had the advantage, pinning him against his car. Somehow Brock managed to shove him inside the open door, pinning him in the seat against the gym bag with Erika's belongings. He wrestled the bigger man in the confining space.

Brock was breathing heavily as he threatened him with clenched teeth. "I've told you over and over. Stay away from Erika." He tightened his hold on Mark's collar, twisting until he struggled to breath. He pinned him tightly against the seat. "Drive away, Mark," he growled. "If I find out you've hurt her in any way, I'll kill you." Brock released him with a shove, catching his breath before he backed away from the door. He moved to the left rear of the car, gesturing for Mark to go.

Pride paid more of a part in his anger than Brock's threats. He straightened his clothes, and Brock watched as he rounded the car and slid in behind the driver's seat. He was smoldering as he watched the smug arrogance on Brock's face. He wanted to tell the man it was too late: He'd lost Erika forever because she was with him and he'd never let her abandon him. He forced his key into the ignition and started the car. He glanced in the rearview. Brock remained standing there, his fists grinding into his waist.

"Stay away from Erika," Brock shouted, and it was enough to make the last bubble of logic in Mark's head pop.

He put the car in reverse and backed out of his space. He glanced up at the rearview again, seeing Brock's triumphant smirk. His rage flashed and he stepped on the gas, flooring the pedal while angling the rear of the car in Brock's direction. The man went flying, his legs the last to be seen in the back window before Mark smashed into a parked car.

CHAPTER 32

James dialed Brock's cell phone but disconnected when the boy didn't answer. Fingerprinting Erika's apartment could wait, because his friend had hit the jackpot when digging into Mark Garing's past. A lot of it was too doctory for James to understand, but Brock would be able to decipher it. For sure he knew Mark was a sick man delivered to two wealthy parents with pockets deep enough to keep their son out of prison.

Mark had spent a considerable amount of time in country-club–type mental hospitals for a variety of disorders. *Borderline personality disorder* was repeatedly referred to in his medical records, but other diagnoses like *paranoia* and *obsessive personality* also appeared. Witness statements from criminal proceedings involving a woman called Jane Doe were consistent, contradicting the medical reports. He was called *suave, charming, sophisticated,* and *charismatic*—all qualities Erika would gravitate toward. Especially at a time when Brock was being such a jerk.

He couldn't believe Erika had taken up with this type of man. But then again, Erika was always naïve, too focused on ignoring people's flaws in the dreamy hope she could save them with a little kindness. Corrine was streetwise, but Erika could never see the bad in anyone. He had had to protect her all her life—until Brock showed up to take over the job.

He dialed Brock's cell again but got no answer again. "Well, boy, you better be doing a damn good job at looking after my baby."

Ginnifer faltered nervously on her heels when she saw Bradley sitting opposite her desk. The man had always been a menace with his moony-eyed stares until he became bold enough to challenge her to go on a twenty-four-hour date designed to change her life forever. She composed herself as she closed her office door, refusing to admit the predatory gleam in his sparkling gray eyes turned her internal thermostat up a notch.

"Our date isn't for another week," she told him as she slipped into her chair, glad for the emotional protection of the desk between them.

"Did you think I would forget?"

She pulled up tight, hiding her sweaty palms in her lap.

"This is about Erika. I've been looking at the security surveillance tapes again."

"Did you find something?"

He told her about Mark's suspicious behavior, his skulking in the corridor outside the clinic and his erratic hours. "It was nothing but a hunch, but I've had to rely on my instincts for years and I did once again. I pulled the tapes from the security cameras at the resident apartments and there was Dr. Garing again—lurking in the stairwell and hallways."

"Could this be innocent on Mark's part? Visiting Erika? Him just looking out for her?"

Bradley scrubbed his chin. "He could make a case."

"But your instincts say otherwise."

Bradley nodded. "My instincts say there's something I'm missing. If you're done seeing your last patient, I thought you'd come to the viewing room with me and go over the tapes. Maybe you'll see something I'm not—since you know Erika and Garing in a way I don't."

"Something like what?" Ginnifer asked, not hiding her suspicion. "Is this a trick to get me alone in a small, dark room?"

"Later." He couldn't hide his sly smile. "I'm thinking you might pick up on a subtle facial expression, or match days when Erika was upset with days Garing was hanging around a little too much."

She contemplated the offer. "If you think it'll help."

"You never know when something insignificant to one person can be a major thing to someone else."

Bradley waited patiently for Ginnifer to finish her work. They locked up the clinic together and walked over to the main building of the hospital where Bradley's security office was situated.

"This is creepy," Ginnifer said, watching Mark's shadow on the screen. "Why would he be watching her . . . like a stalker?"

Bradley glanced at her as if he'd had a sudden, unexpected, and frightening thought. "Let's look at the tapes from today, and then I'll walk you to your car. I should probably walk you every day until this thing with Erika is over." He ejected from his chair, crossing the room with determination. A few moments later, he returned with the day's tapes.

"Have you noticed Mark hasn't been hanging around in the halls since Erika went missing?" Ginnifer asked, now starting to buy into Brock's theory that Mark was involved with Erika's sudden disappearance.

"I did." Bradley's gaze didn't move away from the screen.

"That's Erika's Navigator," Ginnifer pointed out, sitting on the edge of her chair. "Brock's been using it."

"Is he following Garing?"

She looked at Bradley, and they both came to the same conclusion. "He wouldn't do anything to Garing," Ginnifer said. "Brock is the most levelheaded guy I've ever met. Very by-the-book. Stuffy. Never goes against the policy and procedure manual."

They watched in shocked amazement as the scene in the apartment parking garage unfolded.

"They're fighting!" Ginnifer cupped her hands over her mouth, flinching as she watched the blows land between the men.

"Is Mission Hospital WWF a new policy I haven't heard about?"

"Brock's finally had enough."

Bradley scrubbed his chin, reserving his comment until the fight ended. "It's about time he fought for what he wanted. Sometimes you have to pull the girl back to your cave by the ponytail."

Ginnifer rolled her eyes but couldn't fight the tingle his dominance ignited.

Bradley moved in closer to watch the next events on the tape. Ginnifer actually yelped when Mark backed over Brock. "He hit him! Did you see it? Mark ran over Brock. On purpose."

Bradley was already rewinding the tape. "Have you spoken to Brock?"

She squirmed uncomfortably. "Not today. Is he—"

"Call him. I'll send a car to his house." He tapped the bottom of the television screen. "This happened not long ago." He pushed up from his chair, adjusting the belt that held his gun and his radio. "Wait here. Tell the police what we saw, and then one of the guys will follow you home."

"Where are you going?" she called after him.

"To the parking garage."

Ginnifer's mind couldn't process what she'd seen. She didn't know people who committed homicide. Love triangles ending in violence was a storyline for *Law & Order,* not real life. Her alarm turned to raw fear. What would Mark do to Erika if she told him the truth about still being in love with Brock?

"Ginnifer?" Bradley was back, standing over her with a firm hand on her shoulder. "Don't worry. It's going to be okay. Jim here will take care of you." He pressed a firm kiss to her forehead. "I'll call you as soon as I know something."

Mark's fury instantaneously morphed into a nerve-wracking terror when he saw Brock's body sprawled across the pavement, his expensive suit shredded, his body stone still. A cold sweat covered his brow as he navigated his car out of the garage, aimlessly driving to an unknown destination—but at top speed, to escape the scene of the crime.

What the hell was he doing? *I'm a eye doctor, for God's sake. I don't commit cold-blooded murder. I repair little old ladies' cataracts.*

You've just been promoted to murderer, the annoying voice informed him, *because the doctor looked pretty dead to me.*

His hands were shaking so badly he could hardly control the steering wheel. He clamped down on it hard, making a conscious effort to ease his foot off the gas. "Think," he said, forcing himself to calm down by counting backward from twenty.

"This is very bad." Brock being dead, or seriously injured, would land him in jail.

Call your daddy to get you out of trouble like you always do.

He doubted Erika would understand his killing her husband as a way for them to stay together.

She'll leave you just like Sarah and Anne did.

"Or this could be very, very good." He let the dark images flicker through his mind, only briefly, reminding himself of the consequences of running down a man.

If Brock were seriously hurt, he might not remember enough of what had transpired in the garage to name Mark as the driver.

What's the plan? We go back and finish him off if he's still alive? The voice didn't sound horrified by the idea.

"I'm not killing anybody. Listening to you got me into trouble the last time."

If Brock is just scraped and bruised, he'll grab hold of the incident and milk it for all it's worth—winning Erika back, making you look like a psycho, and sending you to prison.

"This was a fight between men—one long overdue—it went bad, that's all. Brock wouldn't go to the police, would he?"

The voice cackled its answer.

Mark slammed his palm against the steering wheel. He needed to explain everything to Erika before Brock was able to put his spin on it.

You need an alibi.

He had to get back to his apartment. She would be his alibi. Besides, he needed to be with her, to see her face, to judge her reaction to what he'd done, to hold her and make her understand.

She'll never understand.

"She will! I'll prove to you how much she loves me. She won't leave me. She'd never turn her back on me."

His hands were still trembling and his mind was racing at a hundred miles an hour when he reached his apartment. He needed to pull himself together before he went inside. He had to appear normal and go about his regular routine. Erika

would help him figure out what to do next. He needed a plan.
He needed a drink.

Ginnifer called Virginia; then Virginia told James and he
went running out of the house. She called the only person she
wanted to be with during a crisis.

"Titus, I need you to drive me to the hospital. It's Brock."

"I'm on my way."

Everyone arrived within minutes of each other: Virginia
and Titus, James with a police detective, and Ginnifer escorted by security. They were ushered into a small family
room reserved for delivering the worse possible news about
loved ones.

"What happened to my son?" Virginia asked the detective.

"I don't know, ma'am. He hasn't arrived at the hospital yet."

"I brought the detective here to hear our story," James told
everyone in the room. "I want everyone to tell the detective
what they know about my little girl going missing, so we can
piece together what has happened to her." He tried to remain
strong, but his throat was thick with worry.

"Someone witnessed Dr. Johnson being hit by a car?" the
detective prompted.

Virginia cried out, falling into Titus's chest where he hugged
her tight.

"We don't know anything yet," Ginnifer said. "Bradley
went to check it out."

"This maniac ran over my son-in-law," James shouted. "I
want police on the streets looking for Erika. No more of this
damned 'she hasn't been missing long enough.'" He waved a
manila envelope through the air. "I have all kinds of proof
here he's dangerous. I want something done, and I want it
done now. Get on the horn and call your chief if you have to,

because you don't want me to start making calls to the people I know. I guarantee you won't like the consequences."

Titus released Virginia and stood united with James. "Young man, we've been working within the law for the past three days, but y'all not working with us. If you don't do something—now—we'll take care of this ourselves, and we don't care about rules and regulations. Make the call."

The young detective looked between the two older men, set in their determination to take action where his hands were tied. These were two powerful men—each in their own way—and ignoring their warning would not go well for anyone. He retrieved his cell phone and made the call.

"Brock's alive," Bradley announced, stepping into the quiet awkwardness of the room. Ginnifer rushed to him and he took her into his arms. "He's banged up pretty badly, but he'll live."

"Take me to him," Virginia said, "I'm his mother, and he's my youngest boy."

Titus immediately moved to her side.

"He's in with the doctor, although he's putting up such a fuss I don't think he's going to let them treat him. The police are waiting to question him. You'll be able to talk to him shortly."

The detective slipped from the room to join his colleagues.

"I need to see my son now."

Titus put his arm around her shoulder and escorted her from the room, ready to make her request happen.

"What happened over there?" James asked, and Bradley filled him in on all the details.

"I'm not going under," Brock insisted. "I'm getting out of here. I have to get to Erika before Mark does something crazier than he already has."

"Your shoulder is dislocated. You have lacerations that

need to be sutured. I'm not sure you don't have a few broken bones," the emergency department doctor explained. "We fix you, you talk to the police, and they go after Mark Garing."

"I'm going to find my wife." He slipped down from the exam table, ignoring the sharp pains and tender aches. He called on his bravado, keeping a blank face against the pain, as he limped to the far wall. He grasped the doorknob with the hand on his dislocated right shoulder and pulled—and pulled—and pulled—baring down and gritting his teeth against the shards of pain piercing his shoulder muscle until he heard the snap signaling his bone was back in the joint.

"That had to hurt like a son of a bitch," the doctor said.

"Not more than not knowing what's happening to my wife right now."

"Dr. Adelman."

Brock turned to see the administrator had joined them. "I don't know how this happened in my hospital. You all right, Dr. Johnson?"

Brock nodded, not wanting to waste time on hospital politics. He didn't know if Adelman's visit was sincere concern for his well-being or advanced planning to head off a lawsuit.

"I want you to know I have the hospital's full resources on this. Your father-in-law just showed me some disturbing reports about Mark Garing. Believe me, everyone involved will be fired and their names turned over to the police for further investigation."

"What reports?"

"You haven't seen them?" Adelman's voice was unreadable, again not giving Brock enough to go on to determine his motives. But he was good at reading people, deciphering their "tells" and knowing what motives lie beneath the surface. Right now, Adelman was interested in saving the hospital millions and protecting the reputation of the caregivers at Mission

Hospital. He couldn't blame the man for doing his job, but right now he had more important things to attend to.

"No, I haven't had a chance to touch base with him."

"Disturbing reports of mental illness and criminal activity."

"How did he ever get a license to practice?" the emergency department doctor asked.

Adelman's expression soured, but he recovered quickly. "We're looking into it. Don't you worry about the details now, Dr. Johnson. Concentrate on getting better, and finding your wife."

"I will."

Adelman made his departing remarks and disappeared out of the front of the cubicle.

"Think he's sweating?" the doctor asked.

Brock went for his shirt but found it ripped and dirty, piled underneath his torn suit jacket.

Knowing what was next, the doctor went into a cabinet and tossed him a green scrub top. "Your family is down the hall, and the police are waiting outside to question you."

He shared a moment with the doctor, calling on his brotherhood as a fellow physician.

"Go out the back of the cubicle. Follow the hall to the doctor's lounge. There's a door on the other side of the sleep room that leads to the parking lot."

Chapter 33

Erika pulled the chain connected to her collar as far as it would go, walking the length of the bathroom to exercise her stiff legs. She had nine hours to explore her small space of confinement. This forgotten room, noticed only for its functionality, became her hidden treasure cove. She searched the cabinets. She pulled out every container and examined the contents.

She found small insignificant objects and dismantled them, relying on her memory of helping her father in the garage as a little girl. He used to show her how to do things. Little secrets they shared between them because it had something to do with his "special" government work he didn't want anyone to know about. She liked to pretend he was one of the cool gangsters who challenged Al Capone, and she was the mafia princess, ruling with total ruthlessness over the territory her father owned. It was a little girl's dark fantasy, such the opposite of her true personality. Today she would recall what she'd learned from her father, draw on the strength of her love for Brock, and use those weapons against her capture.

She almost didn't notice the razor sitting on its charger on the countertop—hidden in plain sight. She couldn't figure out how to break it down into its individual parts, so she struck it against the tub until it fell into pieces. She found the blade, attached it to the tip of a toothbrush, and secured it with dental floss. She tucked the weapon into the crease of her ass, having few hiding places when only wearing a bra and panties.

Still drowsy from the medications Mark had been injecting into her system, she fell asleep wedged against the tub as she formulated her plan. When she woke up, she drank water from the faucet, flooding her system and rinsing away the last effects of the drugs.

She heard Mark when he arrived. He moved quickly toward the bathroom. She was ready. She ignored the strumming of her heart, slowed her breathing, and focused on her goal: getting to Brock. The lock clicked and the door slowly opened.

"Erika?" he asked tentatively as he stepped into the bathroom.

She looked up at him from her place on the floor between the toilet and the tub. She worked hard to hide her disdain for him. She blinked hard but did not answer, afraid she wasn't able to keep it out of her voice yet.

"You're awake. Are you angry?"

"Cold. And hungry."

"I brought some of your things . . . and I picked up a pizza." He answered carefully, trying to read her reaction to what had happened.

She wouldn't give him anything. He didn't love her like Brock did. He wouldn't be able to read her emotions. "Can I change? The floor's really cold."

"Sure. Of course." He ducked out of the bathroom, and Erika adjusted the razor nestled between her bottom cheeks. "I didn't know what to bring. If you're cold, maybe jeans and a T-shirt?"

"And socks."

"I forgot socks." Distress disproportionate to the seriousness of the situation twisted his features.

"I could borrow yours."

His shoulders relaxed and he went for the socks. When he returned, Erika was standing in the same spot where she'd been sitting. The change of position rattled him, and she realized she would have to be extra careful for her plan to work. He handed her a pair of thick white socks.

"Thank you."

"You're welcome," he answered with a tiny smile. "I'll leave and let you get dressed."

"Why?" She stopped him. "You've seen me naked."

"Yeah, but . . ." he hesitated, "you weren't awake and I had to get you out of the dirty clothes."

Her skin crawled. "Yeah, but," she mocked him, keeping her voice low and unthreatening, "when we were in bed, you touched me." She had to know the truth. She was too drugged to remember it, but she had to know what had happened between them.

His face brightened. "You remember us making love? And you're not mad?"

A fine shiver moved across her skin, and she fought the nausea and chills to keep a blank face.

He moved in, squeezing her tightly in his arms. Her ribs collapsed in on her lungs and she had to struggle to breath. "I was so worried. I didn't know how you would react. And with everything I have to tell you—"

"What do you have to tell me?" There couldn't be more.

"Later." He forced a kiss on her lips. "Get dressed and we'll talk over dinner. Maybe you can eat at the table tonight."

She smiled up at him. It was a tight lifting of lips, forced and planned, but Mark adored her adoration. "I should get dressed."

"Yes." He released his grip on her and stepped away.

"Mark."

He turned, expectant.

"Can you release the chain?" She rattled it. "I can't get dressed like this."

He eyed her warily, but another fake smile helped him decide. He ducked out of the room and returned with his key ring. He searched through the keys until he found the right one. He moved to the lock and opened it. The click meant freedom was near.

"Five minutes," he said, leaving the door open behind him.

She only needed three to get dressed. The other two she used to keep herself from crying. *No tears,* Brock would tell her, *get to me and then you can cry.*

Mark escorted her to the dinner table as if they were on a real date in a fancy restaurant, pulling out her chair and everything. He had set the dining room table with his best china for the take-out pizza. Her stomach churned when she thought of Mark violating her during her drug-induced haze, but she forced two slices of pizza down anyway. She needed to rebuild her strength. Every swallow reminded her of the collar wrapped around her neck. Mark had removed the chain, but the collar remained, reminding her she was his plaything.

"You were going to tell me something earlier."

He looked confused.

"You mentioned it in the bathroom."

He swallowed down his wine before answering. "Things have been going so well between us, but Brock just won't go away and leave us alone."

"You've seen Brock?" She toned down her response, hiding the hope in her voice.

"He's been snooping around my office, accusing me of having something to do with your disappearance."

She understood how crazy his mind was working. He believed she wanted to be with him, even though he had to keep her chained to the sink for it to happen.

"What happened?"

"He followed me to your apartment when I went to pick up your things. Bad enough I've got the old guy across the hall in my business, now Brock's on my back." His anger flashed. The intensity of his sudden mood changes reminded her to be very careful with him.

"Brock can be relentless."

"Tell me about it." He gripped the stem of his glass, staring into the emptiness.

"So, tell me what happened."

"It was an accident," he blurted. "I don't know what I was thinking. Sometimes something comes over me, telling me to do things I know are wrong, but I can't stop it. And now everything will be ruined—unless we get away from here."

She wasn't going anywhere with him. Here, she had a chance to learn her environment and plot an escape. If he were to take her on the road, she'd be lost.

"What have you done, Mark?" Her tone caught his attention and he became aware of what he'd said.

"Erika, baby, it was an accident."

"What was an accident?" Fear moved through her body, making her legs go numb.

"We fought. I ran him over."

"Ran him over. With your car?"

He looked away.

"How was that an accident? Is he okay?"

"I didn't hang around to see. I had to get out of there. If I get into any more trouble, I'll go to prison for sure. Then we can't be together."

"I don't want to be with you!" she screamed. "Brock," she

said, fighting a sob. "I have to get to him." She jumped up from the table and ran toward the door, but Mark was there, begging her not to leave.

He attached himself to her arm and groveled. "I've never wanted any woman as badly as I want you. Don't you understand? Do you realize everything I've done to get you?"

"I never asked you to do anything. I don't want you." She fought his hold on her, but he seemed to have ten hands, all reaching for some part of her body like a drowning man needing to be saved.

"Let me explain how it happened," Mark pleaded. "I can explain everything. He threw your relationship away like it was worthless. I'll treat you better, baby."

"I want out of here." She fought him off, going for the razor tucked into the back of her pants.

"You can't leave me. I love you."

"I don't love you," she shouted, inches from his face. "Don't you get it?"

Her harsh words made him freeze. She brought the home-made knife around with fluid quickness, stabbing him in the thigh. Mark howled. She yanked out the knife and stabbed his other thigh. When he collapsed on the floor, she drove the blade into his shoulder, pushing it deep and hard against his screams.

The police be damned, Brock drove to Mark's apartment knowing they wouldn't be far behind. As soon as they realized he'd slipped out the back, they'd be on the way to detain him, afraid he'd hurt Mark if he got to him first. With James's help, he had Mark's address and directions to his apartment. He floored the accelerator, making the twenty-minute trip downtown in ten.

He stopped his car in the street, ignoring the valet drivers as they screamed at him. He could hear sirens in the distance, and he had no illusions about how he would be arrested when the police arrived. He didn't have much time to beat the truth out of Mark, making him confess to what he'd done with Erika.

Residents of the upscale building turned away as he crossed the lobby, battered and bruised, wearing a green hospital scrub top with dirty and torn slacks. They probably tagged him homeless, insulted by his entry into their world. His time would be further limited by their calls to the police to have him removed. He found the gold placard on the wall listing the tenants' addresses. He had no idea if the elevator would allow him to go up, or if he needed to be buzzed, or a security code. He mashed the button, watching the lobby doors for the arrival of the police while a small crowd began to gather.

"Where are the stairs?" he shouted at no one in particular.

No one answered.

He slapped the elevator call button again. The doors finally opened, and Erika fell out into his arms.

The blood wasn't Erika's. There were a lot of hysterics in the lobby of the luxury high-rise until Brock was sure she wasn't physically injured. By the time he had his emotions under control, the police barged onto the scene, pulling him away from her, but not without a struggle that caused his shoulder to dislocate again. If it wasn't for the searing pain, the police would never have gotten her out of his arms.

They were taken to Mission Hospital West in separate ambulances—Mark was taken to the main police headquarters at 1300 Beaubian in a squad car.

Everyone was waiting at the hospital when they arrived: his mother with Titus, James with the police, Ginnifer clinging to

Bradley. Mitchell was there, too, apologizing for not believing
Erika had actually been kidnapped. With Hassan's nagging,
Brock let the emergency department doctor pop his shoulder
back into place—without the use of anesthesia, because he
had to be awake in case Erika called for him. He refused further treatment, slathering antibiotic ointment on his cuts and
bruises himself before tearing through the corridors in search
of his wife.

Ginnifer had been allowed to stay with Erika during her examination and the acquisition of evidence.

"What kind of evidence?" he asked Ginnifer, too upset to
think logically. If he had settled down and tucked his fear for
his wife away to the dark corner that allowed him complete
control of his emotions, his knowledge as an experienced
physician would have answered the question.

"The police are with her now," she said, avoiding a direct
answer. "She can go when they're finished."

Brock entered the cubicle without invitation, going to
Erika's side and placing a comforting hand on her back. His
mother was there, sitting on the opposite side of the stretcher,
her hand on Erika's knee. The officers promised to follow up
with further information about Mark's arrest and left to continue their investigation.

"Are you okay?" Brock asked, but James stepped into the
tiny room before she could answer.

"The police have the crazy S.O.B. locked up," James said,
gingerly taking her in his arms. The gesture told Brock she
was hurting more than she had told him earlier.

"I'm going to leave now," Virginia said, coming to her feet.

"Do you need a ride, Ma?" Brock asked, torn because he
didn't want to leave Erika, but exhaustion was nipping at the
corners of his mother's eyes.

"Titus will take me home. To his place," she added. She

kissed Erika good-bye, did the same to Brock, and left. He had to admit he liked knowing someone would watch over her tonight, because right now he wanted to get Erika alone to begin healing her wounds.

"James, can you tell everyone to go? As soon as Erika gets her discharge papers, I'm taking her out of here. No more visitors tonight."

James nodded, turned to leave, but was stopped by another visitor. At first Brock thought the man was another police detective—someone high in the food chain by the expensive tailored cut of his suit.

"I'm Ben Garing. You're familiar with my son."

James mumbled a curse word, firmly planting himself between the larger man and his daughter. Brock came around to join him, shielding his wife from the crazy predator's creator.

Ben lifted his hands up. "I'm not here to hurt anyone. Quite the opposite. I want to apologize for my son's behavior."

"You've been doing a lot of that through the years," James answered, reminding Brock he hadn't touched base with him to learn what he'd found out about Mark.

Ben didn't blink at the insult. He stood tall and broad, his dark hair with a sprinkling of gray slicked back. He was statue-still, his face a clean chalkboard, showing no emotion, no panic, no anger.

"You've apologized, now go," Brock said. "You think barging in on my wife while she's in the emergency room is the right place to apologize? The only thing sicker is believing you can apologize for what Mark has done."

"I understand your anger—"

The arrogance belonged to the father but had been passed on in a healthy dose to the son. This man's stoic expression along with the haughtiness only reminded Brock of Mark and the harm he'd done to Erika. Mark wasn't available, but his father was, and if he wanted to meet Brock's wrath, he was prepared to introduce them. He made a move toward the man. "You have no idea—"

Erika touched his shoulder, stopping him. "What Mark did isn't your fault. You shouldn't apologize for him. He's not well. He needs help."

Erika's natural kindness would allow her to be forgiving. Brock wasn't as understanding. He wanted Mark inside a jail cell.

"He knows just how sick his son is," James added, his voice trembling with barely controlled anger. "He has the medical evidence to prove it. It started in middle school when the principal called you about your son touching the female students inappropriately."

Ben's shoulders shifted, but his expression remained hard and unmovable.

"You moved him to a fancy private school. Then he became old enough to get real girlfriends, but he didn't understand the meaning of 'no,' so when they tried to leave him, he stalked them. Each time, with each girl, it became more serious—until he locked one—Anne, I believe her name was—in the trunk of his car and tried to run away with her. In between all the little 'incidents' were threats of suicide and visits to the mental hospital." James took a step closer to the man. "What I couldn't figure was how he kept getting off without jail time. And how in the hell did he keep his medical license?"

Brock watched the scene in shock, new terror moving through his body. Erika had been alone with this pervert before Brock even knew he was a threat. This could have turned out much, much worse.

"You've done your homework," Ben said, reaching into the inside pocket of his suit. "I don't know how you managed to get your hands on this information, but—" he shrugged as if it were all meaningless. As if he were so above the law this evidence would not be piled on top of what Erika provided to put his son in prison for a very long time. "I'll worry about that at another time. Right now"—he produced a leather-bound checkbook and gold pen—"we have other business to attend to." He looked from James to Brock, settling on Erika between the frame they made around her. "How much?"

"How much for what?" Brock asked, really ready to put the man down, regardless of his age. After what he'd experienced at James's hand, maybe he should turn him on Ben. It would be a much more even fight.

"To make this go away. I saw the old woman limp out of here. Wouldn't it be nice to get her to the best specialists in the world and make the bum leg go away? What about you?" He jerked his head in James's direction. "Isn't it time to retire in Hawaii instead of playing junior detective?" His cold gaze turned on Brock. "Don't you and your wife want to open a do-gooder's clinic and save the homeless drug addicts from themselves? How much will it take to make all those things happen?"

Brock and James lunged forward together, both having the same thought.

"Brock!" Erika shouted, stopping them. "Help me down. Daddy, step back."

He went to her and held her elbow as she slowly stepped down from the exam table. She looked small and vulnerable in the blue-and-white gown, and it inflamed Brock's rage to think what she'd gone through the past three days and having this man trying to buy it all away. Erika was an emotional person, easily wounded by injustice, but always ready to forgive. She stepped up to Ben, and it hurt Brock to think she would accept the man's bribe to save her family from the turmoil of a long criminal proceeding.

Erika looked up at Ben, him standing with the gold pen poised over his checkbook, waiting for her to name a figure. Erika drew her arm back as far as it would go and punched the man in the jaw with a tight fist. The man staggered, and she advanced with another ready fist. She glared up at Ben with the hunger of a professional boxer going in for the knockout blow. "My husband taught me to do that."

CHAPTER 34

Brock lifted her up into his arms and crossed the hotel lobby, not blinking as he boldly skipped the line and stepped up to the counter. He placed his driver's license and credit card on the counter. "Give me a suite."

Erika knew they were a battered sight, coming straight from the hospital after the night's events. She didn't care about appearances. She snuggled deeper into Brock's hard chest, relishing in the comfort of his hardness as it cradled her softer side. She wasn't able to speak yet, still too traumatized to be comfortable with him alone. So much had happened between them. So much to be fixed. He refused to go home, because he knew the phone would be ringing, the police coming by, curious friends and family stopping over to wish her well. "I want you alone. To myself," he told her in the car on the drive to the hotel.

The registrar grumbled but searched for a key. He ignored the patrons standing in line, preferring to deal with their anger over fighting against Brock's determination. He lifted a finger to the bellhop. "He'll bring your luggage."

"No luggage," Brock said. "Send clothes up in the morning."

The man behind the counter fingered the gold card, his

expression alight with new possibilities. "Yes, sir. Dinner will be up shortly," he added, already starting the spending spree.

At the elevator, Brock took the keep from the bellhop and shoved him out of the private car with a firm hand on his chest. The man staggered back but didn't utter a word as he helplessly watched the doors close.

Erika got a glimpse of the suite's luxurious beauty as Brock moved through the rooms, heading straight to the bathroom. He talked to her in soothing tones, not pushing her to converse with him. He could read her well. He knew what she needed.

He sat her down as he drew a bath in the oversized garden tub. After three days of being chained to a sink, she didn't think she could stand to be in the room—no matter how lavish— until Brock stepped up to her with soft, understanding eyes and began to peel away her clothes. This was about comforting her, not sex.

"You don't have to talk to me right now," he told her, taking his time to undress her, handling her with care. He helped her into the warm, bubbly tub. "You will when you're ready. You're still in shock."

"Please," she said, reaching for him when he turned to leave.

It was the only invitation she would need to give him for the next two days.

Brock stripped out of the tattered green scrub top. He turned his back on pretense of grabbing a towel when stepped out his pants, reminding Erika of their unfinished business. So much had happened over the past three days, including her realizing she could never live her life without him in it—even if it weren't a perfect life together, she couldn't stand to be apart from him again.

Brock slipped into the tub behind her, pulling her firmly against his chest. He lifted the cotton cloth and let the warm water cascade over her shoulders. He washed her entire body, soaping her and rinsing the residue away. He talked to her the entire time, telling her how glad he was to have found her. He let her know how much she had been missed. "I never gave up on you. I knew you wouldn't leave me. Not like that."

Then he got quiet and relaxed back against the tub with her in his arms. He stroked up and down her arms, soothing her without words. She thought of how closely she'd come to losing him, and her heart opened up. "Brock."

He became alert, stiffening a little behind her. "How do you feel?"

"I can't believe I brought Mark into our lives."

"Shh. It's over. It's my fault more than yours. You wouldn't have turned to him if I'd been there . . . like I should have been." He warmed the cloth again, tipping her forward a little to gain access to her back. "Erika, I'm sorry. What I did was selfish. You were right all along. I took all your options away and made you do what I wanted you to do. I didn't respect your opinion or your right to make a decision."

"Brock, I haven't—"

"You did exactly what you should have done. But now I'm asking you. Will you come back home? I love you, and I don't want to let you go. We can fix this. Whatever you want me to do, I'll do. I just need you home with me. You're the soft to my hard. You smooth out my rough edges."

She whimpered and he pulled her back against him, burying his chin in the crook of her neck. "Don't," he softly commanded.

"I'm damaged goods." She shook her head, fighting away the tears. "I didn't want to come back to you this way. I can't."

"Damaged goods?" he asked, clearly puzzled.

She pressed her back into him, absorbing a small amount of his strength. She couldn't look at him when she told him.

Brock was a man of pride, and he wouldn't be able to handle another man sleeping with his wife. "Mark . , ."

"Mark, what?" The edge of anger tainted his voice.

"He—we—"

"Did he touch you?" There was no mistaking the anger now, but he held it in check.

She nodded.

"He forced you to sleep with him?"

"The drugs—"

"Dilaudid, Valium, and Versed were in your system. The ER doctor told me." He was taking the long way around the reasoning process, giving his mind enough time to take it all in. "He drugged you, and then he had sex with you?"

She burst into tears. Not because of what Mark had done, because she had no clear memory of it—only bits and pieces. She cried because she knew Brock would never be able to touch her again.

"Why are you crying?" His hands rested lightly on her shoulders. "Did he hurt you?"

"I don't remember all of it."

"Why are you crying? Are you scared?"

"Yes."

"Mark won't come near you again. I can promise you I won't allow it. We'll see him in jail, or a state mental prison, but he won't ever see you again after we walk out of the courtroom."

She shifted so she could see his face. "I'm not afraid of Mark. I'm afraid of you."

"Me? Why?"

"You're going to leave me now, and I won't be able to stand it when you do."

"Me? Leave? I'm not going anywhere. Not unless you make me go. Why would you think . . ." His eyes widened.

"You think I don't want you because you're *damaged goods*." She turned away, but he brought her back to face him with a grip on her chin. "Let's get out of the tub."

Naked, Brock straddled her nude body to the bed. "This is me now. Damaged goods."

She lay frozen, fearful of her reaction when she saw him for the first time. She loved him and she wanted him, no matter what trauma his body had suffered, or what was to come. But her emotions were still raw, and full disclosure was overwhelming.

"Look at me, Erika. I don't care what Mark forced you to do. Your heart belongs to me, and you only give me your body freely. Can you look at my disfigured body and still want me?"

She watched the hurt move behind his eyes and dropped a stony exterior over her expression. She didn't know what to expect—examining a patient and examining your husband were worlds apart—and she didn't want her reaction to shock or embarrass him.

"Don't do it," he said between gritted teeth. "Don't you dare shut down to me."

Her heart jumped at his warning. He wanted it straight, no sugar coating. Just as she would want. Just as she wanted to give him. She let her eyes move over his body, searching every muscle on the way to his groin. The abdominal incision was healing nicely, but there would always be a faint scar to remind him of his brush with death. He was semi-erect, the mild hardness he always got after a long bath together. He lifted his penis away, revealing his scrotum. The left sac was fuller than the right, noticeable but not horrible. She glanced up at him before reaching out to touch him. He grabbed her wrist.

"Let me touch you," she said softly, her eyes focused on his groin.

He continued to hold her wrist, not as brave as he had tried to portray. She fought to pull away from him, until finally his hand trembled and he released her. She didn't hesitate. She reached out and cupped the right side of his scrotum, watching for signs of pain or discomfort as she kneaded the soft skin between her fingers.

"I'm going to have a scrotal implant," he announced, his voice unsure.

"Why?" She glanced up at him, but her concentration remained on the flattened skin where his testicle used to be. "I loved you before. I love you now. Having one testicle doesn't change how I feel."

His penis began to elongate, shifting upward to his abdomen. Instead of desire, she saw uncertainty on his face.

"What is it?"

"I want to make love to you—"

"Then make love to me."

"I don't know if I can." His knees dug into the bed. "Getting an erection after the surgery wasn't easy."

"You're getting one now."

"I don't know if it will work. I don't know if I'm fully recovered."

"Why don't we stop trying to be perfect for each other? Why don't we just try to help each other heal?"

Brock looked at her with unrestrained amazement. "Heal each other," he repeated. "Start our marriage all over again."

"Now."

"I love you," he said as he lowered his body to hers.

"You don't say it enough, but you've said it twice tonight."

"I love you," he repeated as he pushed her legs apart with his thigh.

"I love you, and I want to spend the rest of my life with you. If you're sick, we'll go through it together. Bad with you is better than perfect with anyone else."

He pressed his hips between her thighs and brought his mouth to her for a kiss. She placed her hands on his cheeks, steadying him so she could control their mouths. She teased his lips—wanting to do this for so long—to kiss her husband, slowly, tenderly, like she had the rest of her life to explore his mouth. She felt him growing, his penis snaking up her body with stubborn purpose. She licked his lips and he opened for her. She found his tongue and relished in the hungry wetness of him.

She needed to touch him to know after all these months they were real again. Her fingertips moved over his back. When he moaned, she pressed her palms into his hard, round ass, pulling him toward her. She reassured him in her purpose when she reached around and took his scrotum in one hand while grasping his penis in the other. She lifted her thighs and he pressed deeper, bringing them closer.

She rolled a condom down the length of his shaft, despite his protests. The nurse in the ER had counseled her on the dangers of unsafe sex until she received all her test results.

She placed the tip of him at the beginning of her opening, and he surged forward unexpectedly. He took her in one long stroke, as if he'd been waiting years, not months to get inside her again. He pushed and pushed and pushed, never stopping until every inch was inside her; then he pressed down, sealing them together. He exhaled a long moan, and she thought he was hurt, until he began to make small circles with his hips. He wouldn't release the pressure, refusing to give up one centimeter.

She looked up into his face. His eyes were squeezed tight, his mouth slack. His hips continued to circle, hard and unyielding.

He collapsed on top of her, bringing his lips to the tender flesh of her neck. He kissed and sucked, but never stopped his hips. The circles grew more vicious, hungry and eager to move into ecstasy. He brushed the tip of her ..ged bud, sending wild shivers down her spine. She jumped and his rhythm faltered. It made her explode, and she carried him along on her tidal wave.

Erika laid her head against Brock's shoulder, tracing his thick eyebrows with her fingertip. "What did it take to make you go to Adelman?"

"It took me realizing I might lose you forever. I don't mean our marriage. I mean losing you to a man who has no morals. I knew you wouldn't be safe with Mark."

"You read people well."

He tipped her chin up, capturing her in the depths of his eyes. "If you still feel the same way—if you don't want to live with me because of the cancer—I'll accept it. I just want you to be happy. I'm hoping your happy includes me."

"When Mark had me chained to the bathroom sink—"

Brock's body tensed. He held her tighter.

"—the only think I could think about was how much time we've wasted. Almost an entire year has been thrown away when we could've been loving each other. I don't want to waste one more minute."

He flipped her onto her back and reigned kisses over every inch of her skin. He remained gentle, but left no doubt who was in charge. They shared the same scent from the bath water, but it smelled differently on his skin—more masculine, primal. She inhaled, trying to take him inside her in any way she could. He gave her hungry eyes, pressed his lips against her ears, and whispered naughty things, telling her what he planned to do with her body. He was good at that, using his words to amp their sex up an unbelievable notch. He kept it clean—just barely—because they were making love, but he promised to use the F-word on her all night when they'd had enough tenderness.

"How will you know when it's time to flip the strip?" she asked, grinning at him.

"You think I don't know your body?" He took her nipple between his teeth, pinning her hands to the bed as he pulled and licked.

"Is this going to be slow and drawn out?" she panted.

He released her nipple, but his finger trailed down her body, stopping at her nest of curls. "How do you want it?"

"Not slow. Not drawn out. It's been too long."

He smiled a rare Brock smile. One that said he loved her and he liked teasing her in bed. "Sorry, I'm in the mood for slow and drawn out, and since I'm in charge, it's what you're going to get."

"Taking my decisions away again?" she asked, but there was no malice, only hope they had moved on enough to be able to laugh at themselves.

"I'm the best at deciding how to make you come. Do your job and lay there and enjoy it."

He kissed her neck, full and wet while his fingers roamed the terrain of her body. He circled her breasts, lifting them, testing the sensitivity as if he had forgotten how to torture her body. He left a trail of goose bumps behind, coaxing her to shift her body so the touch was never ending. He shifted positions and licked her thigh, bowing her back and arching her shoulders. She went up on her elbows to watch him. His eyes rolled up to watch her reaction as he parted her wide and slipped his tongue into the opening. He probed carefully, his tongue mischievously darting in and out but missing its target. The action made her curse.

"So impatient," he said, pulling back. He used his kisses as a weapon on her torso, finding virgin areas to suckle. He moved to her calf, caressing slowly as he slipped each toe into his mouth. The wet heat of his mouth connected to hot, wet places on her body. She didn't want to know where he'd learned this new trick. She only hoped there would be more.

His fingers moved up her legs, kneading the flesh as he went for his target. He kneeled next to her, kissing her thigh and licking the triangle framing her special place. He slipped his longest finger inside, humming at her reaction as he added a second. He went deep, curling his fingers to allow more penetration. When he found her G-spot, she screamed. Her excitement turned him on, and he added pressure, trying to take her as high as she could go. She tried to ward off the winding tension, to push it away so she would last, but she couldn't. She opened her mouth to warn him, but it was too late. She shattered into a quivering mass.

"Mark actually hit me with his car and his father thought he could buy his way out of it."

"I'm sorry." She stroked the pad of hair at his temple, following it down until it framed his jaw.

"Don't apologize for him."

"He's really sick. Maybe we should consider—"

"Consider what? He tried to kill me."

Her finger stilled near the corner of his mouth. "I can't forgive him for that. If something would have happened to you . . . What kind of person does it make me?"

"What do you mean?" His palm curled over her breast.

"What kind of person am I that I can't forgive him? When it wasn't entirely his fault. We both had our parts in causing what happened. Mark is mentally ill. He shouldn't be blamed for it all."

"So you want to take the burden of it on your shoulders? Erika, I love your compassion, but you have to be different about this. Mark is sick, yes, I agree, but it can't be your problem to fix." Before she could protest, he went on, "He's managed to become friends with everyone in the hospital who knows us, and has been questioning them about us. He stalked you, and he's been stalking my mother. I wondered how he knew so much about my medical condition, and it seems he's been hitting on the OR staff to get a look at my records. This is an intelligent man who had to have some idea what he was doing was wrong. You heard about his past. He has to be stopped before he kills someone."

"Leave it alone?"

"Yes. This time, yes."

"I can't save him."

"You can't save everybody. It'll kill your spirit to try." She felt him smile against her chest. "I'm sure we'll have this conversation a thousand more times during our marriage. You want the world to be righteous, but it isn't. Sometimes bad things happen to good people. We do the best we can. We take the good with the bad and we move on. I learned that lesson from trying to shut you out when I found I was sick."

"I have to be a little tougher."

"A little. I'll do the rest. It's my job to look out for you."

"The entire time I knew you'd come for me."

She felt the smile again.

"He'd try any trick to get you, but I'd do anything to keep you. You're my woman—my wife."

The warmth moved through her, heating her body from head to toe. "I love you."

"I love you too." His voice was lazy, he was tired.

She disentangled her body from him, moving down his body. His head jerked up, and she placed soothing strokes on his thighs. "Relax. Let me do this."

She knew he was still uneasy about her seeing his body, but she had to push him past it. She wouldn't let him wallow in doubt just as he hadn't let her worry about what had happened with Mark. She held his penis in both hands, opened her mouth, and took the plunge. She took him too deeply too quickly and choked a bit, forcing her to back up. It had a mental effect on Brock and his penis instantly went rock hard. She took note of a secret fantasy he hadn't yet shared with her.

He balled the sheets in fists, fighting not to grab her hands when she cupped his scrotum. She rolled the left ball between her fingers while her mouth moved up and down on the shaft of his penis. He tensed when her hand abandoned the left ball and went to the area where his right testicle had been. She looked up the line of his body to see him struggling with himself, fighting off the image of what once was.

She found a wet, slow rhythm with her mouth, distracting him. Once he was in the grip of ecstasy, she wound one hand beneath his firm ass cheek. She pulled back on his penis, tortuously slow until she only held the head. She sucked and sucked, making his thighs tremble. When he was on the brink of orgasm, he wound his fingers in her hair and pulled her away. He liked to kiss her when he came from her giving him fellatio. Instead of moving to his mouth, she settled between his thighs and took the soft skin of the right side of his scrotum into her mouth. She rolled it, licked it, and suckled it until he shot a fountain of cream above her head. He jerked upright and dragged her to him, covering her with his perspiration. He was panting too hard to speak.

"Do you have any questions about how sexy I find your body?" she asked him before she pressed their lips together.